They were both transfixed, neither moving

Until the chamber door shut.

Keelin suddenly came to her senses and attempted to cover herself with her hands. Marcus should not be in her chamber. No man had ever seen her unclothed.

He took a step toward her.

"Marcus…" she whispered, unable to keep from wanting what she could not have.

She had no will of her own when he looked at her. Her hands dropped to her sides when he reached for her.

"You are so beautiful," he breathed, taking her hand as she rose from the tub.

Nothing in Keelin's life had prepared her for the surge of emotions that coursed through her now. She felt feverish, though she knew she should have been cold after stepping out of the bath. Instead, she felt heat—nay, 'twas more than mere heat, 'twas a sweltering fire that consumed her….

* * *

Celtic Bride
Harlequin Historical #572—August 2001

Praise for Margo Maguire's previous titles

Dryden's Bride
"Exquisitely detailed…an entrancing tale that will enchant and envelop you as love conquers all."
—*Rendezvous*

"A warm-hearted tale…Ms. Maguire skillfully draws the reader into her deftly woven tale."
—*Romantic Times Magazine*

The Bride of Windermere
"Packed with action…fast, humorous, and familiar…THE BRIDE OF WINDERMERE will fit into your weekend just right."
—*Romantic Times Magazine*

"A wonderful story…experience the emotions and trials of these individuals as they travel on their journey. This one is a must."
—*Rendezvous*

MARGO MAGUIRE

Celtic Bride

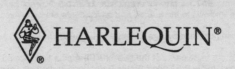

HARLEQUIN®

TORONTO • NEW YORK • LONDON
AMSTERDAM • PARIS • SYDNEY • HAMBURG
STOCKHOLM • ATHENS • TOKYO • MILAN • MADRID
PRAGUE • WARSAW • BUDAPEST • AUCKLAND

ISBN 0-373-29172-8

CELTIC BRIDE

Copyright © 2001 by Margo Wider

This edition published by arrangement with Harlequin Books S.A.

® and TM are trademarks of the publisher. Trademarks indicated with ® are registered in the United States Patent and Trademark Office, the Canadian Trade Marks Office and in other countries.

Visit us at www.eHarlequin.com

Printed in U.S.A.

This book is for Mom, a Celtic Bride herself.
Thanks for the stories of the McCarthys, the Deans,
the Lannens, the Flynns and all the rest of our Irish kin.
And thanks especially for telling me about
Uncle Billy who could charm warts off—but only
under the big oak tree next to the cemetery,
and under a full moon.

Prologue

Early Winter
West Cheshire, England
The Year of Our Lord 1428

The night was a long, troubled one, allowing little rest or comfort for Keelin O'Shea. Plagued by half-remembered dreams and terrible nightmares, Keelin's remarkable intuitive abilities made her aware that she and her uncle Tiarnan were in danger. The Mageean warriors were near. She had no choice now but to take her clan's ancient spear from its hiding place, and by touching the priceless relic, try to gain some clarity of their situation.

Some day, Keelin thought, *some day soon,* she would end her exile. She would return to Ireland and wed the man chosen years before by her father, Eocaidh O'Shea, chieftain of Clann Ui Sheaghda. What a comfort it would be to have a strong and confident champion to care for her, and protect her; what a relief not to be looking over her shoulder at every turn, nor jumping at creaks and shadows. What joy to return to the home she had always called her own.

Tears came to Keelin's eyes as thoughts of her clan pierced her heart. The lonely, isolated existence she and Tiarnan had lived for the past four years had finally worn her down. She could not remain in this foreign land any longer.

'Twas not an ideal time for travel, with winter nearly upon them, but there were precious few coins left of the purse Tiarnan had brought when they'd fled Ireland. If they did not go now, who was to say there'd be *any* left when it came time to buy their passage across the Irish Sea?

Keelin knew she would lose what wits she had if circumstances forced her to stay away from her beloved home for another season. She longed to know how her clan fared after the battle that had killed her father, that final blow that had sent her and Tiarnan fleeing across Ireland with the Sheaghda spear. She desperately yearned for the company of her young cousins and the lasses of the village at Carrauntoohil.

'Twas not that she didn't care for Uncle Tiarnan. Quite the contrary—Keelin loved the old man as much as 'twas possible to love another soul. But there was no youth or vigor left in him. Their survival depended solely on Keelin's abilities, and the task had become far too daunting for a young lass.

Keelin slipped off her narrow pallet and looked over at Tiarnan. The old man was still sound asleep, with eyes closed, his white-bearded jaw slack. 'Twas just as well that he slept. He'd barely recovered from the lung fever and was still weak. It would not do at all for him to get up now, only to fret and worry when Keelin took the spear into her hands and channeled all her energy toward the second sight that had kept them safe during their years of exile.

Keelin's intuition was seldom wrong. In her sleep, she'd sensed that the Mageean enemies were close by, and she knew there was little time to waste. It was of minor importance where they headed—they just had to get away from the abandoned cottage they'd worked so hard to make their own.

Keelin wrapped her shawl about her shoulders, then added more peat to the fire before stepping quietly outside into the chilly morning. The faint glow of the approaching dawn lit Keelin's path and she found her way easily to the back of the cottage where she had fashioned a crude shelter for their mule, and a place to keep the mule-wain and her meager tools. 'Twas nothing fancy, merely an extension to the roof of the cottage, to keep the mule out of the worst of the weather.

By touch, Keelin found the mule-wain and ran her hands across the rough wood, searching for the narrow hiding place she'd made. She could only hope that the support board she'd hollowed out would continue to serve as a secure cache for the precious spear that had been entrusted to her. With luck, no one would ever think to look for the sleek obsidian spear in such an obvious, yet devious hiding place.

Keelin found the metal latch and slid it aside, then reached two slender fingers into the opening to draw out the leather-sheathed spear that was once touched by the goddess of old. *Ga Buidhe an Lamhaigh,* as the spear was called by Keelin's clan, had been given to a Sheaghda chieftain eons ago, in the dark years before the Vikings came, even before the Druids practiced their magic. Over the ages, the beautiful, black spear had become the symbol of Sheaghda dominance in Kerry.

Loss of the spear would mean devastation for the

O'Sheas. And Ruairc Mageean, the sworn enemy of Clann Ui Sheaghda, intended to have it.

Every time Keelin touched *Ga Buidhe an Lamhaigh,* she felt the magic of the spear. Its ancient power surrounded her and swept her into a cloud of sensations, each one stronger than the last, making her intuitive abilities wildly acute, but draining her of her strength.

'Twas her burden, as well as her honor, to be gifted with the ability to use the spear.

Drawing forth all her powers of concentration, Keelin sat down on a bed of pine needles and drew *Ga Buidhe an Lamhaigh* from its sheath.

Chapter One

South of Chester, England
Early winter, 1428

The thick branches of the forest formed a pleasant canopy, high overhead. Dusty beams of sunlight slanted through the barren branches, lighting the dark recesses of the wood. It was late afternoon, and the riders pressed on, anxious to make Wrexton Castle before dark. Marcus de Grant rode alongside his father, tensing as Eldred once again brought up the only subject that could make Marcus tremble.

Marriage.

"There was a bounty of charming, young, *marriageable* ladies at Haverston Castle, Marcus," Eldred de Grant said.

"Father—"

"I am growing no younger, my son, nor are you," Eldred continued steadily. "One day you will be Earl of Wrexton in my stead, and I would wish for you to have a helpmate, a companion…a wife. A worthy woman such as your own mother, my Rhianwen."

That was Marcus's own wish, as well, but he had yet to meet a woman with whom he was at his ease. Except for the wives of a few friends, Marcus found himself tongue-tied and clumsy around women. It was especially true with the young ladies of noble birth, those lovely, preening birds in their velvets and silks, with their maids and servants, their pouting lips, their softly curving bodies and their illogical demands.

They were all so fragile, so delicate. So *mysterious.* Marcus was a soldier, not a courtier, and hadn't the slightest idea how to court a woman. And with his burly build and superior strength, he worried that a mere touch of his clumsy hands could hurt them.

"A wife, Uncle Eldred?" Marcus's young cousin asked indignantly, riding up alongside his elders. The brash eleven-year-old, Adam Fayrchild, had been orphaned several years before, and Eldred, a man generous and kind to a fault, had taken him in, though their kinship was distant at best. "What need have we of a wife at Wrexton? All is in order, is it not? We have Cousin Isolda, as well as cooks and footmen and maids and—"

"A man has need of heirs, young Adam," Eldred said with a chuckle. "One day you'll understand when you find your Eve."

"Find my *what?*" he asked, as his freckled nose crinkled, clearly not understanding the earl's jest. "There was not one girl at Haverston, Uncle, whom I could endure for a single *day,* much less a whole month, or a year!"

Marcus smiled, though Adam's words made him aware of the deep loneliness he felt within his heart. Certainly he shared a warm closeness with his father, and he'd learned to treasure his precocious young cousin as well. But there was an emptiness inside that he'd felt acutely during the marriage festivities at Haverston Castle. More and more of his friends were wed now, and many of the young couples shared a bond that Marcus could only begin to fathom.

And until he somehow managed to get over his terrible shyness with women, he could only look forward to a lifetime spent alone. Marcus knew he was not unpleasant to look upon, but women wanted to be charmed. They wanted to be—

A wild cry from above, followed by a cacophony of barbarous calls, startled Marcus. Bearded barbarians dropped from the trees all around them, with swords and spears drawn. Marcus's warhorse, long unaccustomed to the scent of blood and the fierce clang of iron, reared under him as the Wrexton travelers came under attack by these Celtic warriors. The entire Wrexton party was thrown into confusion, and several men were wounded before they were able to regain control of their mounts and draw their weapons.

The Wrexton men were vastly outnumbered, and struggled desperately to wage battle against their strangely clad, barbaric foes. Swords and spears clashed all around, and Marcus watched with horror as his father was thrown from his horse, and set upon by the savage, foreign warriors who attacked them.

No! Marcus's heart cried out. Eldred de Grant was too strong, too vital to be cut down so heinously. It was impossible for Marcus to imagine a life without his father, a good and just man. He *could not* be dead!

"Marcus! Your father!" Adam shouted. The young boy had used good sense so far, keeping himself behind Marcus and out of the fray, but the attackers came from all sides. The Wrexton knights were surrounded.

Blindly, Marcus dismounted, grabbed Adam and stashed him in the safest place he could find, in the hollow of an old, felled tree. Then he hacked and slashed his way toward his father's unmoving body.

"My lord! Behind you!" one of the men called out before Marcus was able to reach Eldred. Marcus whirled and dealt with the fierce, red-haired attacker, dispatching him quickly. Another bearded warrior replaced the first, and Marcus gritted his teeth and continued the battle as the fight went on all around him.

Wrexton men continued to fall as Marcus battled, and he could see no end to it, no way to get to his father. Even so, the young lord had no intention of giving up. He would fight to the death wielding his own lethal broadsword until he cut down as many of these fierce warriors as was humanly possible.

"My lord! There are riders coming!" one of the men shouted.

"They're Englishmen!"

"It's Marquis Kirkham and his men!"

The barbarians became aware of the English reinforcements, and mounted a hasty retreat as the newly arrived knights gave chase.

When Marcus was free of his last opponent, he hurried to his father's side, where one of the men had dragged him away from the battle. A glimmer of hope surfaced in Marcus's heart as he saw movement in his father's eyes. Marcus knelt beside the older man and took his hand.

"My son," Eldred whispered.

Marcus could not speak. His throat was thick, his tongue paralyzed, and his vision oddly blurred as he noted the severity of Eldred's wounds.

"Temper your grief...in my demise...Marcus," Eldred gasped. "I go now...to join your mother. Know now....that I could not have had...more pride in a son...than I have in you...."

Eldred took his final breath, then commended his soul to heaven.

All was silent. Not one bird chirped, nor a leaf rustled in the still air.

The knights standing 'round knelt and crossed themselves, and gave words of sorrow and condolence to Marcus. The new lord of Wrexton barely heard their words. Only a few short moments before, he and his father had been engaged in their familiar discussion of Marcus's unmarried state. How could all have changed so suddenly? How was it possible that Eldred was gone?

"My lord!" a voice in the distance called. "Quickly!" Marcus turned to see one of his men standing beside the thick, fallen oak where he'd hidden Adam. Dread crept up his spine as he stood and crossed the span.

Either the boy had crawled out of his hiding place, or he'd been dragged out. 'Twas no matter now, though, for the boy lay still upon the deep green moss, with an arrow protruding grotesquely from his back.

Marcus crouched next to him. Never had Adam seemed quite so small, never so vulnerable. "He's breathing," Marcus said.

"Aye, my lord," Sir Robert Barry said, "but if we pull the arrow out, he'll likely bleed to death."

"'Twill be hours before we reach Wrexton!" Sir William Cole retorted. "He'll die for certain if—"

"There is a small cottage nearby, if I remember aright. Down that hill, next to a brook," Marcus said grimly. He looked up at the men of his party. "I will carry him," he said as he carefully picked the boy up into his arms. "Bring my father."

"Be at ease, Uncle," Keelin O'Shea said quietly to her uncle Tiarnan as she lay a gentle hand on his pale brow. His coughing spells were steadily improving, but they still rattled the old man terribly. "I will protect the holy spear. No Mageean hand will ever be touchin' *Ga Buidhe an Lamhaigh.*"

Worry weighed heavily in Keelin's breast. She was shaken and weakened by the sights she'd seen early that morning, and knew 'twas time to move on again. She and Tiarnan could not stay when the Mageean warriors were so close.

It seemed so long since they'd fled Ireland, running from the ruthless mercenaries who had killed her father. Keelin renewed her determination to stay clear of them. She knew that to lose the ancient spear would mean her clan's loss of its right to rule, and allow the ascendancy of the cruel and implacable chieftain of Clan Mageean.

Keelin would never let that happen. She had witnessed Ruairc Mageean's barbarity once too often to allow it.

In order to elude Ruairc's men, and keep *Ga Buidhe an Lamhaigh* safe for her clan, she and Tiarnan had uprooted themselves and moved four times in the years since their flight to England. But wherever they made their home, true security eluded them. Ruairc Mageean's warriors were never far away.

'Twas only Keelin's strange powers of intuition that kept them two shakes ahead of the mercenaries.

"Here, Uncle Tiarnan," she said, lifting the man's head and tipping an earthen mug to his lips. "Have a wee sip."

"Ah, lass," Tiarnan rasped, "Go rest yerself. Ye

touched the spear this mornin' and I know what a strain that puts on ye.''

"I'm fit enough," she said, lying. She was weak and shaky still, hours after she'd seen the sights. But she would not let Tiarnan know, for he fretted too much over her as it was.

"Ye must tell me what ye saw." His poor eyes, opaque now with age, turned blindly toward his young niece, though in his mind's eye, he could still see her fresh beauty. Cream-white skin like her mother's, with a slight blush of roses upon her cheeks. Eyes as green as the fields of home and hair as black and silky as the deepest night. Keelin's was not a fragile beauty, for she was tall, as tall as most men. And she'd grown into a strong and hardy lass.

His poor Keelin had no way of knowing that Ruairc Mageean wanted more than the spear. The scoundrel intended to take Keelin O'Shea herself when he stole *Ga Buidhe an Lamhaigh,* and make her his concubine. Aye, the fiend had lusted after the girl since he'd first seen her, back when she was all gangly legs and big green eyes.

If Mageean managed to abduct Keelin when he stole the holy spear, he would have a much greater chance of usurping Eocaidh O'Shea's heir as high chieftain of all of Kerry. Aye, Tiarnan knew 'twas exactly what Mageean intended.

Nor was Mageean the only man in Kerry lusting after the lass. It pained Tiarnan to know that the girl had been promised in marriage to Fen McClancy, a neighboring chieftain. And *this* abomination had been done by her own father mere days before his death in battle, may he rest his bones and his detestable soul in peace, Tiarnan grudgingly prayed.

Keelin's intended was not only an old man, near as old as Tiarnan himself, but a lecherous old daff, besides. Sure and he might be high chieftain of all that lay northeast of O'Shea land, but Tiarnan knew there were other ways to secure McClancy's alliance without bartering Keelin to the old rascal.

Leave it to his brother, Eocaidh, the strong and capable one, never to see beyond the needs of the clan. He'd have abandoned his young daughter to old McClancy without a second thought. Though he must have known how Keelin would react to the betrothal for he had not informed her of his intentions before his death.

'Twas with sheer luck and a prayer that Tiarnan had been able to convince the elders to send Keelin away as guardian of *Ga Buidhe an Lamhaigh,* instead of staying in Kerry and becoming Fen McClancy's wife. Tiarnan sincerely hoped that in the years since he and Keelin had fled Ireland, the McClancy chieftain had met his death. Nay, 'twas not a malicious wish—Tiarnan truly wished the man a peaceful end, but an end, nonetheless.

And he truly hoped Keelin never learned of her father's promise to Fen. 'Twould break the girl's heart to know how little her father thought of her. 'Twas a miracle she'd never realized it—yet Keelin was surprisingly oblivious to the reality around her. For all her intuitive abilities, she often misunderstood the simplest motivations of others.

Ah, but she was young still. Time enough to learn of the treachery of men.

"Please, Uncle," Keelin said, "save your breath now, and we will speak later. There is nothin'—"

"But there is, darlin'," the old man said as he lay his head back on the soft pillow Keelin had made for him.

"This is important, Keelin, and time is short. Listen to me now."

"What is it, Uncle, that you've got to be saying to me rather than taking your rest?" Keelin asked somberly, pulling a low wooden stool close to the narrow pallet on which the man rested. 'Twas nippy with the late afternoon, though the single room of the cottage was pleasantly warm with a small fire burning in the grate. The aroma of the healing plants and herbs Keelin set out to dry was strong, but pleasing. Later, when Tiarnan was asleep, she would crush the leaves that were ready, and pack them away for their journey.

"The Mageean warriors are comin'," he said without preamble. "I know it with a certainty, even without *seein'* it as you do."

Keelin frowned. Tiarnan was wise, but how could he know what she'd only just seen that morning? The visions had been shattering. Brutal Celtic mercenaries clashing with peaceful Englishmen. Horses screaming, the scent of blood hot and sweet in her nostrils. Mortal wounds, great sorrow. She could not say exactly *when* it would happen, only that it *would* happen, and it would be soon.

"They cannot be far now, lass," Tiarnan said breathlessly, "and ye know it as well as I do m'self. We've been here too long. They must be close to findin' us out."

Keelin quickly assessed the humble cottage. How would she manage to pack their meager belongings, reinforce the hiding place of *Ga Buidhe an Lamhaigh,* and get her weak and ailing uncle away before Ruairc Mageean's warriors came? And where would they go this time? Was it wise to attempt to return home now?

Last time they'd run, Tiarnan had still been able to

see a bit. He'd not seemed so terribly old, nor so feeble as he was now. Would he manage the journey across Wales and down to the sea?

And the visions... Something, Keelin wasn't sure quite what, but *something* was going on at Carrauntoohil Keep. Her urgency to go back was no longer a mere yearning to go home. She was filled with a foreboding that would not rest until she returned the sacred spear to her clan and saw for herself that all was well.

"Listen to me, Keely lass," Tiarnan said calmly, sensing his niece's rising panic. She was young, a mere nineteen years, and though Tiarnan considered her second sight a gift, he knew it was difficult for her. The visions always left her weakened, distraught and drained, even if she tried to hide it from him. "You must take *Ga Buidhe an Lamhaigh* and go away from here before—"

"Nay, Uncle," Keelin cried abruptly. "I will not leave ye."

"Keelin—"

"The warriors have been thwarted for now. I'll not be leavin' this place without ye. I can pack us up," she said quickly, "and you'll ride in the wain when 'tis time."

"Keely," Tiarnan said, closing his eyes wearily. It tried his soul to know that he'd soon send the lass away, to journey on alone, but no amount of prayers to the Holy Virgin or any of the saints had availed him. His chest pained him something terrible, and the cough... Well, he had no doubt the cough would be the death of him.

Keelin's clear green eyes were bright with tears that overflowed their bounds. She took both her uncle's hands in her own and raised them to her cheek. "I will move us to another place, a safer place where—"

"Do ye not understand, love?" Tiarnan said weakly, feeling her tears on his hands. "I am not well enough to travel, and ye must get away before it's too late."

"Nay, Uncle!" she cried. "There is time."

"Keelin," Tiarnan said, "even if there were time, ye don't need an old wreck like me holdin' ye back. Now, go on with ye. Start to pack up yer things and—"

Tiarnan paused and cocked his head slightly.

"What?" Keelin asked, alarmed at the way her uncle had tuned his ear to some distant sound that she could not yet hear. "What is it?"

"Someone's comin'," the man replied. "Horses... men on foot."

"Oh, saints bless me!" Keelin cried, standing up abruptly from her perch. "How could I have been so wrong? They're here? *Now?*"

"I doubt it's them, darlin'," Tiarnan said with the calm that comes with age. "But we've no choice but to wait and see, now."

Keelin swallowed hard. They'd always kept well ahead of the Mageeans before. Never even got close to a confrontation. Yet here she stood frozen in her skin. She was barely able to move, unable to guide her uncle away from the cottage to hide. 'Twas no way for Eocaidh O'Shea's daughter to behave, and she knew it.

"Do ye hear the voices now, lass?"

Keelin gave a slight nod, unmindful for the moment, that Tiarnan could not see her.

At least they would not find *Ga Buidhe an Lamhaigh,* she thought. 'Twas well hidden again, and she would never tell where to find it. Allowing the holy spear to fall into Mageean hands would be the worst possible calamity.

Rage would not serve Marcus now. His desire to accompany Kirkham and his men as they chased down and killed the barbarians in the wood was great, but the need to get Adam to shelter was even more imperative.

With great care, Marcus carried the boy down the hill. The distance to the little cottage was a good deal longer than he remembered, perhaps because of the added burden of the injured boy in his arms. He tried to concentrate only on getting Adam to safety, to a place where his wound could be tended. Any other thoughts of the terrible moments in the wood would bring agony anew.

Four men of their party were dead, and another two seriously wounded. The others had minor injuries. As Marcus walked, surrounded by his men, he was aware that even now, a few of the Wrexton men were gathering the bodies of his father and his other fallen comrades, and would follow along shortly.

Why had they been attacked, Marcus wondered. He could not imagine any reason why foreign fighters would be on English soil, attacking a peaceful English party. It made no sense at all.

It had been fortuitous that Nicholas Hawken, the Marquis Kirkham, had arrived when he did to rout the attackers. As cocky and irreverent as the man was, Marcus knew Nicholas could always be counted upon in a fray. And without Hawken, the Wrexton party would have been utterly doomed.

One of Marcus's men knocked on the door of the humble cottage, which was opened by a young woman who kept to the shadows of the interior. Marcus carried Adam into the room and, with help from one of the men, gently laid the boy on a bed. A white-bearded man lay silent on another bed at the opposite end of the room.

"I'll need hot water," Marcus said as he drew out his knife. He started cutting away the boy's doublet as he spoke. "And some clean cloths. Edward, hold his arms. Roger, take his feet while I pull the arrow."

Keelin pitied the poor wee mite whose body was pierced by the arrow. Nevertheless, she sent up a silent prayer of thanks that it was not Mageean's men upon them. She sensed Mageean's presence strongly, and the turmoil and despair of these men. But no immediate danger.

Keelin stood near Tiarnan's pallet and watched quietly as the English lord took care of his small charge and issued orders. The man was tall, and he'd had to duck as he entered the cottage. Even now as he knelt next to the wounded boy, his size seemed to take up half the room.

His hair was the lightest gold she'd ever seen. With deft fingers, the young lord quickly unfastened his tunic of chain mail, and one of his men helped him remove the heavy hauberk, leaving his broad shoulders loosely clothed in a sweat-dampened, but finely embroidered white linen tunic. He pushed his sleeves up and leaned toward the child lying on the bed, leaving his powerful forearms bared to Keelin's gaze. Then he crossed himself in silent prayer and spoke quietly to the insensible boy.

"I'm sorry, lad, for what I must do," he said steadily, "but we've no choice in the matter, and you must be brave." And then he muttered under his breath, "As must I."

Keelin's heart went out to the young man who was

so obviously shaken. These were the Englishmen she'd seen in her vision this morning, and though she'd not recognized their faces, she understood the measure of their sorrow, their terrible grief. She knew they had lost several of their comrades today, as well as one in particular who held a special place in their hearts.

She could do no less than to help them.

Going to the corner opposite her bed, Keelin opened the small trunk that contained her things. She had a few linen tunics and an old chemise that could be torn into strips. Taking out the items she needed, she made bandages for the boy.

When that was finished, she sorted through her leather pouches and took out the dried plants she would need. She'd learned the healing arts so well from her uncle that she had no need of his advice in choosing her medicines. *Poterium Sanguisorba* to help stop the bleeding, and lady's mantle to keep the wound from festering.

When Keelin turned back to the Englishman, the arrow was out. The boy's back was bleeding freely as Keelin stood beside the lord and placed a white cloth onto the wound. She applied pressure. The child moaned.

"Adam..." the lord said shakily.

Keelin could feel the heat and strength of the man next to her. She looked up at his strong profile—the long, straight nose, his square jaw, and unwavering sky-blue eye—and wondered if there was a man in all Ireland who would give her the care and attention that this man gave to the young boy at hand.

Certainly there was, she reminded herself. The man to whom she was betrothed would care for her as none had ever done before. Eocaidh would have seen to it. Many a time had Keelin asked Tiarnan about her betrothed, but her uncle had always skirted the question, never quite answering her. Keelin had finally given up asking, for 'twas entirely possible he did not know. The council of elders had the final word, and they might not have included Tiarnan in their decision.

"'Tis a good sign, m'lord," Keelin said in a quiet voice. "His groanin'."

He looked at her then, noticing her for the first time. He blushed deeply and his eyes darted away.

"E-Edward," the golden English lord said to the knight who stood near the door, intentionally turning his attention from her. Then he cleared his throat and continued. "See if there is a physician in the v-village down the road and fetch him if—"

"I am a healer, m'lord," Keelin said, spreading her leather satchels on the bed next to the boy. "And I have all I need to tend the poor wee lad." She opened the pouches, pouring some dark powder into a small dish, then adding water. She mixed the two into a paste and then bid the English lord to lift the bandage from the boy's back.

"Ach, 'tis a grievous wound," she said as she spread some of the paste into the deep gash, "made ever more dangerous by its proximity to the spine."

She didn't tell him that the kidney was nearby as well, and that she hoped it hadn't been nicked by the arrow. As it was, the boy would be lucky not to bleed to death slowly, from the inside.

Marcus could only stare at her graceful hands as they worked. In a few short moments, his life had been tossed upside down, his father killed dead in the field and poor Adam gravely wounded and lying in a peasant's hut that was inhabited by an old man and a beautiful woman who was obviously no common peasant.

Nor was she English.

Her presence here made no sense. It occurred to Marcus that she might be connected somehow to the vicious warriors who had attacked them in the wood. Were those men her personal army? Was that why they had attacked? To keep her safe?

He thought it odd, too, that she had not seemed surprised by his arrival with Adam and the others. Was this kind of occurrence commonplace in her experience?

No, he realized. It could not be. They were not so very far from Wrexton now, and Marcus was sure he'd have heard of a band of wild, foreign warriors guarding one small cottage.

But who was she?

The woman wore a simple, but finely made kirtle of wool dyed deep green, and her dark hair lay long and silky upon her back. She moved majestically, with grace and purpose, as she laid gentle, competent hands on his young cousin. She spoke softly to Adam, with her strangely musical accent, even though it was unclear whether or not the boy could hear.

She had the mien of a queen, yet here she was, in this place—this small cottage that was little better than a peasant's hovel. And Marcus felt as tongue-tied and awkward as he'd ever felt in the presence of a lady.

"M'lord," said the grizzled old man on the bed at the opposite end of the room.

Marcus turned and walked toward him, noticing that the old fellow still beckoned. It was then that he realized the man was blind.

"Ye must allow my niece to do what she thinks is best," he said, his words accented even more thickly than the woman's, "for you could ask for no greater healer on English or Irish soil than Keelin O'Shea."

"Is that who she is? Your niece?" Marcus asked, much more at ease now that he was not standing quite so close to the girl. He let out a slow breath as he watched her continue to stitch the wound in Adam's back.

"Aye, Keelin O'Shea of Kerry, she is," the old man said. "And me, I'm her uncle. Tiarnan O'Shea at yer service. Or I will be, once I'm up on m' feet again."

"Kerry... That would be...an Irish province?" Marcus asked, barely listening to the reply. He raked his fingers through his sweat-soaked hair. He was painfully aware that somewhere outside his father lay still in death, his body covered by a shroud and under the guardianship of his men.

Marcus was numb with grief and anger, and did not know how he would function, how he would assume the role of earl, and command these men. How would he get his father and the rest of his fallen knights back to Wrexton and into hallowed ground? And what of Adam? 'Twas obvious the boy could not travel, nor could Marcus leave him here with strangers.

"Kerry's more a *region,* lad," Tiarnan replied, oblivious to the young lord's consternation. "A fierce and proud land of Munster in the southwest of Ireland, wi' loughs and craggy hills galore."

Marcus made no reply, for he was lost in thought. The old man took his silence for worry about Keelin and her handling of the wounded boy. "Truly, ye can trust her, lad," Tiarnan said. "She's got a gift for the healin'."

"I can only pray you're right," Marcus said as he turned away and stalked out of the cottage. Roger and Edward remained within, and Marcus knew he could trust either man to come to him if further trouble arose.

He looked up at the sky and breathed deeply, wondering how such a beautiful day could have been destroyed so quickly, by such ugliness.

'Twas years since Marcus had engaged in battle. Five years, to be precise, since he'd returned home from the French wars to find his mother ill and dying. After her death, he'd stayed on at Wrexton with his father, never returning to France.

Wrexton was at war with no one. The campaign in France had little bearing on what happened here, so far in the west country. There were no border disputes or skirmishes with neighboring knights to account for any violence. He and Eldred had developed good rapport with the Welsh who lived on the land adjacent to Wrexton, and Marcus had had no reason to expect a vicious ambush from foreign knights.

Knights? If that's what they were.

Not even the French were so barbaric. What armor these men wore was primitive. They were unwashed and unshaven, with hair pulled into thongs and hanging down the length of their backs. Their language was strange and guttural, and completely unfamiliar to him. He'd thought them Celts before, and now, knowing that the cottage woman and her uncle were Irish, he wondered what the connection was. There had to be one.

And God help Tiarnan O'Shea and his niece if they were in any way a party to the day's hideous slaughter.

Marcus walked around to the far side of the cottage where the men had set up tents. It was there they would spend the night, where the wounded men would be tended. He did not know how many nights they would stay, or when it would be possible for Adam to travel to Wrexton Castle.

But he would have to get his father home soon, for burial on Wrexton land.

There was a briskly flowing brook near the cottage, and Marcus walked down a beaten path to get to it. He pulled off his tunic and crouched down, dunking his head in the water. Somehow, he had to clear his thoughts.

Keelin finished tending the lad, then put away her medicines and bandages. She washed her hands in a basin of fresh water, then went over to speak quietly to her uncle.

"Sleep awhile now," she told him, knowing that the worry and then the excitement of visitors had exhausted him. "I must go out for a bit, but I'll be back to see to ye soon."

She had to talk to the Englishman.

Stepping outside, Keelin was surprised and dismayed to see so many knights milling about near the mule-wain. She assured herself that there was no danger of one of the men discovering the spear, but it made her uncomfortable to see them standing so close to it.

Keelin calmed herself. With a definite plan in mind, she approached one of the men and asked where the young lord might be found, and was given a direction to follow. She took the path to the brook, skirting a partially hidden nest of baby snipes, and stopped short when she saw him.

There was a strange fluttering in her belly and a heaviness in her chest as she watched this primal young man, standing half-naked on the bank. She felt hot all over, as though her skin were on fire. Her heart pounded as if she'd swallowed some of her own foxglove powder.

If she'd ever seen so well developed a man, Keelin could not remember it. If she'd ever noticed how low a man's chausses hung on his hips, or how the muscles in his arms stood out, the memories were lost to her.

His upper body and hair were wet and he threw his head back as she'd seen wild animals do, half expecting him to shake all over to dry himself. Keelin's mouth went dry as she watched. She forgot to breathe.

And then he saw her.

He took a sudden step back and plopped his booted foot right into the brook. To make matters worse, he lost his balance and fell on his rump. Saints above, the man had a lovely blush, as well as a good deal other attributes, Keelin thought as she rushed down to the water to give him a hand up. He'd gone a lovely pink right to the ends of his ears.

"Well, if 'twas a bath ye wanted..." she said in jest.

Silently, the blond Goliath got to his feet and stepped up and out of the wee river. Keelin realized he was in no mood for humor. Nor was he inclined to be friendly to her. She could understand that. She was Irish, after all, same as the men who'd attacked the young lord's party. Had the situation been reversed, and English mercenaries attacked a group of her father's men... Well, Keelin was certain that no Englishman would be safe from Eocaidh O'Shea's wrath.

"The lad is sleepin' now," she said somberly, breaking the tension his silence created. He'd been full of orders to his men when he'd first arrived, when the boy had needed quick attention, but was clearly loath to speak to her.

"'Twill be some time, though," she said, "before we know how he fares...."

The man nodded curtly and headed up the path toward the cottage. It appeared to Keelin that he wanted nothing to do with her.

This would never do. She had a request to make, an urgent one. This young lord was the answer to a prayer, if only she could get him to agree to escort her and Uncle Tiarnan away. With Tiarnan's health being what it was, this stern giant was her only hope. She'd find a way to leave Tiarnan in this man's care, and then go on to Kerry herself. She needed to know what was going on at Carrauntoohil.

"Wait!" she commanded. And got his attention at last.

He stopped and half turned toward her.

"I am Keelin O'Shea, daughter of Eocaidh, high chieftain of Clann Ui Sheaghda." When he made no response, she said, "I believe 'tis my right to know the name of my guest."

He cleared his throat. "M-Marcus de Grant," he finally said haltingly. "With my father's death this afternoon, I am…I am the new Earl of Wrexton."

'Twas just as she thought. This was no ordinary Englishman, and Keelin was glad she'd given her full credentials. Marcus de Grant was a high nobleman, and a man grieving for his own father. Now, if only she could persuade him to take her and Tiarnan to his lands.

"My condolences on your loss," she said earnestly, walking toward him. The poor man was obviously shaken by his father's death. "'Tis not an easy thing to lose your family."

Marcus doubted he'd ever felt so awkward before. As he stood half-naked on the path, with the O'Shea woman bearing down on him, he wanted to drop his sodden tunic and run. Run from everything—his new position in life, the responsibility he felt for Adam, the death of his father. And he would most certainly run from this exquisite black-haired lady, whose regal manner had him *typically* tied into knots.

At the same time, he sensed that the woman spoke from experience, that she'd known loss herself, and it was that feeling that gave him the impetus to reply to her statement. "No, i-it isn't easy," he said woodenly.

"And the lad, m'lord? Who is Adam?" she asked as they began to walk abreast of each other.

"My cousin," Marcus replied as he moved to keep some distance between them.

"Not meanin' to be impertinent, m'lord," she continued, "but how did all this happen? What befell your party?"

"I had hoped *you* would have some insight into that," Marcus said, surprising himself at his loquacity. He hadn't stammered at all, and somehow had managed to say exactly what was on his mind, in spite of the directness of her forest-green gaze, her exquisitely curved form and the tantalizing spicy scent that seemed to emanate from her.

"Me?" she asked, apparently stunned, for she stopped dead in her tracks.

"Celtic warriors attacked us in the wood north of here," he said. "Another party of Englishmen arrived in time to rout them, but not before they killed four of our men and wounded several others besides Adam."

Keelin O'Shea pressed a hand to the center of her chest, drawing his eyes to her softly rounded bosom. She muttered a couple of unintelligible words, and then to his amazement, she said, "I've been worried somethin' of this nature would happen sooner or later."

"You know about them—the warriors?" he asked, stunned by her admission, even though he'd already made the connection.

Keelin set her jaw and inclined her head and Marcus had the distinct impression that she intended to duck the question. Her evasiveness angered him and he took hold of her arm.

"What of those Celts?" he demanded, his anger rising to the surface again, even as he became aware of her softness. "Will they return? Are there more of them lurking somewhere, waiting for—"

"No!" Keelin replied irritably, pulling her arm away. "At least I greatly doubt it. The Mageean warriors have never split up to search...they've always traveled together, as one...."

"Go on."

"They're Ruairc Mageean's men. And they are after me," she said dejectedly. "They've been chasin' after my uncle and me for the last four years. We've been hidin' out here in England, movin' on whenever the need arose."

Marcus could not afford to be self-conscious or bashful now. Keelin O'Shea had the answers to his questions. She had information about the warriors who'd killed his father, and he intended to find out what she knew. For the first time in his life, he was not entirely tongue-tied and overwhelmed by his nearness to a beautiful woman. Though he still felt deathly uncomfortable, he found he could speak to her—touch her, even—without freezing up like a branch in an ice storm. On the contrary. He felt as if the flames of Hades were consuming him bit by bit. "Who is Ruairc Mageean?"

"Well..." Keelin swallowed hard, taken aback by the lord's anger. Sure, she could see he'd leashed the powerful emotion, but 'twould be a terrible thing if ever he let it free. 'Twas obvious that *now* was not the time to make her request. In fact, she realized belatedly, it might be better to leave the man alone entirely for now. "'Tis a long story, but suffice it to say that Mageean is a rival of my family. A cruel and heartless man who would possess all of Munster if only..."

"If only...?" Lord Wrexton asked, his anger barely concealed.

"If only he had the power to do so," she said uneasily as she turned abruptly and headed up the path to the cottage.

Marcus stood watching as her slender form was swallowed up in the thick woods, but his relief at being left alone was short-lived. Within a few short minutes of Keelin O'Shea's departure, there was a bloodcurdling, feminine scream from somewhere deep in the wood.

He dropped his tunic in the dirt and ran.

Chapter Two

Keelin managed to walk only a short way up the path when she was accosted. Her filthy attacker slapped one hand over her mouth and the other across the middle of her body. Then he dragged her through the woods in the opposite direction of her cottage, away from any help at all.

She kicked and scratched frantically at the villain who hauled her mercilessly across the dense forest growth, but her actions were of no avail. She could not get herself free from the man, except for one short instant when she managed to let out a desperate screech.

The Celtic warrior wrapped her hair tightly around his hand and, speaking in Gaelic, told her in no uncertain terms to keep silent. Pain ripped through Keelin's scalp as the man brutally yanked and resumed his terrible pace through the forest.

Keelin couldn't think clearly, yet a thousand disconnected thoughts ran through her mind as she clawed at the man's hands. Would the warrior kill her? Who would care for Uncle Tiarnan then? What would happen to *Ga Buidhe an Lamhaigh?* Had her cry been loud enough for anyone to hear?

"Let the woman go!"

The Celt suddenly stopped and whirled around. Holding Keelin in front of him like a shield, he faced Marcus de Grant, who appeared like a golden giant out of the woods to challenge him.

"Be still, Keelin," Marcus de Grant growled.

Startled once again by the young earl's sudden appearance, Keelin felt the cold, steel blade at her throat and knew that her life depended on keeping still.

"Give me *Ga Buidhe an Lamhaigh* and I will free you," the warrior demanded.

"Níl!" Keelin cried.

Lord Wrexton's sword was drawn and he was ready to engage the Irishman, but Keelin was afraid the young lord could do nothing while the mercenary held her this way, with one hand tightly tangled in her hair, the other on the knife. If de Grant attacked, Keelin would surely be killed.

De Grant stood at the ready, slightly crouched, and slowly began to circle Keelin and the Irishman. Somehow, in the depths of her distress, Keelin wondered what he could possibly do to free her.

She heard a strange, strangled sound, and realized it had come from her own throat. The mercenary pulled her hair even tighter and turned to keep Wrexton in front of him, though Keelin could feel that he was slightly off balance. She was too frightened to act, and so she moved with him, taking care not to jar herself against the knife.

"You'll never leave these woods alive, Celt!" Marcus taunted. "Let her go and I'll spare you! Drop—"

A loud crack split the air behind her, and the Irishman yelped. Keelin was thrown forward, onto her knees, facedown in the dirt.

Amidst the sudden shouts of men, and confusion all

around her, Keelin came as close to fainting as if she'd just experienced a powerful vision. Heart pounding, blood rushing in her ears, she was helped to her feet, then pulled off them again when her knees buckled. As she fell to the ground, she heard the clash of swords, the grunts of men fighting for their lives. Suddenly, all was silent. De Grant lifted her into his naked arms and carried her to the path that led to her cottage.

The young lord was quiet as he carried her faultlessly through the woods. Trembling, Keelin wrapped her hands around his neck and held on, treasuring the unfamiliar sensations of safety and security. It had been years since anyone had protected her, or helped her in any way. The warrior had killed a man to protect her.

She gazed up at Lord Wrexton, whose eyes were locked straight ahead, and took notice of the short, red-blond whiskers that covered his jaw and neck. She'd never seen any young man up so close, had certainly never before appreciated the strong lines and muscles of a warrior's physique. Yet she'd found herself gaping at this powerful man more than once in the short hours since he'd crashed in on her life. She had never thought a man beautiful before, yet now...

She squeezed her eyes tight as if to shut out the thoughts that would surely cause her nothing but trouble. How the man could have such an effect, and so quickly, was a mystery to Keelin.

Marcus got her back to the cottage and the place where his men were encamped. He eased her down onto the stump of a great oak, and tilted her chin with one hand as his men gathered round. ''You're bleeding,'' he said, oblivious to her appreciative gaze, and astonished that she'd come to no harm. The Celt had been quick to raise his sword against Keelin. 'Twas by the grace of

God that Marcus had been quicker, though he'd achieved little satisfaction in killing the Celt.

With a surprisingly steady hand, Marcus touched the injury on Keelin's neck, assessing its severity.

"The knave cut me?" Keelin asked, surprised. Yet another odd feeling rose in her, much more intense than anything she'd experienced so far, one that seemed to be the result of the earl's gentle touch. But how could *that* be? She'd never heard of such a thing.

"Aye," Marcus replied. "He sliced you when you fell."

"Wh-what happened back there?" Keelin asked. She felt shaky and light-headed now that the threat was done. "How did I... Why did the scoundrel let me loose?"

"We heard your scream," Marcus began. One of his men handed him a clean cloth and a stoppered crock of ointment that he used to daub at the thin slice on her neck. "I came after you, as did Marquis Kirkham—the Englishman who routed the Celts after they attacked our party."

Keelin furrowed her brow and shook her head in puzzlement. "Where did the marquis come from? How did he—"

"I know as little as you, my lady," Marcus replied. "Kirkham arrived in the woods behind you and the Celt, just about the time I got there."

"Aye, my lord," one of the men said. "Lord Kirkham rode up just as we heard the lady cry out."

"I kept the Celt distracted," Marcus continued, "while Kirkham used his whip on the man."

"That was the crackin' sound that made him drop me?"

Marcus nodded. "Kirkham has a fondness for the

whip," he said, "though he's a skilled swordsman as well."

Keelin winced at the stinging caused by the ointment. "Sword or whip," she said as he wrapped a clean length of cloth around her neck. "I'm grateful to the man for comin' along when he did." Then Keelin stayed his hand with one of her own as she looked into his light-blue eyes. "You have my thanks as well, Lord Wrexton."

She saw color burst in his cheeks, then flush down his neck and out to the tips of his ears. His diffidence endeared him to her as much as his strong, powerful presence had done earlier.

Keelin would have touched the bit of golden hair that had fallen over his forehead, but she dropped her hand midway when Marquis Kirkham arrived in the clearing. He was tall and powerfully made, with a visage as fierce and dark as the very devil. Keelin could almost believe the man had routed the Celtic mercenaries single-handedly.

"What say you, Marcus?" the big nobleman said, slurring his words. Keelin realized the man was *drunk!* "I've been mopping up after you all day!"

Marcus did not respond to the man's sarcasm, for he was accustomed to Kirkham's brooding and sarcasm. Instead, he merely finished tying Keelin's bandage in place. Keelin, however, took exception to the drunken newcomer's speech. Such loose and foolish talk would never have gone unchallenged in her father's keep. She stood and faced the man.

"M'lord," she said firmly, "can ye not know of the young lord's loss? His own father was slain this very day, yet here ye jest—"

"Is this true, Marcus?" the marquis asked earnestly.

The captious mischief in his eyes faded and his posture straightened. "Did Eldred fall to those savages?"

Marcus gave a curt nod and turned away. Kirkham followed, and the two men disappeared from Keelin's view.

Keelin sensed a terrible turmoil in the marquis, in spite of his drunkenness, but she was unable to understand any more of the man. Perhaps, she thought, he had good reason for overimbibing, but her intuition failed to give further insight.

She touched the bandage at her neck and thought again how close she'd come to losing her life. What would have happened to the clan then, if *Ga Buidhe an Lamhaigh* was lost? Keelin's urgency to return to Carrauntoohil doubled, though the means by which she was to get there were unclear. Somehow, Keelin would see her uncle safely to Wrexton, and then make the trip to Kerry on her own.

Marcus did not feel the chill of the early evening. He was never one to be subject to the cold, but in the last few minutes, he'd been suffused with heat.

It was entirely the woman's fault.

He would have liked a few moments to himself to savor the experience of holding Keelin O'Shea. He'd have given himself time to think of her softness and the long, elegant lines of her neck, the gloss of her hair and the fire in her green eyes.

Instead, he strode into his campsite beside Nicholas Hawken, and told of his encounter with the barbarian mercenaries.

Nicholas sobered with Marcus's words, and listened attentively, his brooding features never changing.

"I apologize, Marcus," Nicholas finally said, bowing

his head, "for my earlier gaffe. Eldred was a good and just man and I am sorry for your loss."

Marcus acknowledged the condolence. "I sent a pair of men down to Chester to fetch the bishop. As soon as they return to Wrexton, he'll say the requiem."

"When will you leave here?"

"I'm unsure," Marcus replied. "Adam is badly wounded. I expect Lady Keelin will know when it's safe to move him."

"What of this woman?"

Marcus looked up.

"By her own admission, she is the cause of all this grief, is she not?"

Marcus could not deny Nicholas's words, but still, he did not see Keelin O'Shea as the party responsible for his father's death. She was as much a victim as any of them.

"'Tis clear she is in need of protection," Marcus said. "When Adam is able to be moved, Lady Keelin and her uncle will accompany us to Wrexton."

There was silence for a moment, then the marquis let out a bark of sarcastic laughter and gave Marcus a hearty slap on the back. "Ever the chivalrous knight, eh, Wrexton?"

The knights and noblemen of Marcus's acquaintance assumed that his refusal to use a woman for sport was due to a misplaced sense of honor. He'd been the brunt of many a jest over it, but had never seen fit to set them straight on the matter. He'd been dubbed "Marcus the Honorable," but in most instances, 'twas more a slur than a compliment.

Young Adam tossed and turned fitfully. Keelin tended the lad, and saw to her uncle's needs. She had no intention of telling Tiarnan about the Mageean mercenary who'd come back for her, nor did she mention the strange feelings that had come over her ever since the young Earl of Wrexton had entered her life. Her uncle had enough to do, just to get well.

Keelin saw that the men had put up several tents nearby, and they had a fire going. One of them was cooking, while Lord Wrexton stood tall, his golden hair nearly glowing in the firelight.

"Sir Henrie," Keelin heard Lord Marcus say, his voice sending a baffling tingle of warmth through her. "At first light, you and Thomas leave with Arthur Pratt. Return to Wrexton. Inform them—" Marcus paused "—tell all of my father's death. Have the steward begin preparations for his funeral."

Keelin watched as the young man took on the mantle of command, even as he girded himself against the pain of his grief. As she admired Marcus's determined competency, Keelin recalled the day her own father had been killed. With Eocaidh O'Shea's death, Ruairc Mageean had won the day, but Keelin's flight from Kerry with the holy spear had saved the clan.

Again, Keelin wished for the warmth and security of Carrauntoohil Keep, and the company of her people. She'd been away four long years, years during which she'd become a woman, and had little contact with anyone other than Uncle Tiarnan. They had kept to themselves while in England, going into towns or villages rarely, only to barter for the supplies they needed. And though Tiarnan was a wise and wonderful uncle, Keelin missed the camaraderie of young people. She needed to establish a life for herself, not as a niece or a runaway, but as a wife. A mother. Chatelaine of a household.

"What sort of man is he, Keelin?" Tiarnan said, his words breaking into Keelin's thoughts.

"Who, Uncle?"

"The young lord," he replied. "De Grant."

"Well, he's—" Keelin hesitated "—he's tall."

"Aye, I could tell that."

"And quiet, mostly," she added. "Though he's been out there givin' orders to his men since before the sun set."

"A good leader…"

"Aye, I suppose, though I doubt he's been tested," she said. "After all, his father, the earl before him, only passed away today."

"Still and all, lass, a man either has the qualities of a leader or not," Tiarnan said with finality. "What sort of looks has he?"

Keelin shivered, and quickly wrapped her arms about herself. Marcus de Grant had put her in mind of the childhood tales she'd heard of the fierce golden Vikings of old. Aye, his features were most pleasing, but his blush when she got too near, and the gentleness of his manner were most appealing. For all his size and obvious strength, Marcus de Grant was clearly not a cocky, overconfident male.

"Well? Would ye call him a handsome fellow?"

Keelin sighed. "I suppose ye could say so, Uncle Tiarnan."

"What do ye mean, lass? Either he is or he is not. There's no supposin' about it."

Before Keelin could give her uncle a more decisive answer, Adam spoke out.

"Marcus?" he cried weakly.

Keelin went to the bedside and sat down next to the

lad. "He's nearby, Adam," she said. "Do ye need somethin'?" she asked as she sponged his brow.

"Marcus..."

She glanced up at Sir Roger, then sent the knight in search of the earl.

Keelin O'Shea was hiding something. Marcus was as sure of that as he was of his own name. Yet, rather than pursuing his suspicions, he avoided going into her cottage.

His courage—and his miraculous ability to speak to a lovely woman—had disappeared after she'd left him earlier. He doubted he'd be able to put two coherent words together in her presence again. He just hoped Adam and the other wounded men would not need to remain overlong at her cottage. The quarters were too close and Marcus knew it would be impossible to avoid her forever.

He wished he knew what she had *not* told him. He believed her tale that the Mageean fighters were after her, but he was sure there was more to it than a mere family rivalry. What did Mageean want—that he'd go to the trouble of chasing after Keelin O'Shea for four years?

Lust was a definite possibility, Marcus thought, tamping down his own libidinous thoughts. Most assuredly, Keelin O'Shea was capable of inspiring a man to go to great lengths to have her.

But if that were the case, it made no sense for her to withhold that information. Any other woman would have explained the situation, then thrown herself on his mercy and asked for his protection from the predatory Mageean.

Unless Mageean was her betrothed, and she was running from—

"My lord," Sir Roger's voice pierced the darkness.

Marcus turned to face the young man.

"The lady sent me to fetch you," he said. "Young Adam is awake and asking for you."

"How is he?" Marcus asked gravely.

"Better than expected, my lord," the knight answered. "Though the Lady Keelin says he is in a great deal of pain and upset about your father."

Marcus lowered his head. What comfort could he offer the boy? Eldred was dead, and there was no changing that. No going back. At least Marcus had managed to pull the arrow from Adam's back, and had the help of Keelin O'Shea to deal with the wound afterward.

"'Twould be good for him to see you," Sir Roger nudged.

Marcus gave a quick nod and headed toward the cottage. He ducked under the lintel and stood still by the doorway watching Keelin O'Shea gently mop his cousin's brow with a wet cloth. Sitting on a stool next to the bed, she spoke softly to him as she ran the cloth over his forehead and cheeks, smoothing the boy's hair back. Adam seemed completely relaxed.

Marcus knew her touch would tie *him* into knots. Just the thought of those slender hands on his—

"Marcus!" Adam's young voice sounded harsh and strained.

Marcus moved away from the door and went to the boy. It seemed that all color was washed from Adam's face. The bandage on his back was thick and ominous. "You're awake," he said inanely, putting a gentle hand on his head.

"Sit here, m'lord," Keelin said, rising from the stool. She laid a hand on his arm before turning and stepping away, and Marcus nearly knocked over the stool with the shock of heat he felt from her skin.

"Marcus?" Adam asked. Marcus took his cousin's small hand in his. "Is your father...did Uncle Eldred d-die?"

Marcus nodded. "Yes," he breathed.

"It cannot be!" the boy protested feebly. "I loved him!"

"So did I, Adam," Marcus whispered. "So did I."

"When I think of it," Adam said, "I..." He swallowed. "It makes me want to weep."

"Then weep, lad," Marcus said quietly. "You'll feel better for it."

Adam closed his eyes and rested for a moment before speaking again. "Do *you* ever cry, Marcus?"

Keelin stayed by her uncle and tried to give their visitors the privacy the moment required, but it was no use. She could not help but hear the child's forthright questions and she strained to hear the knight's answer.

"Aye, Adam," he finally said, his strong voice wavering as he spoke. "I do."

Keelin resisted the urge to go to Lord Wrexton and wrap him in the peace and comfort of her arms. Earlier, she'd realized that he was ill at ease with her, and she did not wish to discomfit him any further. Yet her heart reached out to these two, whose lives had been shattered by the events of this day. Events caused by the enemies of her clan.

Uncle Tiarnan squeezed her hand and Keelin looked away. After a time, Marcus's faltering voice addressed her. "Lady Keelin, how long before Adam can travel?" he asked without turning away from the boy.

Keelin let go of her uncle's hand and approached the

child's bed. "Two days, m'lord," she said. "He shouldn't be moved for two days."

"How can you be so sure?"

Keelin shrugged. She just knew. "Two days' healin' time and he'll be able to ride for some miles on a soft pallet without breakin' open the wound."

The young lord shook his head. "Two days is a long time. If the barbarian army returns—"

"It won't, m'lord," Keelin said with certainty.

He looked up at her then, his eyes so light, so wary. Keelin sensed no immediate danger, but he had no reason to believe her, especially since the lone Celt had shown up, putting a lie to her earlier avowal that the Celts would never split up.

But Keelin had no intention of explaining her strange talent to Marcus. Being a Celt was enough reason for him to hate her. She would give no cause for him to suspect her of sorcery, too.

Marcus cleared his throat. "Then be ready to leave this place in two days," he said with a tone of command. "You and your uncle will travel with us to Wrexton."

"We'll be ready, m'lord," Keelin said, relieved. This was exactly what she'd hoped for. She could get Uncle Tiarnan settled within the safety of Wrexton's walls, then make the journey to Kerry herself. "How great a distance is it to Wrexton, m'lord?" she asked.

Marcus cleared his throat and backed away from Keelin as he spoke. "'Twould be only a few hours ride if we weren't slowed by the wounded, but now—"

A quiet, but urgent tap sounded on the cottage door. Sir Edward opened it to one of the Wrexton knights.

"My lord," the man said, doffing his helm. "Riders approach."

Keelin gasped and Lord Marcus stood immediately,

one strong, competent hand going for the sword at his side. "The men are ready?" he asked, with utter confidence. There was no faltering hesitation about him now.

"Aye, my lord," the knight replied, "for anything."

"Then let us see who approaches."

"Is it those warriors—coming back?" Adam asked fearfully after Lord Marcus had left.

Keelin went to him. "No, lad," she said, "at least I don't think so." She was sure she'd have sensed danger if any were upon them. Though she did not know who the riders were, she did not feel any threat. "Uncle?"

Tiarnan shook his head. "I've no idea, lass."

"Well, then," she said to Adam as she hugged her arms tightly around herself and sat down next to the boy, "we shall just have to await your cousin's return for news."

Chapter Three

Whoever the riders were, friend or foe, Marcus was glad of the reprieve. He doubted he'd have been able to remain with Lady Keelin a moment longer without some terrible blunder. As it was, he was merely lucky he hadn't trodden on her delicate feet, nor had he said anything inane.

At least he didn't think he had.

The riders hailed the house and approached, identifying themselves in the firelight. They were the last of Nicholas Hawken's men, those who'd been left to deal with the dead Celts. There was nothing new to report, so the knights of Wrexton and Kirkham alike settled down for the night, posting a guard over the bodies, and men to keep watch, leaving Marcus pacing restlessly at the perimeter of the camp.

'Twas his place to sit at Adam's bedside for the night, but he was loath to return to the close quarters of the cottage. Spending the night with Keelin O'Shea—

He blushed with the very thought, even though there was nothing in it.

Marcus cursed silently. He was earl now, and it was time he took control of his ridiculous shyness whenever he was near a woman. Somehow, he had managed to speak coherently to Keelin O'Shea today. He could do it again.

He *ought* to be able to do it again.

Marcus heard the quiet voices of the men in camp, the horses nickering, the fire crackling. The sky was black and without stars. Rain tomorrow, he thought, knowing he was putting off the inevitable.

Finally, he picked up his saddle pack, gathered up his blankets, and his courage, and headed for the cottage.

Keelin gave Adam a draught of her precious valerian, then sat at the young boy's bedside, watching over him as he drifted off to sleep. It was serene and peaceful in the little cottage, with her uncle's quiet snores brushing softly over the silence. She could hear men's voices outside, and knew there'd been no confrontation with the riders.

Marcus would soon return. She sensed no need to fear him, aware that he preferred to keep his distance from her. She did not blame him for despising her race—after all, her people were responsible for so many undeserved deaths that day. She only wished…well, at the very least, she wished he wouldn't shrink away from her so blatantly.

The sudden presence of Marcus de Grant made Keelin realize how very alone she'd felt these last few years. Sure, she'd had Uncle Tiarnan all along, but it wasn't the same as having her peers about. And it was not at all the same as having a man like Marcus de Grant.

Not that she had him, exactly. But Keelin had never felt so alive as she had when he'd held her in his arms.

To be sure, he'd carried her only because he was a man who understood chivalry, and she'd been as unsteady as a leaf in the autumn wind. Keelin knew she could expect nothing more from him than mere civility. Yet his very masculine touch, and his concern for her well-being touched something deep inside her, arousing feelings and sensations Keelin had never experienced before.

It made her yearn for something she could not have—or perhaps she would have it, she thought hopefully—once she returned to Ireland and learned what plans her father had made for her before his death.

In the flickering light from the hearth, Keelin unpacked her comb and a shawl. She loosened the laces of her kirtle, then slipped it off, keeping on a linen under-kirtle. Wrapping herself up in the thick woolen wrap, Keelin was satisfied that she was decently covered for the moment when Marcus de Grant returned.

For years, Keelin had managed to keep the ache of loneliness at bay but now it threatened to overwhelm her. She'd taken care of Tiarnan, moved them when the need arose, gathered food, bartered for goods in towns and villages, and kept as isolated as possible to avoid the Mageean mercenaries.

Never once had she allowed herself to think of what might have been, of the marriage her father had arranged for her, or the children she would already have borne. To think now of the years lost was too painful to bear.

She promised herself she would not succumb to tears now, not when her duty was so clear. She had Tiarnan and Adam to care for, and plans to make and packing to be done. There was no time to wallow in any foolish self-pity.

Marcus ducked to enter the cottage and found all was nearly as it had been when he'd left. The only difference was that now, he and Lady Keelin were essentially alone. No other knight guarded Adam, and the old uncle was asleep.

And the lady was missing a layer of clothes.

The scent of herbs filled the place, and the fire was warm. Lady Keelin looked soft and sleepy, with her dark hair flowing loosely about her shoulders. Her manner was subdued, quiet. There was an essential sadness about her that he had not marked before.

Marcus handed the blankets to her, fumbling awkwardly when their hands met.

"M'lord?" she whispered.

"You can make up a pallet by the fire," he explained, faltering when he looked into her deep-green eyes, thickly framed by dark lashes. "I—I'll sit up with Adam."

Keelin took the blankets. "All is well, then?" she asked softly. "The riders posed no threat?"

Marcus shook his head somberly, concerned about the suspicious brightness in Lady Keelin's eyes. Not tears, he hoped. "Just Kirkham's men returned from chasing Celts."

"And...did they find any?"

"I've been assured that we will encounter no more of your countrymen." Marcus sat down next to Adam's bed. He did not see Keelin wince at the word. "How's the lad?"

"I gave him a tonic t' help him sleep," she replied.

Marcus touched Adam's brow. "There is no fever."

Keelin agreed, but did not state what was obvious to both of them. Fever would come later. Discouraged, Marcus brushed Adam's hair from his forehead. Life was so fragile, he thought, as the enormity of his loss became more real than it had been all day. His father lay lifeless outside, beneath a shroud on the hard, cold earth. If he lost Adam, too...

No. Marcus could not bear to dwell on that possibility. The day had been full of too much pain already.

He ran one hand across his face, then looked up as Lady Keelin spread a blanket on the hard earthen floor. She sat down upon it, arranging her legs modestly beneath her, then took a comb and ran it through her long, dark tresses.

More than willing to be distracted from his dismal thoughts, Marcus sat mesmerized, watching as the stiff tines caressed her scalp, then crackled through the dark silk of her hair. He could practically feel her soft locks caress his skin, and his body tensed in reaction to the sensations conjured by his mind. She was fully covered, but in her long-sleeved undershift covered by a simple woolen shawl, Keelin O'Shea seemed all but naked.

Shocked by the direction of his thoughts, Marcus cleared the inexplicable thickening from his throat, and turned away. It would be well for him to consider his plans for the future rather than lusting after Keelin O'Shea.

In two days, they would return to Wrexton where Adam could recover in his own bed, with ''Cousin'' Isolda Coule and the other women of the castle to tend him. The Bishop of Chester would say Eldred's requiem, and the first of the de Grants would be laid to rest in the Wrexton crypt, for his father had inherited the earldom from Edmund Sandborn, a distant cousin.

Then somehow, life would go on. Winter would soon be upon them and—

''M'lord,'' Keelin's soft voice broke the silence.

He turned to see that she'd finished combing her hair

and was now struggling to untie the bandage at her throat.

"It seems to be knotted," she said in a low tone as she stood and walked over to Marcus. "It's chafin' somethin' fierce and I'd have it off if ye'll help me."

Marcus rose from his seat, aware that he ought to do more than nod his agreement, but she stood so close that his throat closed up. His hands burned, felt as though they were blistering even as he raised them to the cloth at her neck.

"I think some o' the threads must have unraveled," she said in a small voice as he finally touched her, "and tangled in the knot."

She was tall for a woman, the top of her head reaching as high as his nose, so he hardly had to bend to reach her. Marcus trained his attention fully on the knot, but could not avoid noticing a slight trembling in her chin. His fingers stilled and he ventured a look at her face, enthralled as she blinked one crystal tear from her eye.

She began to turn away to cover her tears, but Marcus cupped her chin and kept her from moving. The sense that she was just as vulnerable as he, was overwhelming. He rubbed a thumb over the errant tear, and drew his head down toward hers, unerringly seeking her lips, as if he were a well-practiced lover who had kissed a hundred maidens.

Their mouths met tentatively at first. Marcus kissed her softly, then pulled back slightly to allow a small space between their lips. Then the wondrous contact occurred again and Marcus deepened the kiss, enthralled by the amazing heat and sensual pleasure in this simple touching of mouths.

Yet it was anything but simple. Keelin made a sound, deep in her throat, and Marcus felt her hands slip up his chest, then around his neck, and into the long hair at his nape, causing an unparalleled torrent of sensations. He slid his arms around her and pulled her to him, crushing her breasts to his chest, sharing the chaos that was merely the wild beating of their hearts.

Every muscle clenched. Every bone turned to ash. Marcus wished there was no barrier between them, that he could feel her soft, warm flesh pulsing against his own. He could go on forever like this, tasting her, craving more. She was like a fever, raging in his blood, heating his flesh, burning his soul. He'd never experienced anything like it, nor—

He pulled his mouth away suddenly. This was insane! Adam lay here wounded, and there was Eldred...

Keelin.

She stood perplexed, looking into his eyes. Both remained silent for a long moment, then they both spoke at once.

"I apologize, my lady."

"M'lord, I—"

Then, except for Tiarnan's soft snores, there was silence again.

"Why do you weep?" Marcus asked when he'd regained a measure of control.

Keelin turned away shakily. "'Tis nothin', m'lord," she said casually, as if handsome young lords arrived at her door and kissed her senseless once a month. "Only the day, and the terrible things in it."

Marcus could still see the hurt in her eyes. And something more. Bewilderment? He was mightily bewildered himself, after sharing that kiss. It had been utterly intoxicating. Bewitching.

Her perfect skin was flushed with color now, and the

devastating sadness gone from her eyes. Now, her delicate brows arched with wonder.

Keelin's blood felt as though it were on fire. As she struggled to compose herself, she tried to understand Marcus's withdrawal, and his apology for kissing her. She did not know how he could be sorry for such a kiss, unless, by her inexperience, she had somehow made it unpleasant for him.

He did not look displeased, though, Keelin thought as she looked up at him. His chest moved as if he'd just run a race, and his eyes were still intent upon her. The touch of his lips had been entirely unexpected. Soft, yet firm and warm, too, as warm as the sun in midsummer.

His chest, when it was pressed against her, was so very different from her own soft form, that it had pleased her beyond anything she'd ever known, and shaken her senses as thoroughly as any vision she'd ever had. Marcus de Grant was truly the most fascinating man she'd ever encountered, in England or Ireland. She could fasten her attention on his fine features for all eternity.

But as Keelin stood gazing at Marcus, her vision began to cloud. She blinked her eyes rapidly, and gave a quick shake of her head, but the haziness only increased. With utter dismay, Keelin realized the sensations were the same as those she experienced when a vision was upon her. She bit back a cry and backed away from Marcus, struggling to regain her proper senses—her senses of *this* world, not the misty, unreality of her intuition.

'Twas no use. Instead of Marcus's handsome face before her eyes, she saw her cousin's, the fierce and deadly Cormac O'Shea, chieftain of Clann Ui Sheaghda. And though Keelin could still dimly discern the walls of her snug English cottage and the meager furniture within, the gray skies of Kerry began to show more clearly than her true surroundings. Marcus's comely face began to fade from her vision....

She heard the clang of steel meeting steel, and knew she was witnessing a battle, though whether past or future, she could not say. She watched as Cormac fought ferociously against his opponent, his formidable muscles bulging with every strike of his blade. He lunged and strained, ducked and spun, but his enemy soon gained the advantage and knocked Cormac to the muddy ground.

"No," she whispered, trembling. The little cottage was gone from her sight now, only the landscape around Carrauntoohil Keep remained. The smell of blood was thick and there were mournful wails to be heard. Black smoke billowed from the huts in the village, and choked Keelin's lungs.

Cormac was violently disarmed. Keelin heard a satisfied grunt, then watched as a shiny steel blade pierced through Cormac's leather-clad chest, killing him instantly.

Keelin shrank from the sight of Cormac's murder, but could not shut out the images, the sounds, the smells. She'd have run far away if her feet would have carried her, but they were rooted to the ground where she stood.

Two powerful hands grasped the hilt of the killing sword. One strong leg moved, and a booted foot stepped on Cormac's lifeless chest as the sword was yanked out.

Then Keelin heard a Gaelic shout of victory, and saw the face of the man who'd shouted, the one who held the bloody sword high above his head.

'Twas Ruairc Mageean.

Chapter Four

Marcus caught Lady Keelin as she fell, and carried her to the blanket on the floor. Unconscious now, she continued to shake violently, as if she had fever and chills combined. Marcus covered her with one of the blankets.

He did not understand what was wrong. One moment, they were both standing stunned by their kiss, the next, her eyes were wide, and dilated to black, and she was trembling and whimpering. He was not so naive to think it had been his kiss that had affected her so, but he could not imagine what had come over her.

He frowned as he shook her gently, and rubbed her hands to revive her, but his efforts changed nothing. She was deeply unconscious. And the longer she stayed that way, he felt the worse it would be for her.

Seeing no alternative, Marcus reluctantly arose and stepped to the bedside of her uncle. Quickly, he roused the older man from a deep sleep.

''What is it? Keely?'' Tiarnan asked groggily. ''Are ye—''

''Wake up, old man,'' Marcus said, keeping his voice down. ''Something came over Keelin a while ago. She was fine one moment, and the next...''

"The next?" the man prodded, frowning with worry.

"I don't know," Marcus replied. "Her eyes went black and she stood there, staring...."

Tiarnan coughed fitfully, then struggled to a sitting position, holding his chest all the while. "Did she start tremblin' and whimperin'?"

Marcus nodded, thanking heaven that the man seemed to recognize what had happened, though he did not care much for the look of concern on Tiarnan's face. "She did."

"Ach, no. 'Tis too soon for another one," he muttered dejectedly to himself. "'Twas a vision she was havin'," the old man said to Marcus. "Was she holdin' the spear, or just—"

"What spear?" Marcus asked, frustrated by the old man's riddles. Beautiful Keelin was lying near death, and her uncle could only ask foolish—

"Oh, saints, 'twas straight from Keelin herself, then. And the power of it knocked her flat?"

"The power of *what?*" Marcus asked frantically, glancing back at Keelin's trembling form under the blanket. "I don't understand, O'Shea."

"Nay, ye wouldn't, lad," Tiarnan replied, shivering. "'Tis cold tonight. Best ye wrap the lass up in blankets, then hold her close and give her some o' yer own heat. And I'll be explainin' as well as I can."

More than happy to comply with the man's instructions, Marcus wedged his big body down between Keelin and the wall, then pulled her up into his arms and wrapped her snugly in the blankets. Her color was deathly pale and she felt cold as a wintry night. It was difficult for Marcus to fathom that this was the same hot, vibrant body he'd held only a few minutes before. "Speak, then, O'Shea. Tell me what ails her."

Tiarnan succumbed to another coughing fit, so it was a few moments before he was able to begin his tale. Finally, though, he cleared his throat and spoke while Marcus sat holding Keelin, sharing his warmth.

"The lass has a 'gift,' ye might say," Tiarnan said, "though she doesn't quite see it that way."

"What gift? Speak plainly, old man!"

"'Tis the sight," Tiarnan explained. "Ever since she was a tiny lass, she's been able to see what others cannot. In my clan, it's called the 'second sight.' Here in England, ye may call it by another name.

"But whatever words ye use for it, Keelin has a powerful intuition that tells her of things that are to come. And when she touches *Ga Buidhe an Lamhaigh*, the power increases beyond anything ye, or even *I* could understand."

"What's this *Ga Buidhe*—"

"*Ga Buidhe an Lamhaigh* is our clan's sacred spear. Many years ago—even before Saint Patrick trod on Irish turf—'twas given to an ancient O'Shea chieftain by Diarmaid, consort of the sun goddess. And don't ye be thinkin' 'tis a pagan thing. 'Twas blessed by Saint Bridget herself when Cathair Sheaghda was but a lad."

"Enough childish fairy tales, O'Shea," Marcus said, annoyed and frustrated that the man would not get to the point. "What ails Lady Keelin? How can I help her?"

"Ach, there's nothin' ye can do, but keep her warm now, and hear the tale so ye'll understand what's come over her."

"Get on with it then, and be clear about it."

"Keelin has always been able to see and know of events before they ever happen," Tiarnan said. "Just like her mother, she is. She 'sees' danger comin'—

whatever it may be—and gets us quickly out of harm's way.''

''Do you mean to say that Lady Keelin is be-witched?''

''Nay, lad,'' Tiarnan said with aggravation. '''Tis not bewitchment at all! The lass is *blessed!*''

Marcus looked down at Keelin's deathly still features. *Cursed* was more like it, though he had no wish to be-lieve her soul possessed by the devil.

Yet she had certainly bewitched *him*. Suddenly, he realized why he had been able to speak to Keelin, touch her, *kiss* her, when in all his previous twenty-six years, he'd hardly been able to look at a young woman without tripping over himself to escape her presence.

'''Tis a rare gift, one that Keelin's mother possessed before her, and *her* mother, and on from ancient times.''

Marcus had never heard such a far-fetched tale. Yet he knew there were strange things in the world, things he had not personally experienced. There could very well be an ancient, magical spear that possessed some unexplained power, a power that Keelin somehow used.

He pulled Keelin closer into his embrace, as if to pro-tect her from further harm. She was not as cold now, but her body was trembling. Tight coils of desire wrapped around him even now, as she lay unconscious in his arms.

Was it witchery? Or a blessing, as her uncle had said.

Marcus could see nothing but innocence now in Kee-lin's delicate features, feel only vulnerability in her soft form as he cradled her under the blankets.

''She must have seen something momentous,'' Tiar-nan mused.

''Why do you say that?''

''Well…'tis not so easy a thing to explain,'' the old

man said. He rubbed his chin and chewed his lower lip. "In all the years since Keelin's been me own true responsibility, only twice before has she been benumbed by a vision she's seen without the aid of *Ga Buidhe an Lamhaigh.*"

"Benumbed?"

"Aye," Tiarnan replied. "Made senseless. As ye see her now."

Marcus nodded as he shifted Keelin in his arms.

"The first time was when the lass was a mere child," he said, "and her brother was drowned."

Marcus cringed. "What happened?"

"Aw, it pains me fiercely to recall the day when Brian O'Shea died," Tiarnan said. "'Twas early spring. As elegant a day as we'd seen in many a week, with the sun burnin' high and new greenery shootin' up all around. Keely and I were within the walls Carrauntoohil Keep, with me at me work, and the lass playin' with her rag babe.

"Most of the able-bodied men went out to hunt early that day, and the lads were left with more time than sense. They left Carrauntoohil and went to the river, swollen by then with the spring floods, and rushing faster than any of them realized."

Marcus listened as Tiarnan O'Shea described the sudden pallor that had come over Keelin, then the violent shaking and unintelligible speech. Then the girl had lost consciousness, only to weep uncontrollably when she was finally roused.

"She'd seen Brian's death," Tiarnan said. "The vision had come upon her without warning, without so much as a touch of the spear."

"And this had never happened before?"

"Nay," the man said. "Not even to her mother. But

Keelin's gift is strong. None before her ever had the same clarity of visions that Keelin experiences.

''She saw as clearly as the lads who were there—poor Brian as he fell from the boat, tumbling into the rocky passage....''

Marcus was appalled at the thought of the child Keelin witnessing such a thing, but Tiarnan went on.

'''Twas death again that took hold of her...when her father, Eocaidh, was slain by Ruairc Mageean.''

''And you believe it's happened again? That she's seen another death?''

''Aye,'' Tiarnan replied. ''Without touchin' the spear, the lass senses things. She has premonitions. But when she actually holds it in her hands, there are visions. Colorful. Vivid.''

Marcus made no reply. He gazed down at the limp figure in his arms and tried to imagine how Satan could possibly do his evil work through Keelin and her visions. No answer came to him.

''If ye would be so good as to keep her warm, lad,'' Tiarnan said, ''just till the worst of it passes...''

Marcus had plenty of heat to spare. He glanced up at Adam, who lay still in the bed, and then slid down to make himself more comfortable with Keelin. He enveloped her in a cocoon of warmth, and waited.

Keelin regained full consciousness at dawn. She'd had moments of awareness through the night, when Lord Marcus rubbed her back and her shoulders and whispered quiet, soothing words to her, but she had been unable to respond.

Her mind was still muddled, and she could not piece together all of the events of the previous day, nor did she know how she'd come to be resting in the arms of Marcus de Grant.

He still held her close, though Keelin believed he dozed. His chest, pressed against her own, moved deeply and regularly. His strong arms still embraced her, though loosely, and Keelin, fully aware now, relished the feeling of security they brought.

Her face was eye level with the hollow where his neck met his chest, and the small hairs of his chest tickled her nose. Without thinking, Keelin burrowed her face in.

"Umm..." Marcus grunted. His arms tightened around her.

Keelin shivered, not from cold, but from an altogether strange sensation, unlike anything she'd ever experienced before. Oddly compelled, she moved against him, eliciting another groan. Marcus's muscles flexed against her, and one of his hands made circles on her back, pulling her closer to him. She knew he was not quite awake as she breathed in the scent of him. The smell of fresh river water, his chain hauberk, his linen, and something altogether different...something that was distinctly...Marcus.

Her body felt every inch of his where they touched, and she had the inexplicable urge to taste him. Her mouth was a mere breath away from his chest and she could easily—

Shocked by her own wanton whimsy, Keelin would never be so bold as to attempt such a thing. No matter how strong the impulse.

She sensed the moment when he came fully awake. His body tensed and he pulled slightly away from her.

"Ah, you're awake, then?" he said awkwardly, clearing his throat as he spoke.

Keelin nodded. It was still unclear how she'd come to

be lying among these thick woolen blankets in Marcus de Grant's arms. She remembered parts of the previous evening, Marcus's hands working on the knot at her neck—his kiss, and the way her bones had seemed to melt....

Cormac!

Oh, dear God and all the saints, she suddenly remembered. Cormac O'Shea was slain! And the deed was done by Ruairc Mageean.

Keelin pushed herself up from their cozy nest and became dizzy with the sudden movement. She went back down on her knees.

"Easy," Marcus said as he helped to lower her down.

"Keely lass?" Tiarnan questioned from his bed.

"Aye, Uncle," she replied. She kept her head down. She could not bear to look up at Marcus and see the revulsion she knew he must feel. She remembered clearly now. He'd kissed her, and then she'd "gone to black" on him. What must he think of her?

"How are ye, now?" Tiarnan asked, propping himself up on one elbow and facing her as if he could see her.

"I'm all right, Uncle Tiarnan," she answered as she moved to stand again. "The lad...is he...?"

"Still sleeping," Marcus replied. "I checked him not long ago."

"No bleedin' from the wound?" Keelin asked, finally looking up at him. She did not see revulsion, but that could mean only one thing. That he had a rare gift for hiding his emotions.

"No," Marcus replied to her question. "And there's no fever yet, either. Whatever you gave him made him sleep soundly."

"'Tis a blessing indeed," Tiarnan interjected while Keelin studied Marcus surreptitiously.

She recalled how he pulled away from her as soon as he'd awakened, and knew how he must feel, having been forced to spend the night sharing his heat with an aberrant woman of questionable sanity. No man outside Clann Ui Sheaghda could possibly understand the "gift" that was passed from mother to daughter in her family for generations.

Keelin stepped away from Marcus and went to Adam's bedside. She knew that Tiarnan was anxious to know what she'd seen, but the vision was still too raw to speak of those things. She would talk to him later, after her heart and mind settled down.

She lit a tallow candle and listened. Adam's breathing was soft. There was no unhealthy sound or irregularity to it. His forehead was not hot when she touched it, but seemed to be of normal temperature. She pulled the blanket down and peeled the dressing away from the wound. It looked just as it had the day before.

As Keelin made a new paste of lady's mantle and spread it over the wound, she heard sounds of the men outside rousing themselves. There were wounded men out there, too, she remembered, men whose injuries she should tend.

After viewing Adam's wound, and seeing that all was well in hand, Marcus let himself out of the cottage and went out to the area where the men were camped. No changes there, so he went on to the river where he sat down with his back against an ancient willow.

He felt shaky this morn. 'Twas not so much from lack of sleep, but from hours of lying thigh to thigh, and breast to chest with Keelin O'Shea. The most alluring woman he'd ever met, she was the only one he'd ever slept with—and 'twas a far more intimate experience than the one shared with a harlot years before when he was with King Henry's army in France.

They'd been camped at Troyes, just before King Henry signed the treaty that should have brought peace to the two countries. Marcus and all the rest of the English knights were jubilant. Victory was theirs. Henry would wed the daughter of the French king, and be made king of France upon Charles's death.

The wine flowed, and women made their way into the victors' camp. Marcus drank more than he ever had before, and more than he had since. And, he allowed himself to be seduced by a woman who wanted his coin.

Marcus had not been entirely naive. He'd spent a whole night learning what a woman expected of a lover, from a cocotte who did not particularly care for him, nor he for her. Though he had experienced a great deal of physical pleasure, he'd gone away with an intense emptiness inside. He had chosen not to share himself so cheaply again.

Until Keelin O'Shea, not that any sort of conjugal sharing with the Lady Keelin would be a cheap affair.

Chapter Five

Marcus sat at the river's edge. He washed and shaved, just as he'd done every other morning of his adult life. But today there was a significant difference. Now, he was Earl of Wrexton. Eldred was dead.

A new wave of anguish swept over him. His father had always been solid as one of the ramparts of Wrexton Castle. Eldred and Marcus had been as close as a pair of friends, yet Eldred had clearly been Marcus's mentor. They'd worked together to repair Wrexton—the castle as well as the estate—after the death of the last earl. They'd wrought wonderful changes and Wrexton was more prosperous than ever before.

Yet the holding had just lost its true master.

Marcus dropped his head into his hands and allowed the sorrow to flow through his soul. If only Adam hadn't been injured as well, he thought, then this grief would not be quite so hard to bear. As it was, he did not know if Adam would survive. He did not know when he'd be able to return to Wrexton. Nor did he know if he would ever wear the mantle of earl as well as his father had done.

A soft footfall interrupted Marcus's dismal thoughts.

He got to his feet and turned to see Nicholas Hawken approaching on the path.

"'Twas a quiet night," the marquis said.

It had been anything *but* quiet, but Marcus said nothing of the way he'd passed the hours. He still didn't know what to make of it himself. Besides all else that troubled him, his blood still burned for the woman whose body had been pressed so close to his through the night, but he dared not pursue that chain of thought.

The two men walked together, surveying the area for signs of intruders. Celtic prowlers.

"There doesn't appear to be anyone lurking about," Marcus finally said. "No signs of a fire, no tracks."

"My men must have gotten all of those rotters," he said. "All but the one who doubled back here yesterday."

Marcus shrugged. 'Twas often how it went in battle. Amid the confusion of battle, one man could slip away with ease. Certainly that was how the lone Celt had managed to elude Hawken's men.

A chill wind blasted through the trees. Marcus glanced up and saw heavy low clouds in the distant sky. 'Twould begin raining soon. Perhaps a freezing rain, for it had turned so much colder during the night.

Talk around Wrexton town was that they were in for a particularly harsh winter. 'Twas the reason Eldred had gotten his party on the road so soon after the wedding at Haverston Castle, rather than staying for the lengthy festivities planned by Lord Haverston. Eldred dreaded getting caught away from home in an early storm.

Eyeing the ominous clouds above him, Marcus wondered how long the poor weather would last and whether or not it would interfere with their return to Wrexton.

''Marcus,'' Hawken said. He bent his head and folded his hands behind his back as he spoke. ''My men and I will be heading back to Kirkham today. We can easily go by way of Wrexton. I would be honored to carry your father...and the others...home if you wish.''

Marcus was astonished by Nicholas's offer. The man was usually rude and crass, with little consideration of aught but his own amusement. Yet Marcus knew the man was plagued by his own inner demons which drove him to excesses.

His offer was well-timed. Marcus realized it might not be possible for him to escort his father's body as he'd intended. Better, perhaps, to get Eldred transported within Wrexton's walls and go on with the solemn requiem even if Marcus became waylaid.

''I appreciate your offer, Nicholas,'' Marcus said. ''Perhaps 'twould be better if you carried my father home.''

Nicholas glanced at the sky and Marcus could read the other man's thoughts. He'd have to hurry in order to stay ahead of the storm.

The two men walked back to the riverbank where Marcus had left his leather pack, and found two of his men gathering reeds and rushes in large burlap bags.

''What are you two about?'' Nicholas asked.

''Lady Keelin bade us collect stuffing to make pallets for the wounded men,'' one of the men replied.

''She said it's too cold and damp for them to remain in tents,'' the other said, ''and she'd rather have them indoors where it's warm and dry, where she can tend them.''

Nicholas but raised an eyebrow, then headed up the path to where his men were camped.

* * *

"Move his bed here," Lady Keelin said to the men who'd come in to help rearrange the cottage. The weather had turned cold, and a piercing rain had begun to fall, so she'd made up pallets for the two wounded Wrexton men and had them brought inside where they'd be warm and relatively comfortable.

She had not seen Lord Marcus since he'd left the cottage much earlier, nor had she spoken yet to Tiarnan about the devastating sights she'd seen the previous night.

She sighed. He would not allow her to avoid him forever.

While organizing the cottage so there'd be room for the men, she pondered her moments under the blankets with Lord Marcus, dwelling on the strange sensations caused by his close proximity, by his scent and by the touch of his big hands stroking her back. She'd never experienced anything so exhilarating, and at the same time, confusing.

She was strongly attracted to the young man, but Keelin knew her destiny was in Ireland. Not only was she betrothed to the man her father had chosen for her in Kerry, but after seeing Cormac's fate in the vision, Keelin knew she had no choice but to return to Carrauntoohil. Whoever became chieftain would have desperate need of *Ga Buidhe an Lamhaigh,* in order to prevail over Mageean.

Keelin renewed her vow to see Tiarnan settled at Wrexton Castle, then somehow get herself across the Irish Sea before the snows began. She would ignore the confusing feelings and sensations that coursed through her whenever Marcus de Grant was near.

'Twas time to return home to see what could be done about Mageean.

* * *

The cottage should have smelled like an infirmary.

Instead, the pleasing aroma of herbs and spices met Marcus's nose as he entered the hut. A kettle of stew simmered over the fire, and men slept on soft, stuffed pallets near the hearth.

Old Tiarnan was awake and propped up somehow, and Keelin sat next to Adam, speaking quietly to the boy.

She wore the green kirtle again, laced tightly against a narrow waist and full, high breasts. The linen under-kirtle, with which Marcus was so familiar by now, was visible above the low neck of the green wool, and her fine white skin showed above that. Delicate bones slashed across both sides of her shoulders. She was exquisite.

''Oh, aye,'' Keelin said, after halting a moment when Marcus entered, '''twill be a mighty warrior's scar. And if ever yer tunic's raised, all who see your back will know you've seen battle.''

''Who is come?'' Adam asked weakly.

'''Tis Lord Marcus,'' Keelin replied, ''come to see how ye fare.''

''How *do* you fare, lad?''

''Lady Keelin says I am perfect, Marcus,'' Adam replied weakly. ''She said I am stronger and braver than any lad in Carrauntoohil—that's her village in Ireland.''

''I daresay the lady is correct,'' Marcus replied. ''Though I don't know the lads of…Carrauntoohil.''

''Lady Keelin told me that the Marquis Kirkham took Uncle Eldred to Wrexton.''

Marcus nodded as he put his hand on Adam's forehead. The boy was hotter than before. He looked over at Keelin, who nodded slightly. Fever.

"Will we go to Wrexton for the requiem?" Adam asked.

"We'll try, Adam," Marcus replied. "For now, just concentrate on getting well."

The boy acquiesced and lay quietly as Lady Keelin got up and went to the hearth. Here, she picked up a long wooden spoon and stirred the steaming contents of the cookpot. "How many of your men are left here, m'lord?" Keelin asked quietly.

Marcus stifled a yawn. The last twenty-four hours had taken their toll. When Nicholas Hawken left, he'd taken most of the Wrexton men with him. Marcus and the remaining men made a thorough search of the surrounding area, making certain that no enemies or other intruders were near. "Four, in addition to these men," he replied, indicating the two on pallets near the fire. "They're keeping watch."

"You must be weary, m'lord," Keelin said, "after the night ye had. There's room enough for ye to stretch out your blankets here and rest awhile."

Marcus blushed at the mention of the night he'd had. He thought there was a brighter tinge of pink on Lady Keelin's face, too, and wondered what she thought of the whole incident. He hadn't heard any description of the vision she'd seen before her collapse, nor had either of them discussed the fact that they'd spent the night entwined in each other's arms. As though by *not* speaking of it, it hadn't happened.

There was, however, no doubt in Marcus's mind that it had very much happened.

He took a pair of blankets from the table and settled himself down by Adam's bed. Too weary to think any more on it, he fell quickly asleep.

"Keely lass," Tiarnan said, "sit yerself down half a minute and have a talk with yer old uncle."

Keelin glanced around the cottage and saw that everyone except Tiarnan was dozing. She could put it off no longer. She pulled a stool up next to Tiarnan's bed and told him all she'd seen when the vision overtook her.

Marcus opened his eyes to the sound of a fierce wind lashing around the cottage. Surprisingly, it remained snug and warm inside. He sat up, wondering how long he'd slept. The men outside needed to be relieved of their watch and a chance to come in and warm themselves.

He watched as Lady Keelin knelt beside one of the knights and wrapped a clean length of cloth around his shoulder wound. She spoke quietly to him, reassuring the man that the wound was clean and he'd not lose the arm to putrefaction. She was gentle and kind with the knight, and fully aware of his worries. She bolstered his spirits with her smiles and kind words.

Then she turned to the other fellow who lay in front of the fire and wiped his brow with a cloth from the water bowl next to him. Her kirtle molded to her breasts as she moved, and Marcus could practically feel her long, graceful fingers as they moved along the knight's skin.

His mouth went dry.

Keelin leaned over to wet the cloth again, and stopped short. Her body jerked suddenly, as if she'd been hit from behind. Then her eyes darkened, and she knelt unmoving, her attention concentrated on some unseen thing.

An instant later, she was in motion again. She got up from her knees and began to rearrange things, making more free space before the fire. Then she helped one of the wounded men to shift one side.

"What is it, Lady Keelin?" the fellow asked.

"Oh, 'tis nothin'," she said. "Just makin' a wee bit more room for...for..."

Marcus cleared his throat just then, and got to his feet.

"Oh, Lord Marcus," Keelin said, stepping carefully through the cottage to reach him. She put one hand on his arm. "I'm afraid there's to be more bad news...." She spoke so quietly that the other occupants of the cottage would not hear.

He looked at her skeptically.

"One of yer men has been thrown from his horse," she said, her brow furrowing with concentration. "He's hurt...I'm not sure...I think he's..." She shook her head. "Two men are carryin' him even now toward the cottage. They could use more help—"

Suddenly, voices were audible outside the cottage and Marcus turned and pulled open the door. Just as Keelin had said, Sir Edward was being carried between two men, his left leg hanging limp between them.

A shudder ran through Marcus that had nothing at all to do with the frigid air and freezing rain that blew inside. He turned and gazed at Keelin with perplexed, narrowed eyes.

"Here," Keelin said, quickly turning away from the look Marcus gave her. She felt as if she'd been struck. "Put him down here near the fire."

The injured man groaned with pain as the two knights eased him down to the floor by the fire. "His horse slipped, my lord," one of the knights explained. "The ground is icy in spots and with the rain coming down in sheets it's difficult to see."

"His leg's broken," the other knight said.

Marcus used his knife to cut away the man's hose and occupied himself looking at the leg while Keelin mixed one of her powders into water. How could she have known? It was impossible, yet he had not imagined the way she'd been *physically* struck by the premonition. Nor could he forget the words she'd said just before the three men had come into the cottage.

Keelin took the mug to Edward and held it to his lips, helping him drink. "'Tis but a wee bit of valerian to ease the pain and help ye to relax while the bone is set," she said. "'Twill make it easier. On all of us."

She helped him to lie back, then knelt opposite Marcus. "We'll be needin' two splints," she said to the men. "There's wood behind the cottage near the mule wain," she added. "Somethin' back there's bound to work."

Sir Edward groaned when Keelin ran her hands along his leg. To Marcus, she seemed to have the gentlest touch, though his mind was still spinning with what he'd just witnessed. How could he trust *anything* he saw or heard anymore?

"Have ye any leather strips, m'lord?" she asked, looking up at him.

Marcus gathered his wits and replied in the affirmative.

With help, Keelin had set Edward's leg. Then she managed to get him to eat some of the hot stew. The other men would remain inside now, even though it was close quarters. There would be no intruders on the prowl in this weather, no good reason to keep men out in the cold and wet.

Marcus had to get out, though, to get some air. He needed to gain some distance between himself and Keelin O'Shea. He pulled a warm woolen tunic over his linen shirt, and quickly dug his cloak out of his pack.

"Marcus?" Adam asked.

"Yes, Adam," Marcus replied, ashamed that he'd considered skulking out without speaking to the boy who had been awakened by Edward's groans of pain.

"Where are you going?"

He bent toward the boy. "I'm just—just going outside to have a look around. To see that the horses are secure." He patted the boy's head and let himself out.

The Wrexton knights had extended the mule's shelter with canvas from their tents, and the horses were tethered there, out of the worst of the rain.

There'd been no signs of interlopers, and Marcus thought it unlikely that the Celts would be wild enough to attempt travel in this weather. Even the animals of the forest sought shelter when it was this foul.

Marcus trained his thoughts on "normal" things. The horses, the weather, the provisions. He hoped Nicholas Hawken managed to stay ahead of the storm. He wondered if the bishop of Chester had left for Wrexton yet, or if the storm had held him up.

Mayhap he should ask Lady Keelin.

Damnation!

He could not avoid thinking of it any longer. What Tiarnan had said about Keelin's uncanny ability was true. She had premonitions, and they were accurate.

What sorcery was this? Or was it sorcery at all? Could Keelin's power be a blessing, as Tiarnan had claimed? Was it a gift from God, or was she cursed?

Marcus had seen nothing to indicate bedevilment. Nothing in any of Keelin's actions smacked of witchery. She had been caring and kind with Adam and the wounded men, then had gone so far as to make the sign of the cross before attempting to set Edward's leg bone. Would a woman who was an instrument of the devil do such a thing?

Marcus did not know what to think.

One thing was certain. His reaction to her was anything but commonplace. She had somehow managed to enthrall him quickly and completely. But how had she done this, if not by sorcery? Why was he unable to remember the faces of any of the young women at the wedding he'd just attended? Surely his memory was not so poor that he'd forget them in the course of a day. And how had she contrived to make it possible for him to speak to her without stammering? To touch her? Kiss her, even, and hold her body close to his through the night?

He still felt her presence acutely—a few minutes ago, he'd felt as if he were smothering in the close quarters of the cottage. He'd had to get out of there, to get away from her.

Marcus disliked the idea of bewitchment, but there was no reasonable, rational explanation for his wild attraction to the lovely black-haired lady who, even now, carefully tended his men's ills.

"Ye realize, of course," Tiarnan said, "I won't be goin' back with ye."

"Back? To Ireland?" Keelin asked as she spooned more stew into her uncle's bowl. Lord Marcus's men lined the floor, wrapped in blankets. Some were dozing, some sleeping deeply. Snoring. Keelin kept glancing toward the door, expecting Marcus to come through at any time.

Expecting to see disgust and distrust in his eyes.

"Aye," he replied. "Even the distance to Wrexton Castle may be too far for an old wreck like me."

"There'll be no more talk of leavin' ye behind, Uncle."

"Keely lass, ye must be reasonable about—"

"Nay," she said. "There's nothin' reasonable about leavin' ye here alone to fend for yourself."

"Keelin—"

"Besides, I've a feelin' about Wrexton. And you."

"Oh?" Tiarnan asked, curious about Keelin's "feeling."

"'Tis only an inklin', mind you," Keelin said, her eyes losing their focus and turning inward, "but I see contentment for ye at Wrexton. A lovely, wee garden...with a stone bench. Sunshine...and you, Uncle. Ye're sittin' on that bench and it's springtime. All the green things are the tiniest shoots...."

Tiarnan lay back and closed his eyes on the vision Keelin presented him. 'Twas enough to give him the hope he needed to go on.

Night fell, and Marcus de Grant did not return. Keelin wrapped up in a blanket and made herself comfortable against the wall near Adam's bed, in case he should need her. She was weary after a long day of tending the wounded and injured men, but unable to sleep.

Marcus did not return until well into the night. Rather than having to withstand his scorn once again, Keelin feigned sleep, keeping her breathing steady and even so that he would not discover her wakeful state. She watched as he pulled off his sodden cloak and hung it on a peg by the fire. Keelin knew his tunic had to be wet, too, but Marcus left it on as he stepped back to Adam's pallet and checked on the boy.

Apparently satisfied to find Adam sleeping soundly

and his fever no worse, Marcus removed his woolen tunic and the linen he wore underneath. He took a cloth from his pack, then made his way through the men to stand by the fire, drying himself.

Keelin watched as Lord Marcus bent over the kettle that hung in the fireplace, then found a bowl and spoon, and ladled a serving of the stew that still simmered there. He pulled on a dry tunic, then crouched near the fire to eat.

To Keelin, he appeared as weary as she felt.

This is how it would be when she had her own husband, she thought. Her man would return late from his labors and find the food she'd left him. He would eat, then remove his clothes and crawl into bed with her. The movement of the bed, and mayhap the heat of his body, would wake her. Perchance he would even rouse her with a gentle touch, and then...

Would it be as wondrous as the feelings Marcus had roused in her the night before? Could the touch of *any* man kindle the wild sensations he'd wrought in her? This, Keelin would soon discover, for when she returned to Kerry, she had no doubt she would wed the man her father chose for her.

Tiarnan had always insisted he knew nothing of her intended bridegroom. Keelin suspected that was not quite true, but no amount of pestering had gotten her an answer to her query. She was still as ignorant as ever about the man her father intended for her.

There were several prosperous men around Carrauntoohil—any one of whom would be a suitable husband, Keelin thought. Though she could not imagine the caresses of any of them, she trusted that her father had chosen the best man for her. After all, the daughter of a mighty chieftain could not wed for love or mere attraction. 'Twas her duty to strengthen the clan, especially now that Cormac was dead.

Keelin wondered how her clan would survive now. Her vision had not shown her whether Mageean had taken over Carrauntoohil Keep, or if the Sheaghda clan had held him off.

Keelin sighed with frustration. For all that she'd seen in her vision the previous night, it had not been nearly enough. She could not keep from dwelling on Cormac's death, and the questions regarding the fate of her clan. If only she could get back to Kerry now, and return *Ga Buidhe an Lamhaigh* to her people, then Clann Ui Sheaghda might have a chance of withstanding another attack by Mageean.

Keelin knew her wish was unrealistic. She had to force herself to be patient. She did not know when they would leave for Wrexton, or how soon thereafter she'd be able to leave Tiarnan. No matter how desperately she strained to "see," she could not force a vision. It had never worked that way.

Chapter Six

'Twas four days before the weather permitted Marcus and his entourage to leave Keelin O'Shea's cottage in the woods.

In many ways, Marcus felt he'd miss the little house. It had been warm and snug against the cold, and the sharing of close quarters with his men would come to an end once they reached Wrexton Castle.

So would his proximity to Keelin O'Shea.

He had tried to keep his eyes off her, to keep his mind from returning to those moments when he'd held her. But countless times he found himself following her graceful movements as she cared for Adam and the men. More than once, she caught him watching her, and her lovely green eyes held his.

Heat permeated Marcus's body in those moments and it was all he could do to keep from taking her outside to find a bit of privacy where he could mold his body to hers, and explore her mouth again with his own lips, his teeth and tongue.

Luckily for them both, the frigid rain never abated.

On the fourth morning, when the sun finally broke through, Marcus decided it was their best opportunity to try to get to Wrexton. Normally, it would be only about a two-hour ride. But with the mule-wain and the wounded men, they'd be lucky to make it in four.

Lady Keelin packed her herbs into the trunk that held her belongings, and one of the men tied it to the back of the wain. She packed nothing that resembled a spear, though Marcus could not imagine Keelin leaving behind something so precious to her.

It was there somewhere.

"M'lord, will ye carry Adam to the wain?" Keelin asked when all was ready.

Marcus carefully lifted Adam from the pallet where he'd lain these past four days and carried the boy to the mule-wain. He knew it would be a rough ride, but Keelin had done all that was possible to make it comfortable for the injured child.

"Do you think we'll be back for Uncle Eldred's funeral?" Adam asked. Keelin had given him a draught of something that would make him drowsy throughout the ride, but he was still awake.

Marcus hugged the boy closer as he carried him. "I don't know," he said. "I sent Sir Roger on to Wrexton to tell them our plans. If the funeral has not yet been said, the bishop will await our arrival."

Marcus placed the boy carefully into the wain alongside Tiarnan. The other wounded men, and Sir Edward, with his broken leg, occupied the rest of the space, leaving no room for Keelin. She had no choice but to ride one of the wounded knights' horses.

The destrier was impossibly huge. Keelin did not know whether she would be able to mount the massive beast, much less ride him. She'd never done a lot of riding, and had not mounted a horse at all in the years since she'd come to England.

As they made ready to leave, Keelin stood eyeing the horse, oblivious to Marcus's curious glance.

"Do you ride?" he asked, startling Keelin.

She turned slightly, keeping the horse in her sight, and replied, "A wee bit, back home. But it's been several years."

"If you, er…" Marcus turned and looked at the mule-wain as if to remind himself that there truly was no more room for Keelin. "If you are uncomfortable with… er…you could ride with me," he finally said.

She would have liked nothing better than to ride within the security of his capable arms, but knew she could not. Not when he had taken such pains over the last few days to keep his distance.

She'd told herself repeatedly that it did not hurt. That his aversion to her made no difference.

"Thank you, m'lord," she said quietly, ignoring the thickening in her throat. "If you'll but give me a boost, I will ride this beast all the way to Wales if I must."

Again, Marcus hesitated, and Keelin knew he was loath to touch her. She felt tears burn the backs of her eye sockets and turned away. Quickly gathering the reins in her hand Keelin led the horse to the stump where she'd sat when Marcus had tended the cut in her neck. She would mount this animal, she thought, and Marcus de Grant could keep his precious distance.

"My lady," Marcus said, standing as big and bold as you please, in Keelin's way.

"Please do not trouble yourself, m'lord," she said. "I can manage this way."

She saw him blush to the tips of his ears before she turned to step up on the stump. Then, before she knew what was happening, Marcus had her by the waist and was lifting her onto the destrier.

The air went out of her as she landed on the horse's back, and Marcus handed the reins to her. ''Can you...? Er, this saddle is—''

'''Twill serve,'' she replied breathlessly, settling her legs on one side of the horse. ''I thank you, m'lord.''

Marcus had never felt so exposed. Riding with a wain-load of wounded men, a woman who was ill at ease on horseback, and only two other capable knights, he kept one eye on the trail ahead and the other on the trees above. An attack by the Celts now would be fatal.

He and Roger had scoured the territory just after dawn and had found no signs of recent travelers in the area, so Marcus had deemed it safe to leave the cottage. The sooner he got Adam and the others to Wrexton, the better.

He had not forgotten the feel of Lady Keelin's supple body beneath his hands as he'd lifted her onto her mount. Nor had he missed the ease and grace with which she moved, arranging herself sidesaddle, in the manner of a lady.

Though she was well covered now in her hooded cloak, Keelin had not worn a veil or wimple these last days, leaving her hair long and free, and visible to his appreciative eye. Marcus had never realized how sensual a woman's hair was, or how his hands could itch with the desire to touch it.

Marcus knew he had to rein in these thoughts. Lady Keelin's hair, her gentle hands and her appealing feminine form were not his concern. He had only to concentrate on getting them safely to Wrexton. When that was accomplished, he could mount his attack on the Celts who had killed his father.

He had considered using Lady Keelin and her uncle

as bait to lure the Celts to Wrexton, but quickly realized that would not be necessary. As long as the Celts believed Keelin possessed the magic spear, they would continue to seek her.

They would eventually find her at Wrexton, and fall into Marcus's trap.

Keelin would be fully protected. Whatever her connection to the spear, whether it be bewitchment or blessing, Marcus intended that she come to no harm with his plan. It was not up to him to judge her worth, or the state of her soul. He would provide shelter for her and the old Irishman, and when all was resolved, she would be free to go.

Keelin shifted in her saddle.

The ride was grueling, especially for one unaccustomed to it. Keelin could see that the men in the mule-wain were in pain, though Adam slept for most of the journey. Every time the wooden wheels of the wain went over a bump in the road, Sir Edward went white, and groaned in agony as the movement jarred his leg.

The sight of Wrexton Castle in the distance did not come too soon for any of them.

Much larger and grander than the Sheaghda stronghold at Carrauntoohil, Wrexton Keep stood solid and strong within its high curtain walls. A wide, swift-flowing river bordered one side of the castle wall, and a small village lay beyond. It was a welcoming place after hours of riding in the cold and damp.

As they approached the village, people came out of their homes and greeted Marcus, giving words of condolence and encouragement. He dismounted, directing the rest of his party to continue on through the castle gate, while he stayed to speak to the villagers.

Marcus reminded Keelin of her father just then, big

and burly, with a commanding presence and a demeanor fit for a warrior king. She had seen a gentle side to Marcus—something her father had not possessed—but she knew it would be a mistake to think it meant he was soft.

Marcus de Grant could be as hard and unyielding as Eocaidh O'Shea.

They rode past several wooden buildings before reaching the keep, and Keelin observed everything she saw with a keen eye. Stables, barracks, storage huts and several low buildings she could not identify were laid out in the upper bailey, as well as a chapel and other sturdy timber structures in the lower bailey, nearer the keep.

She recognized Sir Roger as he approached, along with several of Wrexton's other knights. Immediately, they set to moving the wounded men to the barracks, and carrying Adam to his quarters. As soon as Sir William had assisted Keelin from her horse, she helped Tiarnan from the wain, then took his arm and supported him as they slowly climbed the stone steps of the keep. Lame since birth, his gait was even more unsteady now with age and infirmity. Lack of sight did not improve matters, either.

"Sir William," Keelin said, "where will my wain and mule be kept?"

"Why, my lady," he replied with some surprise, "your mule will be stabled with the other mules—opposite the knights' horses."

"And…the wain?" she asked, not wanting to sound too anxious, but determined to know where she'd find *Ga Buidhe an Lamhaigh* when she returned for it later.

She preferred to keep its existence secret and would not risk taking it out now, where anyone could see it.

"'Twill be stored with the other carts and wagons in yon low building next to the stable," he replied. "But you needn't worry—I'll have men carry your trunk to your chamber as soon as the wounded men are settled."

"My thanks, Sir Will," Keelin said, satisfied that the man had taken her interest in the wain as concern over her belongings. When she found a suitable hiding place within her chamber in the keep, she would make her way to the storage shed and take *Ga Buidhe an Lamhaigh.*

"The place has a massive feel to it, lass," Tiarnan said.

"Aye, you've got a good sense about you, Uncle. 'Tis massive," she replied. "I've never seen the like."

"Bigger than Carrauntoohil Keep is it?"

Keelin stole another look around as she reached the immense carved oak doors. "Aye," she said. "And well-tended." Then she added quietly, "The Wrexton lord must have wealth to spare."

The oaken doors opened just then and Keelin was greeted by a young, well-dressed woman.

"Lady Keelin," Sir Will said, tipping his head in the direction of the woman, "Lady Isolda Coule, chatelaine of Wrexton."

Isolda greeted Keelin graciously, in spite of the plain introduction, and bid her to enter. Keelin wondered who Lady Isolda was—whether an impoverished relation of Marcus de Grant, or perhaps more…. A widowed sister? His betrothed?

"Chambers have been made ready for you and your uncle, my lady," Isolda said as she led them through the great hall. Keelin was struck by Isolda's proprietary air underneath her benevolent manner. "I will have refreshments sent up as soon as you are settled."

"I thank ye," Keelin replied. The subtle hostility in Isolda's attitude should not have troubled her. It had no bearing on anything to do with Keelin. As soon as Tiarnan was settled, and Adam healed, she intended to leave Wrexton Castle and make her way west. She could only pray that, when she arrived at the coast, the weather would permit her crossing.

Thoughts of her journey to Ireland receded to the back of Keelin's mind as she followed Isolda. Wrexton was magnificent, overwhelming. Keelin had never seen a dwelling as formidable, or as welcoming as Wrexton Castle. She was so in awe over the colorful wall hangings and the lush appointments of the great hall that she nearly stumbled over her own feet.

Carrauntoohil Keep was a cold, mean place when compared with this. With only a modest layer of rushes covering the cold floors, and no wall hangings, Carrauntoohil was more a military stronghold than a home. 'Twas a difference Keelin had never noticed until now. It had always been home to her, but she knew she would see it through different eyes when she returned.

In the meantime, she would observe everything here at Wrexton, from the way the hall was kept so clean and pleasant-smelling to the training of the knights at the quintain.

Keelin turned her attention to Isolda. The chatelaine was some years older than Keelin, but certainly not past her prime. She was still young, and lovely, with auburn hair and the large, soft eyes of a doe, with long thick lashes framing them. Her nose and cheeks were sprinkled with velvety freckles, reminding Keelin of the pretty lasses of Kerry.

Her hair was partially hidden by a clean, pressed linen wimple, and she wore a bright-blue surcoat over several colorful underlayers. Elegant sleeves flowed past her knees, and a jeweled brooch graced her neck.

Keelin pulled her drab cloak tightly around her. It had been years since she'd thought much about her own appearance, her clothes, her hair.

"Lord Marcus was detained?" Isolda asked as she climbed the stairs at the end of the great hall to the private chambers above.

"A bit," Keelin answered. "People from the village came out to speak to him and he stayed on."

Isolda did not reply, but Keelin thought she saw a quick pursing of the woman's lips that was gone before she could be sure she'd actually seen it.

Tiarnan grasped Keelin's arm and they climbed the steps slowly together. "I doubt he'll stay long," Keelin remarked. "He was very anxious about Adam and getting the lad to bed."

"Ah, yes," Isolda said. "Adam. Was he badly hurt?"

"Oh, aye," Keelin said gravely. "He took an arrow in his back, next to his spine. 'Twas a grave injury."

"But he'll recover?"

"'Twould seem so, though your prayers would not be amiss."

Isolda made no further response and Keelin was struck again with curiosity about this woman. Should she not have shown more concern over Adam and his wound? "Ah, here is your chamber, Lord Tiarnan." She opened the door to a room illuminated only by the fire in the grate. Crossing to the far side, she opened the heavy curtains and let in some light from outside. "I hope this meets with your needs," she said.

"'Tis a fine room, indeed, Lady Isolda," Keelin answered. "We thank ye." She led Tiarnan to the bed and helped him get into it, knowing that the old man was fatigued after the long, arduous ride to Wrexton. "Rest awhile, Uncle, and I'll be back to see to ye soon. Is there anything you'll be needin' before I go?"

"Nay, Keely lass," he said, turning onto his side. "Just let me sleep fer a bit and I'll be good as new."

Keelin doubted that, but took one of the tapers from Isolda and followed the other woman to another bedchamber nearby.

"You sent for us, my lord?"

Marcus loosened the buckles of his hauberk and slipped it off. A tub of hot water awaited him, his bath before his father's requiem. But first, business.

He looked at the young knights he'd summoned to his chamber and knew his choice had been correct. These two would be able to accomplish what was needed.

He pulled his linen tunic over his head and tossed it on the bed. "I have a special mission for the two of you," he said.

"Aye, my lord?"

"You will travel to the land of the Irish," he said as he sat and pulled off his leather boots. "Once there, you will make your way to a kingdom called Kerry. I would have you learn all there is to know of Keelin O'Shea and her uncle, and a warrior-chief called Ruairc Mageean."

If the two knights were surprised or chagrined by Marcus's orders, they did not show it. Each man merely nodded his agreement to take on the task assigned by their lord.

"Is this a matter to be kept secret, my lord?"

Marcus hesitated. He did not want the populations of Wrexton and Wales made aware that he was actively seeking information on these Celts, yet some discreet questions once they reached Ireland would not be amiss. After all, he could not tell them exactly how to get to Kerry, nor did he know how his men would be received if they galloped into Carrauntoohil without making their connection to Lady Keelin known.

After saying as much to the men, and giving further instructions, the two knights departed and Marcus sat down and removed the rest of his clothes. He had no sooner dropped down into the tub near the hearth when Isolda burst into his chamber, followed by a pair of maids carrying towels and clean garments.

"Do not say me nay, Marcus," Isolda said before Marcus could utter a sound. "I would serve you now in your mourning."

"I-Isolda," Marcus said, angered by this intrusion. He'd have stood and ushered her out of the room, but he was naked and unaccustomed to being in such a state in the presence of a lady. The fact that he was blushing profusely and that she could see it annoyed him immeasurably. "We have b-been over this before. I am in need of n-no assistance when I bathe."

"But—"

"Leave me," he said, and then he repeated the order more forcefully, so that there could be no mistaking his intentions.

Isolda stood rooted in place for the moment, her soft brown eyes traversing where they would, making Marcus grit his teeth with vexation. She had tried this ogling game five years before, when Eldred had become earl and they had moved into Wrexton Castle. Marcus had made it perfectly clear then, and on several occasions since, that he had no intention of becoming entangled with the former earl's glorified housekeeper.

Nothing had changed.

He knew Isolda had illusions of becoming the Countess of Wrexton. She'd hinted as much to Eldred all those years ago, and in fairness, Eldred had posed the question to Marcus. At the time, Marcus had been flattered but not at all ready to take a wife. Certainly not Isolda, whose cool, controlling manner did not appeal to him in the least.

Later, Isolda's all-out attempt to inveigle a proposal of marriage had done nothing more than make Marcus acutely uncomfortable in her presence. Over the years, he had done everything in his power to keep his distance from the woman, just short of rudeness.

Marcus did not understand why his father's predecessor had not found a husband for Isolda. As her only relative, it was the former earl's duty to have made arrangements for her. Instead, he'd kept her at Wrexton as chatelaine.

After Marcus had made his disinterest clear, Eldred attempted to make a match for her, but Isolda refused all suitors. Clearly, she was not about to settle for anything less than Wrexton.

Marcus sighed. With Eldred's death, there was no doubt in his mind that Isolda's efforts to win him would be renewed.

Chapter Seven

Smoke and incense filled the chapel.

The body of Eldred de Grant, Eleventh Earl of Wrexton, lay on a pallet outside the sacristy where the Bishop of Chester and the chamberlain celebrated the requiem.

Keelin gave thanks for the bright sunlight streaming through the colored glass of the windows, creating a luminescence that made her fairly breathless. The sacred figures in the glass seemed to glow, to move with the shifting light. It was as magical as anything Keelin had ever seen. In a gallery high above her, voices chanted music in such rich harmonies, it echoed through the vaulted ceiling of Wrexton Chapel and touched her soul.

She dearly wished she could have held *Ga Buidhe an Lamhaigh* while she experienced this Mass, but knew such a thing would be construed badly.

Marcus stood with his back to her, his shoulders broad and straight, his light hair gleaming. The other lord—the marquis who had escorted the body back to Wrexton—stood beside him on one side, and Isolda Coule on the other.

The chapel was jammed with people. Keelin observed that some weeping was going on, though not by the principal mourners. She supposed it was the village women, and perhaps some of the castle servants who wept for the fallen nobleman, though Keelin saw many a man with a teary eye. Clearly, Marcus's father was well-loved if only quietly mourned.

Realizing that Irish funerals were nothing like this solemn, highly dignified Mass, Keelin wondered what chaos had broken out at the funeral of her own father. She and Tiarnan had fled before Eocaidh had even been laid in his grave. They'd had no choice but to go, for the ruthless Ruairc Mageean had been primed to carry off *Ga Buidhe an Lamhaigh* before Clann Ui Sheaghda had had a chance to recover from the shock of Eocaidh's death.

Luckily, they'd foiled Mageean that time, and all during the four long, lonely years since then. Now, with Cormac's death at Mageean's hand, the clan would be foundering. It was imperative for Keelin to get *Ga Buidhe an Lamhaigh* back to Carrauntoohil to provide the confidence the spear would bring. Unfortunately, she could not leave immediately.

Adam's condition had worsened during the journey to the castle, and Keelin knew she would be needed here for the next few days, at least. Perhaps even a week. She would not be able to leave the boy until she was certain he was healing.

Tiarnan needed her for the time being, too, although his condition was better than it had been before the arrival of Lord Marcus and his men. Keelin could only pray his health would continue thus, especially once she was away and no longer able to care for him.

She forced her attention back to the Mass, clearing her mind of all thoughts of her journey to Kerry. Centering her awareness and her prayers on the man whose body rested on the bier in front of the congregation, Keelin could not help but remember her own father. And as she bowed her head, she offered prayers for Eocaidh O'Shea—the man whose funeral she had not been able to attend.

It had been four distant years ago, Keelin told herself. Time enough for the grief to have abated. Yet it had not. She felt the sorrow rise from her chest and take hold in her throat, burning there, just as it had on the day she'd watched Ruairc Mageean cut Eocaidh down.

There'd never been time to mourn her father. Tiarnan and the elders of the clan had met and conferred hastily. Within hours of Eocaidh's death, Keelin and Tiarnan were on horseback, racing toward the coast and a ship that awaited them. They'd sailed immediately, skirting the southern coast and heading east. Landing finally on the English coast, they managed to elude Mageean's men for months.

Keelin blinked away the tears she was not even aware were present and looked up.

Though Mass was over, the bishop continued with the prayers for the dead and the chamberlain gently swung the censer over the body. The tang of incense was strong, the somber chanting of the choir haunting.

Wrexton's men-at-arms lifted the body and carried it to the back of the chapel, with the Church dignitaries following. Marcus and Marquis Kirkham walked behind, and Keelin was near enough to see that Lady Isolda had placed her hand on Marcus's arm.

The sight of that touch should not have disturbed Keelin. Her own connection to the young earl was merely a peripheral one, as opposed to Isolda's. Keelin was a temporary resident of Wrexton and would take her leave as soon as it was feasible.

Besides, there was a bridegroom awaiting her at home, in Kerry. The kiss she'd shared with Marcus de Grant had been nothing but an aberration, a moment's diversion from life's cruelest realities. The connection she'd felt between them was merely her imagination.

Keelin looked down at the floor anyway, unwilling to let her eyes rest on that contact between Marcus and Isolda any longer than necessary.

'Twas past midnight and Marcus was glad of the few hours sleep he'd managed before being awakened by a footman. The days of cramped quarters in Keelin O'Shea's tiny cottage gave him a new appreciation for his spacious chamber and the large comfortable bed upon which he was currently sprawled.

After dressing quickly, Marcus hurried to Adam's room to see why Lady Keelin had summoned him. He entered to find the room brightly lit with extra candles. Adam lay prone, and unconscious, with Keelin standing at his bedside. The boy's wound was uncovered, and Marcus winced when he looked at it.

"Praise God and all the saints," Keelin said quietly. She seemed more than pensive. She was worried. "The wound has festered, my lord. I'll need your help when I drain it."

She wore the same deep-green gown he'd seen her in earlier, at his father's funeral. Her hair was unbound as he was accustomed to seeing it, and the silky, dark curtain made Marcus's fingers burn to touch it.

God's teeth! He'd just buried his father, young Adam was lying near death, and here he was thinking of Keelin O'Shea's hair! He curled his fingers into his fists and subdued the inappropriate urge.

Marcus wondered if Keelin had gotten any rest at all

since coming to Wrexton, and denigrated himself for neglecting her. The discoloration of the fine skin under her eyes only added to his guilt. He realized that while he'd spent the afternoon playing host to the bishop, conferring with Wrexton's steward, and seeing to his falcons in the mews, Keelin had been attending his family as well as her own.

Keelin had kept to herself all day. 'Twas true, she had come to his father's funeral, but she'd disappeared immediately afterward. She'd been moved by the ritual— he'd seen her wipe away tears more than once, but he detected a deep sorrow within her, something she'd managed to keep well hidden until then. Clearly, Keelin O'Shea kept her own counsel. Marcus had never known anyone like her.

"M'lord?" she asked. "Mayhap I should have summoned an—"

"No, no," Marcus said, looking down at Adam. "What would you have me do?"

"Go on up near his head," she replied quietly. "Hold him gently, and speak to him. I doubt this will be a particularly agreeable experience for the lad."

Her brogue rolled pleasantly over him as it had done over the past days. Mayhap she was no more than she appeared—merely a displaced Irish noblewoman who had a talent for seeing the future. He could only pray that it was so.

Marcus rubbed the rough planes of his face with his hands, then knelt next to the boy. "Adam," he said. There was no response, so he looked up at Keelin.

"I gave him somethin' to ease the pain," she said as she pulled her lower lip through her teeth. "He'll be drowsy, but speak to him anyway."

Marcus gave a quick nod. "Adam," he repeated, touching the boy's head. "He's burning up!"

"Aye. The wound has festered and now it's causin' fever," she said. "That's why I must drain the poison out."

Lady Keelin seemed to have things well in hand, so Marcus spoke quietly to Adam while Keelin did what was necessary to the wound. The boy squirmed and moaned weakly, but did not seem fully coherent.

Still, Marcus held his shoulders and arms, and talked to him, giving the kind of reassurances he'd seen Keelin give him and the injured men over the last few days. Keelin did what was necessary, then finally cleaned the wound and slathered a green paste over it.

"How's he farin'?"

"Fainted, I think," Marcus replied.

"'Tis better that way," Keelin said. "It had to hurt him somethin' fierce." She washed her hands, then began to wrap clean linen around Adam's torso. 'Twas an awkward task. "Would ye mind helpin' to lift him, m'lord?"

Marcus moved to the opposite side of the bed and slipped his hands under the boy, reaching to take the roll of bandage from Keelin. He did not expect the shock of heat that flashed through him when their hands touched.

He looked up and met her eyes, and saw the same kind of awareness there. Quickly, she pulled her hands out and reached for the bandage that he was ready to hand her, acting as if nothing had passed between them.

'Twas for the best, of course. She was merely a visitor at Wrexton, a woman whose very presence would lure the Celtic assassins. And when they came, Marcus planned to be ready for them.

There was that strangeness about her, too. He knew

'twas her odd powers that made him so uneasy. He still had not figured out how the lady could seem so devout in her prayers, yet keep him so completely in her thrall. For enthralled, he was—utterly and completely, which was one of the reasons he'd stayed away from the keep all afternoon and evening.

Keelin tied the bandage in place, then dipped a clean cloth into a basin of water. Uncovering one of Adam's legs, she wiped it down with water. She repeated the process on the opposite side, then again with his arms.

"What else can I do?" Marcus asked.

"Naught, m'lord," Keelin replied. "I was just wantin' ye nearby in case he awoke fully and needed ye. Yer presence gives the lad comfort."

"Then let me bathe him," Marcus said, walking around to where she stood. "You should find your bed—" he blushed and floundered "—er, you must be weary."

He stood near enough for her to see the fine green lines that rimmed the blue of his eyes, and the golden tips of his lashes. "Aye," she said breathlessly. "I am. But I'll be stayin' 'til I'm sure the lad's improvin'."

"I am grateful to you for your tireless care of my cousin," he said. The utter formality of his tone made him sound insincere, as if he spoke out of courtesy, and not from his heart.

"Aw, he's a dear lad," she replied, "and I don't like to see him laid so low. Besides, 'twas my people who caused—"

"Lady Keelin, you know that I do not hold you responsible for Adam's injuries, or my father's death."

Keelin turned away. She knew no such thing. How could he not blame her, she wondered, when it was her very presence in England that had caused Mageean's mercenaries to be in the vicinity.

He was merely being kind.

Marcus took the cloth from her hand and repeated the motions he'd seen her perform just moments before. While Adam remained asleep through these ministrations, Keelin blew out most of the candles that illuminated the bed. Then she curled herself up in a big chair next to the hearth.

She looked soft and vulnerable and Marcus wanted nothing more than to pull her close and hold her until she slept. Instead, he ran the wet cloth down Adam's legs again and concentrated his thoughts on his young cousin's plight.

"You've got a gentle touch, m'lord," she said, breaking into his thoughts.

A shudder ran through Marcus with her words. "Hmm," was all he said. He ran the cloth down Adam's other leg.

She burrowed deeper into the cushions of the chair, unaware of Marcus's discomfiture. "Would ye say 'twas unusual for a man of your size and strength to have the patience to tend the sick?"

Marcus cleared his throat. 'Twas unsettling to be the object of her perusal, though he had to admit 'twas pleasant in some odd way. There might even be a hint of admiration in her tone. "On the battlefield, we men tended each other when necessary."

"Battlefield?" Keelin asked.

Marcus nodded. "I was with King Henry in France."

"But King Henry's been dead more than six years," Keelin said. "Ye couldn't have been more than a lad yourself then."

Marcus shrugged. "I was barely twenty when he died."

Keelin said, "What was it like? Bein' in a foreign place and fightin' fer your life, over land that's of no consequence to ye?"

He hadn't considered it much in the past few years, though it had occupied much of his thoughts when he was in the muddy trenches, wearing armor that was heavy and hot, eating rations that were maggoty as often as not. "'Twas not pleasant," he said, "but *you* should know something of that. You're here in England, and fighting for your life."

"Ach, but not on the battlefield," she countered. "There're no warhorses neighin', or swords clashin' around me."

"But there could have been—there could still be yet," he said, and then regretted his words when she appeared stricken. "Rest easy, Lady Keelin," he said quickly, "you're safe here at Wrexton."

He watched as she covered her dismay with a shrug. She was a proud one and didn't care for being beholden to him. He could see that she was rankled by needing his protection now.

In truth, Marcus wasn't sure she *did* need his protection.

Nevertheless, she had it for now, and her presence at Wrexton would bring the Celts.

"How did you learn the healing skills?" Marcus asked, turning the discussion from himself. He preferred to listen to her speak rather than being the topic of the conversation.

"From Uncle Tiarnan," she replied. "He was my father's elder brother, and would have been chieftain after their father, but he was born lame."

"So he could never lead your clan in war."

She nodded. "But he was my father's most trusted advisor. When my mother died, Uncle Tiarnan took me under his wing. He taught me all he knew."

"So Tiarnan is the healer."

"Aye," Keelin replied. "I'm merely his pupil."

They were silent for a few moments while Marcus continued to sponge Adam. "He feels cooler now."

Keelin got up from her chair and went to Adam's head. She placed one hand under his arm, the other on his head. "I believe you're right, m'lord," she said, as a small smile teased her lips. "The bathing seems to have worked."

Marcus watched her form the words, but did not hear. His attention was riveted on Keelin's mouth and the perfect white teeth exposed by her smile. He could take comfort from a touch of those lips on his own, and momentarily escape the trials and demands of his circumstances.

They were mere inches away. He could smell spearmint on her breath, feel the heat of her body next to his. He lowered his head and saw her eyelids drift closed as she leaned toward him.

What is happening to me? he wondered as he suddenly straightened. He was not in a panic and ready to bolt, nor were his hands sweating. He had not stuttered once, but had carried on a more than passable conversation with her.

Bewitchment. It could be nothing else.

Keelin blushed and quickly stepped away.

"Mayhap I will find my bed, m'lord," she said quietly, her eyes downcast. "Send for me if he worsens and I'll see if aught can be done."

Chapter Eight

Keelin fell into a deep, dreamless sleep, and when she awoke, she felt more refreshed than she had in ages. Not since her early childhood, before Mageean had begun his onslaught, had she felt so safe. She knew she owed this utterly foreign sense of peace to the security of Wrexton Castle.

The other feelings—the restlessness and yearning—she owed to Marcus de Grant.

He'd been about to kiss her when he'd changed his mind and drawn away from her. She'd felt his breath on her lips, smelled his familiar masculine scent, and seen a yearning and desire in his eyes that matched her own.

Yet he'd pulled away.

She swallowed hard and turned over in her bed. There were many reasons for the man to have pulled away. For one, he was now an earl. And by the looks of things at Wrexton, he was a powerful man. Marcus would likely begin his search for a wife who would bring further wealth or political power to Wrexton. He would have no interest in a romantic entanglement with an Irish nobody.

Besides, this Irish nobody was responsible for Eldred de Grant's death. And though Marcus denied holding her responsible, she knew he would always associate her presence in England with his father's death. Her own father would have done so, as would any number of other warriors. Marcus would be no different.

And then there was Keelin's gift. Even the people of her clan, those who had known her since infancy, had difficulty accepting her second sight. If not a gift from the very devil himself, then surely 'twas an ancient curse heaped upon her family by the *Tuatha De Danaan*—the ancestors of the little people.

And if the O'Sheas themselves were doubtful of her, why should she expect anything more of Marcus de Grant?

'Twas still quite early. Birds were chirping in the courtyard, but the sunrise was a cold and gray one. More rain to come, Keelin thought, dismissing the vestiges of wishful thinking from her mind.

Ready now to face the day, she threw off the warm, woolen blanket and stood in the chilly room. She washed and dressed, then slipped out quietly to check on Tiarnan.

One of Cook's helpers came to sit with Adam, and since the boy was resting quietly, Marcus took the opportunity to get out of the child's sickroom and stretch his legs. Instead of making a clean escape though, he found himself lingering near the stair, waiting.

He did not wait long, for the object of his interest soon appeared in the dim gallery. Keelin O'Shea closed her own door quietly and made her way to another— that of her uncle—and went inside.

Marcus did not intend to speak to Lady Keelin. Nay, he had no idea what he wanted to say to her, though he had every confidence that something would come to him.

Words had come last night, just as they had during the days they'd been stuck in her cottage with Adam and the men.

Marcus just stood on the stair until she'd gone, waiting for the usual flush of uneasiness to appear as it always did when he was confronted with a beautiful woman. It did not happen. Not this time, or any other time he'd been with Keelin O'Shea. Not since that first day.

Leaving strict instructions with the servant, Marcus left Adam's room and headed out to the mews. 'Twas there he would clear his mind. Gerald, Wrexton's falconer, had gone off to break his fast, so there was no one to disturb Marcus's quiet time with the birds.

The pungent odor of the mews assailed him as he entered the large room. He lit several lamps, then walked across the gravel to where his largest birds, a pair of gyrfalcons, were perched.

"Good morning, ladies," he said. "Bit off your jesses again, Guinevere? And you, Cleo. Have you grown lazy in my absence?"

He stroked the birds and talked to them while he assessed the condition of their wings and talons. Gerald kept the birds—the entire mews—in excellent condition. He was one of the best falconers in all of England, and Marcus valued the man immensely.

He walked past peregrines, sparrow hawks and merlins, then looked over his goshawks before arriving at the perch where two prized nestlings were situated. They had recently been captured and brought to Wrexton. "A fine set of merlins, you are," he said, crouching down to the perch. Marcus had no doubt that a buyer would appear, once they were trained to the glove.

However, he would leave the training of these two to

Gerald. There were too many other demands on Marcus at this time, from his new responsibilities as earl, to the intensification of his knights' training. They had to be well prepared when the Celtic mercenaries arrived.

Marcus had no idea how long it would take before the Celts discovered Keelin's location. With luck, the weather would deter them for a time, but Marcus had several precautions in mind, in case they reached Wrexton sooner rather than later.

Adam's fever was worse. The boy was drenched in sweat and groaning and muttering incoherently.

Luckily, Tiarnan seemed to have recovered from the previous day's long journey, and was enjoying the comfort and company afforded by his new residence. This gave Keelin the freedom she needed to attend Adam.

Keelin sent for Lady Isolda to help her with the boy, but word came back that Isolda was unavailable. Marcus was on the training grounds with his men. Keelin knew no one else in the castle, no one else to call on for help.

She looked up at the cook's helper who was still in the room, and smiled ruefully. "'Tis you and I, then, Kate," Keelin said. "You'll have to hold him while I deal with this."

Keelin opened the wound again and drained it while Kate struggled to hold him still. Partway through the procedure, Adam lost consciousness, so Keelin finished quickly, then dressed the wound. With Kate's help, she bathed him, hoping to cool the fever, and pulled the soiled linens off the bed.

"Stay here a bit, Katie," Keelin said, "while I take these down to the laundress."

"Oh, no, my lady!" Kate protested. It was not the

place of a noble guest to cart dirty linens to the back kitchens. "I'll carry these."

Keelin gathered them into a pile and overruled the young helper. "I'd like ye to stay here with Adam for the moment, Kate," she said, "while I get a thing or two that I'll be needin' from the cook. Then I must speak to my uncle. I won't be long."

With that, she carried the bundle out of the room and down the steps. She got instructions from a footman on where the laundry was to be taken, and headed toward the back of the great hall.

"Lady Keelin!" Isolda cried from her chair next to the great hearth. "I do not know how it's done in Ireland," she said indignantly, "but servants fetch and carry here at Wrexton."

"Aye. Well…I'll be speakin' to the cook and since I was headin' this way anyway—"

"Nonsense!" Isolda protested. "You there! Bill! Come and take this—this—" She wrinkled her nose as she looked at the blood and other discolorations. "Help Lady Keelin."

The young footman rushed to take Keelin's burden. "I thank ye, Bill," she said as the young man rushed off, then turned back to Isolda. "Would ye direct me to the kitchen, please?"

Isolda gave her a dubious look, then pointed toward the oaken door that led to the cook's domain. "That way."

Keelin nodded once then left her hostess, puzzling over the woman's disdainful attitude. Surely Lady Isolda had not been so cold last night when they'd arrived? Keelin did not know what offense she had committed—other than having carried soiled linen through the hall.

A flurry of activity met Keelin's eyes as she entered

the main kitchen. Preparations were underway for all the meals of the day, and Wrexton fed a multitude of people. Keelin hated to interrupt the cook, but saw no other alternative.

"Good mornin' to ye," she said.

"And to you, my lady," the cook replied. He was respectful, but not cowed by the presence of a noble visitor. "Is there aught I can do for you?"

"Aye, there is."

Keelin spent some time working with Wrexton's cook, getting what she needed for Adam, and for Tiarnan. By the time she left the kitchen, she was laden with clean linens, and a tray containing a light meal for her uncle, as well as a special broth for Adam.

She had also gained the respect of Wrexton's formidable cook.

"Let me get one of the boys to help you carry—"

"Nay," Keelin said, sailing out of the room. "'Twill be quicker this way. Besides, they all have their own work."

Wrexton's cook scratched his head as his puzzled gaze followed her. He'd never known one of his betters to perform a task that could be done by another. This Lady Keelin was a rare one, he thought, watching her as she turned and backed out of the doorway.

Marcus entered with Sir William and Sir Robert just as Lady Keelin backed her way into the hall. She smiled at young Bill, the footman who pulled the door open for her, but graciously refused his offer of help.

Isolda stood near the hearth with a maid who was cleaning away some of the soot and ashes; both women seemed oblivious to Keelin, though Marcus could not see how they missed her. She had laughed aloud—her pleasing voice echoing through the cavernous hall.

Keelin looked up and saw him as she walked, their eyes meeting for one exhilarating moment. He'd not heard her laughter before, and the sound lightened his troubled heart. And seeing her look at him that way, from across the—

Keelin suddenly tripped. The tray she carried flew up into the air, along with all its contents. Keelin herself fell to the floor amid the clanging of bowls, spoons and knives. Marcus rushed ahead to help her while Isolda began to scold the maid for leaving her broom in Lady Keelin's path.

Marcus vaguely heard their argument as he reached Keelin and helped her to her feet. "Are you hurt?" he asked.

Shaken and embarrassed by the fall, Keelin frowned and shook her head. "What a mess. I'm sorry to have caused such a fine ruckus, Lord Marcus. I'm not usually so—"

"'Tis naught," he replied, motioning to footmen to help clear up the mess. He turned and spoke to Bill. "Go back to the kitchen and have Cook replace what was ruined."

He led Keelin to a chair before the hearth and made her sit.

"Truly, m'lord," she protested, "I am fine. And I must return to Adam. The poisons are back in his wound and he's feverish again."

Lines of worry creased Marcus's forehead. He glanced at the steps at the far end of the hall, then back at Keelin. "If you're certain you're unhurt…"

"Stupid maid," Isolda said after she'd finished dressing down the girl whose carelessness had caused Keelin to fall. "Let me see your hands."

Keelin lifted her hands and Isolda turned them palms up. She hovered over the small scrapes on the heels of Keelin's hands and when she began to fuss over supposed injuries to Keelin's knees, Keelin stood abruptly.

"I thank ye for your concern, Lady Isolda," she said, "but 'tis nothin'. Please trouble yourself no further on my account." She started to walk away before Isolda could further detain her and realized that Marcus followed right behind her.

"Is Adam awake?" Marcus asked. At least he would allow her to go on and forget her embarrassment.

"Nay, m'lord," Keelin replied, oblivious to Isolda, who stood where they'd left her, looking after them with her hands on her hips. "He was, for a short while this mornin', but the pain and the fever..."

Marcus took Keelin's arm as they climbed the stairs. His touch was as much a shock as the look they'd exchanged when he'd come into the hall. She kept her eyes down, however, and walked carefully, unwilling to repeat her clumsy performance in the hall.

She would never understand how she'd neglected to notice the broom handle in her path. She could have sworn the way was clear.

"I've done all I know how to do for Adam," she said. "I've used lady's mantle and germander, but the wound continues to fester."

They reached the top of the stairs and Marcus released her arm. They went into Adam's room together. "Ah, my lady," Kate said, rising from her crouch by the fire. "He hasn't stirred a bit, though he's hot."

Keelin brushed one hand over Adam's forehead and frowned. Turning away, she poured water into a basin and handed it to Marcus. "Would ye mind bathin' him, m'lord?" she asked, then went to her satchel to pull out several leather pouches. Finding the one she wanted, she poured a gray powder into her hand, then dumped it into a cup. Adding water, she stirred it, then went to the head of Adam's bed.

"Adam, can ye hear me?"

A quiet moan was the only response.

"Take a sip, lad," Keelin said as she spooned some of the mixture into his mouth. He swallowed and she sighed, relieved that at least she would be able to get this medicine into him. With luck, it would help to cool him.

An hour later, the fever still raged. If Adam's condition did not improve, and quickly, the boy could die.

"I need my uncle," she finally said.

Marcus heard the quiet desperation in Keelin's voice and forced himself to stay calm.

"Shall I get the priest, my lord?" Kate asked.

Angered by the suggestion that Adam would need the Last Sacrament, Marcus snapped at the girl. "No! Go and see to it that Lord Tiarnan is escorted here, at once."

"Yes, my lord," Kate replied, cowed by Marcus's uncharacteristic show of temper.

"Surely there's no harm in askin' the priest to come," Keelin said gently, putting one slender hand on Marcus's brawny one.

Though her voice remained steady, there were tears in her eyes and Marcus knew he would be a fool to ignore her plea.

Kate waited long enough to receive a quick nod from Marcus, then fled the chamber. Marcus stood still, struck by the enormity of what he had just admitted to himself. Not since the attack had he allowed himself to consider that Adam might not survive his wound. Now, though, he had no choice but to face that dire possibility.

Impulsively, Marcus pulled Keelin into his arms. He sensed that she needed comfort as much as he, and as he wrapped his arms around her, he felt one shuddering sob escape her.

It had been a long, monstrous day. Adam was unconscious now, his fever down, the wound freshly cauterized. Drastic measures had been taken upon Tiarnan's suggestion, and carried out by Keelin and Marcus under the old man's direction. Never before had Keelin held the balance of life or death quite so closely in her own hands.

Never before had she felt such a need to escape. There had been a strong, nearly overwhelming sense of foreboding in Adam's chamber, that grew as the day wore on. Keelin tried her best to get a clear grasp of it, but 'twas no use. She could not see exactly what misfortune would occur, though she sensed that, whatever 'twas, it did not directly involve Adam.

Keelin considered going to the building where her mule cart was stored and pulling *Ga Buidhe an Lamhuigh* out of its hiding place. With one touch of the spear, visions would come to her. She knew, however, that the experience would drain her strength and keep her from caring for Adam.

Mayhap 'twould be better for now, to wait. After all, she and Tiarnan were safe at Wrexton. There wasn't a Mageean soldier alive who could penetrate the castle wall without raising an alarm. And even if a whole company of Celtic mercenaries arrived inside Wrexton's walls, Marcus de Grant and his men would meet them, arrow for arrow, and sword for sword.

At least Adam was in good company now. Tiarnan was ensconced in a comfortable chair next to the bed, Kate stayed on to keep up the fire, and to run any necessary errands, and Marcus was there to keep watch over his young cousin.

It gave Keelin the opportunity to go outdoors for some badly needed fresh air, and to put a wee bit of space between herself and Lord Marcus, the man whose presence was becoming far too important to Keelin.

Young Kate had kept all the servants apprised of Adam's condition every time she'd left the boy's chamber, and told of all that was being done for him. When Keelin withdrew through the hall and into the kitchen, she was met by all who worked there—the servants who had known and loved Adam for years.

Cook asked Keelin about Adam and all the kitchen servants gathered 'round to hear her report. They shook their heads and clucked their tongues, saying they were grateful the boy had as gifted a healer as Keelin O'Shea to attend him.

Keelin was humbled by their confidence in her. And afraid. She was doing all she could for Adam, but knew it could very well not be enough.

She wrapped her cloak snugly around her, then slipped out of the castle and found her way to the gardens. She wanted a few moments of quiet and solitude to gather her thoughts, to compose herself.

Keelin did not want to become attached to these English people at Wrexton. For days, she'd fought against becoming emotionally entangled with them, fearing that any deeper involvement would make it wildly difficult to leave, to return to Ireland. But it was no use. She was losing the battle.

Recollections of her homeland were fading. Thoughts

of her betrothed—an Irishman she did not know—paled when compared to the reality of Marcus de Grant. Keelin thought she would burst this morning when he'd wrapped her in his strong arms and comforted her though it was his own kin who lay near death. He had understood her frustration as well as her sadness.

Later, when Uncle Tiarnan had come to help with Adam, Marcus had worked with her as if they'd been partners forever, sensing what she needed before she even spoke. All his movements bespoke of size and power, as well as competence and efficiency. He spoke to her with respect and consideration, lending credence to his denials that he held her responsible for the Celts' attack.

Keelin observed Marcus's every move with a fascination that bewildered her. She noticed small things about him—the way his eyes turned slightly down at the corners, the scar that creased his lower lip, the soft, smooth skin of his earlobes—things she would never have thought about twice in another man. And then there were his hands, large and well formed, and heavily sprinkled with red-gold hair. She wondered—

"Lady Keelin."

Keelin whirled around at the sound of the familiar voice, deep and rich in timbre. She was certain he could read her thoughts just by the flush on her cheeks. His wonderful hair was bound at the base of his neck by a short leather cord, making the sharp angles of his cheek and jaw stand out prominently.

"M'lord?" It came out more of a croak than anything, though a tingling warmth surged through Keelin when the gaze of his light-blue eyes pierced her.

"I, uh…" He clasped his hands behind his back. "I

wondered if aught was amiss. You...left Adam's chamber so abruptly.''

"No, m'lord," she replied. "All is well. A-as it can be, at least. I just...well, I was just needin' some air.''

Marcus closed the space between them. "There's a frigid edge to the night," he said, looking up at the sky. "Snow is coming.''

"But not today.''

"Some say we're in for a harsh winter.''

Keelin nodded. She'd seen some of the signs herself.

"You're not thinking of making the journey to Ireland yourself, are you?'' Marcus asked after a moment's hesitation. He seemed to surprise himself with the question as much as he took Keelin off guard.

"W-well, aye, m'lord," she stammered. "'Twas my thought to go as soon as Adam is well enough....''

"And your uncle?'' Marcus asked. He took hold of the edges of her cloak and pulled them together so that his hands—those big, gentle, hair-roughened hands—hovered over her heart.

"I m-meant to have him stay h-here," she said, feeling the heat of his body, the intensity of his eyes, "with y-ye, m'lord.''

Chapter Nine

Marcus's eyes never left hers, and Keelin was certain he could feel the pounding of her heart under his hands. She leaned forward, as if pulled by some unseen magnetic force, needing his touch as much as she needed her next breath.

"'Tis not a good time of year for travel," he breathed.

"Aye, sure and I know it, m'lord, but—"

Words and thoughts halted abruptly as Marcus's mouth touched hers. Keelin's eyes closed to savor the featherlight touch. Her hands slipped out of her cloak and came to rest on Marcus's waist as he deepened the kiss.

Keelin's heart pounded as Marcus opened his hands. His palms skimmed her chest, grazing her collarbone, moving lower, setting every nerve on edge, until he reached the sensitive peaks of her breasts. At the same time, his tongue invaded her mouth, sending Keelin to another level of sensation.

Somewhere in the recesses of her mind, Keelin was aware that her back was pressed against a tree. Marcus's body, hard and solid against her own, caressed the soft length of her. She felt his heat and power with every shift of his muscles, every movement of his hands.

Keelin's arms went around him, pulling him tightly against her. She could not think, but only feel the exquisite sensations pulsing through her, and wish that it could be more, that her skin could be bared to his touch, and his mouth could follow the path of his hands. She moaned her frustration, entirely caught up in the moment, oblivious to anything but Marcus.

Marcus's mouth dipped to the exquisitely sensitive flesh below her ear, then traveled down her neck, feasting on the notch where her collarbones met. His hands stopped their gentle assault only once, to push her cloak back off her shoulders. Loosening the laces to her kirtle, Marcus slipped one hand inside and stroked her until she whimpered.

Keelin bit her lip to keep from crying out both her pleasure and the astonishment it caused. Never had she guessed that the touch of a man's hands could make her brain wither and her bones melt. Incapable of conscious thought, instinct gave Keelin the desire to please him, too. She slid her hands down until they rested on his buttocks. The muscles were firm but yielding to her touch, and Marcus gave out a harsh sigh of his own when her fingers tested his brawny form.

A sharp intake of breath on a muffled cry from somewhere behind pulled them from their sensuous haze. Keelin's hands dropped to her sides, while Marcus turned slightly to see who stood behind them. After a quick glance, he turned back to Keelin and pulled her cloak back over her shoulders to cover her disheveled clothes.

Keelin felt like a naughty child, caught in a thoroughly wicked act. And, while her emotions were certainly in turmoil, Keelin knew down to the roots of her soul that kissing Marcus could never be wicked.

The woman who stood glaring at Marcus and Keelin was much older, Keelin thought, peering around Marcus's broad shoulder to see. Her hair and neck were fully covered by a white linen wimple, but her eyes gave away her age. Her hostility was palpable, Keelin thought, but the woman finally had the good grace to look away. After a moment she turned in a huff and stalked away.

Embarrassed once again, Keelin fumbled with the laces of her kirtle. When Marcus moved her hands aside and tied them, she could feel the tension in his body. The look in his eyes was at once forbidding, yet intriguing.

He did not speak, only kept his eyes locked with hers, his hands steady on the fastening of the laces. Clearly, a struggle was going on within him. Keelin did not know the cause of his discontent, only that he was mightily displeased.

She could only guess whether or not *she* was the cause of his displeasure. She doubted it, at least not this time. All had been well—more than well, she thought with a sigh—until the old woman had interrupted their tryst. Keelin could only conclude that the woman in the headrail was the cause of Marcus's ire.

His eyes suddenly softened. Rather than speaking, his customary reticence prevailed. He raised one hand to cup her head, and caressed her cheek with one thumb, sending shivers of delight through Keelin.

It was over all too quickly. Marcus dropped his hand and took her arm. Together, they started walking through the garden toward the castle keep.

"Who was that woman?" Keelin asked as they approached the door of the back kitchen.

"That was Beatrice. Isolda Coule's maid," he said, scowling. "A companion."

"I don't understand," Keelin said. "Is Isolda your kin? Your—"

"Nay. She is no kin of mine, but a distant cousin of the man who was earl before my father," Marcus replied. "She came to Wrexton several years ago, with Beatrice, and has never left."

"Yer father was a kind man, Marcus," Keelin said quietly, "to give her leave to stay."

Marcus did not reply, but his expression showed his appreciation for her insight. Eldred *had* been kind, taking pity on the impoverished gentlewoman to whom he owed nothing. Marcus did not know if he would ever be as beneficent a lord.

He did not feel particularly beneficent at the moment. In fact, he could have wrung Beatrice's neck. He had a suspicion that Isolda knew he had found Keelin in the garden and had sent Beatrice out to intercept them. Interrupt them.

Marcus did not understand why Eldred had not insisted that Isolda marry one of her suitors. Surely Eldred would have preferred to get her out from underfoot at Wrexton. Though he felt unkind and petty for thinking these thoughts, Marcus did not have the same level of patience and charity possessed by his father.

As soon as possible, Marcus would see what could be done about marrying her off.

"Marcus," Keelin said, stopping. She put a hand on Marcus's arm. "Do ye smell smoke?"

Marcus stood still for only an instant, then looked up sharply. "The stables!"

* * *

Keelin was right behind Marcus as he ran through the courtyard across the lower bailey to the source of the dark-gray smoke that was billowing up and away in the wintry breeze. Men were already throwing buckets of water on the stacks of burning hay stored behind the stable. Keelin took an empty bucket and ran to the well where she waited in line to refill it.

"My lord!" Boswell, the stable marshal cried when he saw Marcus. "Your stallion and the pregnant mares were moved out right away. The lads are getting the rest of the horses now."

Grateful that Boswell had seen to his prized mares and the stud, Marcus ordered men to splash the wall of the stable with water to keep sparks from taking hold. But it was already too late. Sparks flashed up on the thatched roof and the fire was rapidly spreading.

The marshal and several grooms were leading horses to safety. Keelin could hear the frantic neighing of the panicked animals, and she left her place near the well to go help.

The marshal was preoccupied, so Keelin did not bother to speak to him. Instead, she entered the smoke-filled stable. Pulling a corner of her cloak up to cover her mouth and nose, she ran to the farthest stall and opened the door. Speaking calmly to the frightened horse, she quickly slipped a bridle over his head and led him out to safety.

Confusion reigned in the bailey. Men and women were shouting and running in all directions, and animals milled about while the stable marshal tried to establish a holding pen for them. The ground was a muddy mess now, from the water being poured over the building and all the feet and hoofs trampling through. Everyone pitched in to help wherever they could.

A young boy took the horse's reins from Keelin's hands and she returned to the burning building. She discovered her own mule in a stall, far to the back of the stable, rearing and baying in terror. Using her voice to calm him, Keelin approached cautiously, even though it was imperative that she hurry. She had no intention of being trampled by her own mule, and she knew how to handle him.

"My lady!" a man's voice called. "Quickly!"

"Aye," she called back, keeping her eyes on the mule. There was no choice but to be quick about it.

Knowing full well 'twould be now or never, Keelin unlatched the gate to the stall and went to step in, but before she made another move, a sharp crack across the back of her head made everything go black.

There were too many timber buildings in the bailey. If the fire spread, 'twould be a disaster, especially as they approached the depths of winter. Supplies would be burned, as well as living quarters for the soldiers and servants of Wrexton.

Marcus could only be grateful there hadn't been more damage. Most everything but the stable remained intact. No humans had been seriously injured, and his mares, Frieda and Isabella, both about to foal, had been spared. As had Gregor, the sire of many a fine warhorse.

Marcus had not seen Keelin for some time, not since she'd left the water carriers to help move the horses to safety. There'd been no hesitation about her actions as she'd pitched right in to help wherever she was needed.

She'd done the same when he and his men had arrived at her cottage, and again here at Wrexton, when Adam's condition had worsened. Quite unusual for a noble-woman. He'd certainly not seen Lady Isolda in the vicinity of any of their recent troubles.

Marcus turned his attention back to the shovel in his hands. A battalion of knights worked alongside him to dig a ditch around the yard where the burning hay had been stored. He'd been told that all the animals were freed from the stable, so they'd given up on the fire that burned its roof. If they could just contain the area of damage, they would rebuild when they were able to obtain supplies.

Luckily, a light drizzle had begun, squelching the fire in the thatch. Marcus knew that it would likely smolder for hours, even with the rain, but at least it would not spread.

"Lord Marcus!" The tone of Alan Boswell's voice was alarming. Boswell, the stable marshal, was a man not generally given to excited outbursts.

Marcus dropped his shovel and met the man partway. "'Tis your lady, my lord!" he said, grabbing Marcus's arm and leading him to a storage shed well removed from the fray.

"My lady? Keelin O'Shea?"

"Aye, my lord," Boswell replied. "She's been hurt. Knocked unconscious by a falling beam or some such. One of the lads found her and we carried her here."

Marcus entered the shed. His heart lurched as he dropped to his knees next to Keelin, who lay unmoving on the dirt floor. Her eyes were open, although she looked dazed. There was blood in her hair.

He took her hand in one of his own. "Keelin," he said quietly, his tone belying the concern he felt.

"Marcus?" she asked, her eyes finally coming into focus. A sudden spasm of coughing overtook her. "What happened?'' she asked once she was able to catch her breath. She suddenly thought of the spear that had been so well hidden. ''Oh! The fire! Did the sheds burn? Was anything…?''

''Nay, Keelin,'' Marcus said, alarmed by her panic. ''The fire was confined to the stable.''

She relaxed visibly, then asked about her mule.

Marcus glanced up at the groom.

''One of the other lads got it out,'' he said.

Without discussion, Marcus lifted Keelin into his arms and carried her toward the keep. The fire was under control, and besides, there was nothing more important at the moment than getting Keelin safely into her bed, where the cut on her head could be tended.

''I'm capable of walkin', m'lord,'' Keelin admonished, wrapping her arms about his neck, the action contradicting her words. Her eyes seemed soft and sensual, though Marcus knew the effect was the result of the blow to her head.

Still, he drank in the tantalizing sensation of her arms clasped around him as he walked, and would have prolonged the contact if it had not been quite so urgent to get her somewhere warm and dry. He would see to the cut on her head himself, he thought, as there was no healer at Wrexton besides Keelin herself. Even Tiarnan could not help her since he could not see.

Marcus carried her through the hall and before they reached the stairs, Isolda Coule caught up to them.

''Marcus!'' she cried. ''What happened?''

''Lady Keelin was hurt in the fire,'' he replied without stopping. ''Walk ahead of us, Isolda, and open Keelin's chamber door.''

Isolda did as she was told, although she cast a disparaging glance at them as she went. She entered the room, then pulled open the bed curtains, giving Marcus the space to lay Keelin gently on the bed.

"Bishop Delford awaits you in the solar, Marcus," Isolda said. "He has been expecting to see you all afternoon but you were—"

"Detained, putting out the fire that destroyed our stable," Marcus said with some impatience. Good God, could these people within the keep have had no idea of the catastrophe in the bailey? "Get some water and clean cloths, Isolda," he said. "And tell Delford that I shall attend him after I've seen to Lady Keelin."

Isolda sniffed at his curt tone, but turned and left Keelin's room in a flurry of displeasure.

"Marcus, I can tend myself," Keelin protested, pushing herself up from the bed.

A wave of dizziness overtook her and she dropped back to the bed, wincing as her injured head landed.

"Lie still, Keelin," Marcus said as he sat on the bed next to her. An overpowering sense of protectiveness overcame him. It was intensely disturbing to see her hurt. It went beyond the kind of caring he should have had for any guest, yet he could not understand how this depth of feeling had come to pass in such a short time.

Bewitched he might be, but he felt no grasp of Satan's hand in it. On the contrary, whenever Keelin O'Shea was in his arms, Marcus felt he was in the hands of God and all His saints.

Keelin was worn-out. She knew she should try to sleep, but the day's events had stirred her emotions into an uproar. Light-headed though she was, she climbed out of bed and made her way to the fireplace. Marcus had stoked the fire nicely before leaving, so it was blazing cozily. Keelin sat down on the chair near the hearth, and drew her feet up under her. She wrapped her hand around the short leather cord that had bound Marcus's hair earlier.

Somehow, it had wound up in her hand.

Marcus had taken excellent care of her. The thought warmed her thoroughly, even as it caused a wild turmoil within.

She had to return to Ireland. It was time to return *Ga Buidhe an Lamhaigh* to her clan.

Keelin pulled her knees up to her chest and rested her chin upon them. Her silky black hair spilled around her shoulders, trailing down her back and her legs. The leather cord heated in her palm.

Just the very thought of leaving Marcus made her ache inside, but Keelin knew her duty. Her first allegiance had to be to Clann Ui Sheaghda. She was compelled to wed the chieftain her father had chosen for her, to help ensure the security of the clan. 'Twas not hers to decide.

She brushed a tear from one eye and pushed her hair back behind one ear. 'Twould not do at all to allow her feelings for Marcus to grow into anything more than what she already felt for him. Which was considerable. Though she had little experience with matters of the heart, Keelin did not believe she would ever encounter another with as noble a soul as Marcus de Grant. He was kind and considerate, strong in his heart as well as his body.

'Twas no matter, Keelin told herself ardently. As soon as she was able, she would leave Wrexton. Tiarnan would be in good hands, and content here in Marcus's keep. In spring, she would see that men were sent out from Kerry to escort him home, where he could live out his last years with his clan.

In the meantime, Keelin had to retrieve *Ga Buidhe an Lamhaigh* from her mule-wain. The fire in the stable had shown her how precarious her current hiding place was. It could have been the storage building that had burned in addition to the stable, and *Ga Buidhe an Lamhaigh* along with it.

Keelin's only choice was to get the spear and bring it to her chamber in the keep, where it would be safe until she was able to leave. Surely no fire nor any other untoward event would endanger the spear if it were well hidden in her chamber.

'Twas unfortunate she was unable to hide her heart as well.

Chapter Ten

The damage to the stable was extensive. The roof was gone, and only the support beams of the building remained standing, along with a few of the horse stalls. The inside stank of smoke, and Marcus decided it would be necessary to rebuild entirely.

Marcus's eyes scanned the bailey, assessing all the buildings and the potential for fire. Too many of them were made of wood. 'Twas never seen as a problem before, but now that the stable had burned, Marcus did not care to have that kind of disaster repeated. Come spring, he would have workmen begin to replace each building with stone.

Marcus poked around, pondering the fire and its probable cause.

"For the life of me," the stable marshal said, "I cannot figure how it began, my lord."

Marcus walked alongside the man as they inspected the ruins of the stable.

"I was just out back not five minutes before, answering nature's call, and there was nary a sign of anything amiss."

Of course there wouldn't have been, Marcus thought,

or Boswell would have dealt with it before the fire had had a chance to grow to such a magnitude. Still, it was worrisome. A fire that started and spread that quickly…precautions had to be taken.

By the light of a few well-placed torches, men were sweeping up as much of the mess as possible. "Gordon," he called to one of the grooms, "where did Lady Keelin fall?"

"Back here, my lord," Gordon replied, leading Marcus and the stable marshal to the stall where her mule had been boarded. "Best watch your step."

"Aye, I will." Marcus walked around, noting that the area was remarkably clear of debris. There was one piece of charred wood on the ground, and when Marcus picked it up, he saw that it was sticky with what must have been dried blood, and a few strands of long, black hair. 'Twas the beam that had knocked Keelin out.

The roof was gone, but the side of the building remained intact, along with the support beams overhead. Marcus wondered where the joist in his hand had fallen from.

"'Tis truly amazing that no one was more seriously injured, my lord," Boswell said. "Except for Lady Keelin. How is she, by the by?"

"She'll do," Marcus answered. "No thanks to this," he said as he tossed the heavy piece of wood into the pile of debris.

"Will you oversee the rebuilding, my lord," Boswell asked, "or shall I?"

"I'll leave that to you, Boswell," Marcus replied. "My only stipulation is that the new stable is to be made of stone."

"Aye, my lord," the stable marshal replied approvingly. "'Twas by the grace of God this disaster was no worse."

Marcus returned to the keep and asked that a bath be made ready for him in his chamber. He stopped in to see Adam first, and found Tiarnan sitting near the boy, dozing. Adam slept, every breath deep and clear. Marcus put one hand on his forehead and was relieved to find it merely warm. There might still be fever, but at least it no longer raged out of control.

"Ah, yer back," Tiarnan said, sniffing at the charred, smoky odor Marcus brought into the room with him. "And did ye learn anything new?"

"Nay," Marcus replied. "The fire started in a hay-stack behind the stable and spread from there. 'Tis likely someone was careless with a torch and is afraid to come forth and admit to it."

Tiarnan did not reply right away, but waited for Marcus to continue looking Adam over, and satisfy himself that the boy's condition continued to improve.

"Keely says ye took fine care of her," he finally said, "and I thank ye fer it."

"I only wish I had kept her out of it," he replied. "She would not have been hurt if—"

"Ah, but stoppin' my Keely lass isn't always an easy thing," Tiarnan interjected. "She's got a mind of her own, just like her father before her." The old man crossed himself as he mentioned Keelin's father.

Marcus nodded, forgetting that the old man could not see the gesture. He wondered if Tiarnan knew Keelin intended to leave him at Wrexton and return to Ireland.

The thought of her leaving caused an ache in Marcus akin to what he felt over the loss of his father. He could not say exactly what his feelings for Keelin were, but knew that not once in his life had he ever felt this way about any woman.

And if he allowed Keelin to leave, chances were he would never see her again.

"Tell me, m'lord," Tiarnan said. "How badly was Keelin hurt? She will never say when aught ails her, and tonight is no different, though I could hear from her hoarseness that she swallowed a lungful of smoke and soot."

"Yes, she did," Marcus said. And the huskiness of her voice had seared him clear to his toes. "It's likely she'll have quite a cough for a few days."

Tiarnan nodded. "And the cut on her head?"

"'Twas deep, but the bleeding stopped and she wanted no fuss," Marcus replied, "so I did not stitch it."

He was glad he had not been required to sew the wound. Needlework was not one of his particular talents and he was loath to hurt Keelin any more than she had been already.

"Well, she's a hearty lass," Tiarnan said. "She'll mend."

Marcus supposed so, though he still wished she'd not gone into the stable. He did not understand how she had managed to be struck by the one beam that had fallen in her vicinity. An ugly suspicion reared its head, but he quickly discounted it. Isolda would never venture into the stable for any reason.

"How is Adam?"

"Better tonight," Tiarnan replied. "The fever's down and the wound is not quite so putrid. I had young Katie mix some valerian and the lad swallowed it. He'll sleep a good while."

"His color is better," Marcus said.

"Take yerself off to bed, lad," Tiarnan said. "Katie and I will see to young Adam tonight. And if we've need of ye, we'll call."

The prospect of a bath and a few hours' sleep was too compelling to resist, though he did not believe the old man was well enough to stay up all night. Nor should Katie have to do so, either, since she'd already spent the day doing Tiarnan's bidding. The girl, who was nodding in a chair near the hearth, needed her rest, too.

"Kate," he said, waking her. "Go to bed."

"But—"

"One of the footmen will spell you for the night."

"Yes, my lord," she said sleepily. She stood up a little unsteadily, and left the room.

"Tiarnan, I'll send someone to help you to bed as well," Marcus said. "Adam's sleeping comfortably now. If he needs us, we can easily be summoned."

Tiarnan did not protest as Marcus bid him good-night and left Adam's chamber.

He did not go far before Lady Isolda waylaid him.

"Marcus," she said, "I've been looking for you."

"What is it, Isolda?" he asked wearily.

"As you know, Bishop Delford plans to leave on the morrow," she replied. "I persuaded him to delay his departure one more day, and I intend to serve a suitable feast for him. 'Twould be well for you to preside at the meal."

"My presence will depend on Adam's health, madam," Marcus said, "and whether I am needed here."

"Marcus," Isolda sighed impatiently. "The bishop is an important man. You met with him only briefly after the funeral, and again for a terribly short time this evening. You cannot snub His Eminence in this manner. The bishop has a great deal of sway at court and—"

"And if he is such a dolt that he cannot understand the gravity of my other commitments, then I give him leave to return to Chester without the pleasure of my company."

"Marcus!"

Isolda could not have been more surprised by his words and tone than Marcus himself. Never before had he spoken to her in such a fashion.

However, it was not just the fatigue that drove him, nor the events of the day. He was earl now. He had the power and authority of his station and he intended to put it to good use.

"Send one of the grooms to Adam's room," he said to Isolda. "Have him help Lord Tiarnan to his chamber, then return to Adam to keep watch for the night. If Adam's condition changes in the least, I wish to be summoned immediately."

"But Marcus—"

"Unless you prefer to sit with Adam yourself. In that case—" Marcus began, but Isolda gathered her skirts and stalked away. Marcus felt only a twinge of regret for calling attention to Isolda's particular shortcoming. She had no stomach for illness, and Marcus knew she intentionally avoided contact with the sick or injured.

He continued on his way until he reached his chamber, where he entered, untying laces and shedding his smoke-damaged clothes as he went. Keelin's gown had been ruined as well, and Marcus doubted she had many more to choose from.

He sank into the tub that awaited him, exhausted yet unable to relax. Keelin O'Shea was very much on his mind.

She planned to leave.

Marcus did not care for the empty feeling that came with that thought. He had never known anyone like Keelin O'Shea—not in west England or Wales, not in London or anywhere in France.

Marcus hadn't realized until now what a difference her size meant to him. She was not one of those soft, petite ladies who seemed as if they would crumple under the least pressure. Nay, Keelin was more like Cleo, his magnificent gyrfalcon. Soft and sleek outside, Lady Keelin was strong and fierce within.

She was tall for a woman, tall enough that he had hardly needed to bend to kiss her. He recalled that her long, lithe form had fit him well, and his body had ached to make it a more intimate fit.

Marcus ducked his head in the water in a futile attempt to clear it, and to settle his body's runaway urges.

She would return to Ireland as soon as she was free to do so, he told himself again. That was where her heart, as well as her allegiance lay, though if he knew how to change that, he would not hesitate to do so.

Marcus suddenly thought of the spear Tiarnan had told him about. He hadn't thought much about it before, but now he realized that Keelin must have brought it to Wrexton with her. Where had she stored it on the journey? Marcus was certain he'd seen everything that had come on the mule cart, and there had been no spear. She had not carried it on horseback, either.

The spear was obviously something of great importance to the O'Sheas, Marcus thought, judging from the way Tiarnan had spoken of it. He could not imagine that Keelin had left it at her cottage, not when she knew the Mageean warriors would soon return.

No, it had to be somewhere here at Wrexton.

Keelin was up early the next morning, before anyone at Wrexton stirred. She dressed and threw her cloak over her clothes, then made her way down the stairs and out of the keep. It was still dark but her eyes quickly adjusted to the shadows in the predawn light. She did not need much light, anyway. She knew the location of the storage shed where her mule cart had been stored and she hoped the power of the spear would draw her to it.

Letting herself inside the shed, Keelin let her eyes adjust to the deeper darkness. She had to pick her way through a mound of equipment that had been salvaged from the stable and tossed inside, but she soon found her wain mixed in with those that belonged to Wrexton.

'Twas strange…she could not feel the presence of the spear. For some reason, it did not draw her.

Regardless, she slipped her hand along the frame of the wain, and searched for the hollowed-out length of wood that sheathed the spear. Sliding her fingers along the wood, she bit back a cry of discomfort as a sliver of wood jabbed into her flesh. She stopped her task to pull it out, then went back to her search.

Finally locating the small metal latch that held the cover in place, Keelin flipped it open and reached two fingers inside.

'Twas empty!

Ga Buidhe an Lamhaigh was gone!

No, that could not be right, Keelin assured herself. She must somehow have chosen the wrong wain in the dark, no matter how certain she'd been of her choice.

Before true panic could set in, Keelin lit one of the candles by the door, and started to look around more carefully. *There must be a good dozen wains in here,* she thought. *No wonder I've chosen wrong.*

But even as she thought it, she realized that no other wain would have a hollow chamber in which to store an

object as long and thin as *Ga Buidhe an Lamhaigh*. Her
heart sank as the truth of the matter hit her.

She'd lost her clan's precious spear.

How would she ever find it if it no longer possessed
the power to make its presence known to her?

Surely no thief would own up to taking it, for the
punishment would be severe. But what would she do
now? She could not return to Carrauntoohil without the
spear, nor could she stay here at Wrexton while her clan
was suffering the chaos that had certainly resulted from
Cormac's death.

Keelin lifted the tallow candle and looked around.
Mayhap she was mistaken about *Ga Buidhe an Lamhaigh* going missing. Was it not possible that someone
had discovered the spear and then put it away somewhere, not knowing what else to do with it?

She checked every wall to see if the spear had been
propped up or laid down. When that failed, she looked
inside and under every cart and wagon, in every pile of
leather harnesses and behind every tool that was stored
there.

It was all to no avail. The spear was gone.

Chapter Eleven

Marcus played the dutiful host to Bishop Delford all morning and through the noon meal. He did not see Keelin during that time, though he was told she was tending Adam. That did not come as any surprise.

Isolda sat next to Marcus through the meal, chatting with Delford as though she were the princess of Wrexton. Her attitude irritated Marcus, although there was no reason why she should not feel so proprietary. Neither he nor Eldred had ever said or done anything to discourage her.

Today, however, Marcus resolved to speak to her. He would see to it that she understood his intent to find her a husband.

The opportunity for this discussion did not present itself until the late afternoon, well after the bishop had settled into a long ecclesiastical debate with Father Pygott, Wrexton's chamberlain. Marcus excused himself as the two clerics strolled toward the chapel, deep in discussion.

"You wished to see me, Marcus?" Isolda asked as she entered the solar.

Marcus folded his hands behind his back and stepped

over to the window. He was unsure how to go about this, but hoped he would somehow manage to make the discussion agreeable for both of them. It felt strange to have summoned this woman—*any* woman—to his presence. He'd never done such a thing before, much less been required to take charge and direct the conversation.

But he was earl now, and this was only the beginning of his obligations to all who dwelt at Wrexton.

"Sit down, Isolda," he said more calmly than he felt. She took a seat near the fire and smoothed her skirts over her lap. Marcus sensed an unusual nervousness about her.

"I, er, I don't believe I've ever known where you are from," he said, uncomfortable with bluntly saying what was on his mind.

"Wh-why, I was born in Lancashire, near Manchester," she replied warily. A crease appeared between her brows. "My father was Baron Geoffrey Coule of Ellingham."

Marcus nodded. He paced away from the window, and then back to it. "So...you were raised on an estate?"

"Yes, in sheep country," she said. "Ours was the best wool in the county."

But Marcus did not care to speak of sheep or wool. He wanted to establish Isolda's need for a husband and a domain of her own. Somewhere *outside* of Wrexton. "Ah. And the estate?" Marcus asked. "What happened to it upon your father's death? Who holds it now?"

"Marcus, I am not sure I understand your reason for these questions," Isolda said, her arched brows wrinkling in puzzlement. "You've known me these last five years. I have no connection now to Ellingham. It has not been my home since Edmund Sandborn brought me here to Wrexton nearly ten years ago."

"I realize that, Isolda," Marcus said, fully aware that he needed to change his tack. Mayhap the roundabout method was not the best. "Sandborn was a cousin of yours?"

"Our mothers were cousins," she replied. "And he apparently recalled their fondness for each other…"

Marcus remembered Edmund Sandborn well, and could not imagine the former earl respecting any fondness his mother may have had for anyone. He'd been a spiteful, vindictive man and Marcus doubted any saintly motive for taking Isolda in. Still, Isolda was not to blame for Sandborn's flaws.

"A distant cousin holds my father's estate now," she said, standing. "He and his wife had seven children when he inherited, and no need for an eighth—*me.*"

Marcus did a quick calculation. Isolda must have been seventeen or eighteen at the time of her father's death and her displacement from her home. Marcus was not insensitive to her plight. 'Twas a difficult age to be left alone and friendless, without a protector. Why had Baron Coule not made any plans to get his daughter wed? Marcus could not understand how Isolda's father could have been so remiss.

"And—" he cleared his throat as he got to the point "—was there no young man, er…a suitor perhaps? Someone who…" That thought drifted when Marcus noticed Isolda's stricken look.

She shook her head. "Nay." Her voice took on a breathless quality and Marcus was sure he heard a slight quavering. "Once my father died, I was completely alone. I h-had no one."

Marcus felt like a beast for making Isolda feel so vulnerable. That had not been his intention at all.

"I thank God every day for Edmund Sandborn, and for Wrexton Castle," she added. "Your father—"

"Isolda." Marcus turned and stalked away. "Some day you might wish to marry," he said, "and if—*when*—you do so, I will provide a dowry."

"But Marcus, I have never wanted to live anywhere but Wrexton—"

"I'm not suggesting that you leave…." Well, yes, that was exactly what he had intended, but the conversation was not going the way he'd planned. "Isolda, you must know you will always…have a home here at Wrexton if need be. But if—*when* you should decide—"

"Thank you, Marcus. That is very reassuring," she replied in a tight little voice as she walked to the door of the solar and put her hand on the latch. Clearly, she sought to avoid any unpleasantness, and thought to escape before Marcus had an opportunity to voice her worst fears. "But I have no—"

"Isolda," Marcus said, stopping her from leaving. "Please sit down. I have yet to finish what I intended to say." He raked one hand through his hair as Isolda abruptly turned and tramped to the chair she had just vacated.

Marcus was vastly uncomfortable but he pressed on, in spite of the exasperated look on Isolda's face. He knew he had to take charge of the situation now or he would never manage to make his intentions known to Isolda. "I feel 'tis time to find a husband for you," he said finally.

The exasperated look changed to astonishment and her face went white. Marcus turned around so he could not see her, and thus be put off his purpose. "You have managed Wrexton well," he continued, "but there will come a time when…er, when I will take a wife."

A sharp intake of breath stopped him momentarily, but he went on.

"It would not do to have two ladies—" he paced away from her "—I mean, my own lady wife would naturally become the Lady of Wrexton—"

Marcus was cut short by Isolda's gasp, and her abrupt flight from the room.

Well, there was nothing to be done about it. Marcus had certainly never given Isolda any hope that he would have her to wife, although he suspected his father allowed her to stay at Wrexton as a last resort. Eldred likely assumed that if Marcus did not manage to find his own wife, he would settle for Isolda.

And, to Eldred's thinking, Isolda as a wife would have been better than none.

Marcus disliked hurting Isolda, but he felt 'twas better to say something now, and allow her to become accustomed to the idea of leaving Wrexton. He would send messages to Chester with Bishop Delford, and to the counties beyond, informing prospective bridegrooms of Isolda's availability, and the dowry she would bring.

"Where is Keelin?" Marcus asked when he went to see Adam a short time later. The boy was conscious, but so weak that he was unable to sit up unaided, unable to feed himself.

"She left here nigh an hour ago," Tiarnan replied. His brows were furrowed into a frown. "She said nothin' about where she was goin' though somethin' was troublin' the lass."

"What was it?"

Tiarnan shook his head. "That, I don't know," he replied. "And I asked her, too, but she told me 'twas nothin'."

"What do you think, Tiarnan?" Marcus asked. "Has she...*sensed* something she doesn't want to tell you?"

"That may be, lad," Marcus said. "Though, what it might be is a mystery to me. She's never held back from me before."

Marcus knew she intended to leave. Perhaps that's what it was. Her plans to leave Tiarnan at Wrexton and go on to Ireland alone were making her anxious.

Those plans made Marcus anxious, as well, though he forced himself not to dwell on it.

Instead, he talked to Adam, who responded weakly, and answered the boy's questions about Eldred's funeral. 'Twas a long and dismal interlude.

Keelin searched nearly every building in the bailey, but found no sign of *Ga Buidhe an Lamhaigh*. She did not want to have to return to the keep and tell Tiarnan the spear was lost until she had turned Wrexton Castle upside down with her searching.

At dusk, she found herself entering the mews, the building where all of Wrexton's hunting birds were housed. She felt a bit like a thief in the night, sneaking into the mews as she'd done at Carrauntoohil, for her father would never allow anyone but his handlers near his precious birds.

She had loved them, those fierce, majestic creatures of the sky. She never felt sorry for their captivity, except during the training, which Keelin felt was unduly harsh. Otherwise, they were petted and fed, and well rewarded for their hunting prowess.

"Evening, my lady," Gerald Falconer said, taking Keelin by surprise. She had not seen the man in the shadows.

Keelin greeted him, and, realizing she was not going

to be chastised for trespassing where she was not wanted, she turned and looked around.

This building was much larger than the mews at Carrauntoohil, and was home to a great many more birds than her father ever kept. There was gravel underfoot—another difference. At home, her father had had coarse sand brought in to cover the floors. It had been necessary for Keelin to cover her tracks whenever she'd sneaked out, so no one would notice that a small intruder had invaded the birds' sanctuary.

Everything here was in perfect order. A workbench lined one wall where leather-working tools were neatly arranged. Linen socks and bells sat on the table, while leather jesses and leashes were looped and hanging on hooks above the bench.

Keelin looked beyond the bench. The birds were magnificent and in her admiration of all that she saw, Keelin momentarily forgot about her search for *Ga Buidhe an Lamhaigh.*

''D'ye think Lord Marcus would mind if I went along inside?''

Gerald shook his head. ''I doubt it,'' he said. ''The birds are well trained. They're not easily ruffled.''

Keelin walked to the far end and spoke quietly to the gyrfalcons, perched together at shoulder height. They eyed her curiously, but she put them at ease with her soft, musical voice.

Resting on other perches of various heights were peregrines and sakers, as well as the smaller goshawks and sparrow hawks. ''Oh, my,'' Keelin whispered, spying a pair of nestlings. She crouched down to the nest where the two looked at her with stunned eyes. ''Look at you. How lovely ye'll be when you're grown.''

''I had hopes of them growing to be fierce, rather than

lovely,'' Marcus said as he approached, his footsteps crunching the gravel.

Keelin smiled. ''Ach, and they will be, m'lord. Just look at them!''

But Marcus preferred looking at her.

She was disheveled, and had spots of dirt on her clothes and a smudge on her cheek, as if she had been helping to clean up the stable mess. Marcus wouldn't put that possibility beyond her.

She must have washed her hair, for it shone darkly in the gloaming, and showed no signs of the blood that had matted it the night before. His hands ached to touch the silky mass, left loose and uncovered just to tempt him.

''Your pardon, my lord,'' the falconer said.

Marcus and Keelin turned in unison.

''I'll be going now,'' Gerald said as he pulled up his hood and wrapped his cloak tightly around. ''We hunt tomorrow, then?''

''Yes,'' Marcus replied. ''At first light if weather permits.''

Gerald gave a quick nod. ''Likely to be cold, but no snow yet.''

Marcus agreed that snow was unlikely, but gave no further thought to Gerald or the morrow. Keelin O'Shea occupied his full attention. He enjoyed watching her with the falcons. He felt completely at ease with her, though that did not surprise him now, as it would have a mere week ago.

Her body was slender and graceful, her hands kind yet able. Her eyes sparkled with intelligence and interest and Marcus could think of nothing but touching her.

''Your head…'' he said. ''The wound does not trouble you?''

"Nay," she replied. "At least, not much. Did I thank ye for helpin' me yestereve?"

Marcus nodded, her smile rendering him speechless.

"My own father kept birds at Carrauntoohil," she said, standing up again. She smelled spicy, like the herbs she kept in her leather pouches. Her lips were full, moist. It seemed more like a week rather than a mere day since he'd kissed them.

"Did you ever hunt with him?" he asked just to keep her there, to keep her talking.

"Nay," Keelin replied with a sour laugh. "He was not one to allow a woman—or me, a mere lass—near his birds." Then a thought suddenly dawned on her and she sobered. "Do *you* mind, Marcus? That I'm here among your fine falcons?"

He shook his head. "Of course not," he replied, then thought of a reason to keep her at Wrexton, if only for a few more days. "Mayhap you would care to join us on the morrow?"

"And hunt, ye mean?" Keelin asked, her eyes sparkling with delight.

Marcus nodded.

"Oh, aye, Marcus!" she said. "There's nothin' that would please me better."

"Then it's settled. What is it?" he asked, noticing a sudden change in Keelin's joy.

"Ach, 'tis a grievous matter," she replied, her delicate brows furrowing in a troubled frown, "and I nearly forgot." She turned away from him, wringing her hands before her.

"I've lost something precious that belongs to my clan," she said.

"Ah...would it be the sacred spear your uncle spoke of?"

"Aye, Marcus, and it's missing," Keelin said with surprise. She had not realized Tiarnan had told him of the spear. "I thought I hid it so cleverly, yet someone found it and—"

"Luckily, 'twas *I* who found it," Marcus interjected.

Keelin looked stunned. She made the sign of the cross and muttered a quiet thanks to Saints Bridget and Patrick.

"I knew you must have brought it to Wrexton, so I checked your mule cart and found it there," Marcus said. He had reasoned that the cart was the only place it could be. When he found it, he'd considered withholding it from her, just to keep her at Wrexton. But that would not have been an honorable thing to do. Marcus would not keep her at Wrexton by coercion. "'Twas hidden quite ingeniously," he said.

"Oh, I've been so worried," she said, placing one hand over her heart. Her relief was nearly palpable. "I was sure a thief must've taken it, and I'd have to be tellin' Uncle Tiarnan what a dolt I was for leavin' it in that storage shed."

"'Tis safe in my chamber," he said. "It can remain where it is, or I can give it to you to keep."

"Aye, I thank ye, m'lord, but I will take it myself, if ye don't mind."

Marcus *did* mind, though he knew it was foolish. Keelin was accustomed to trusting no one but herself. It should not be construed as a personal affront that she wanted the spear in her own keeping.

Marcus lit several tallow lamps to ward off the growing darkness. He wanted to be able to see her.

"Will you be puttin' socks on these chicks soon?" Keelin asked as Marcus came back to where she stood.

"Yes." They would cover each bird in a linen sack

that was open at both ends for their heads and feet, and begin the chicks' training. "Gerald will start the training within the next few days," he added as he set his lamp down and crouched next to the nest. "We got them when they were newly hatched, so they've had time to become accustomed to us. They're quite tame."

The baby merlins tipped their heads and cheeped as Marcus came nearer. Keelin watched as he picked one up in those big hands of his.

"Males or females?" Keelin asked, a little breathlessly.

"Females are the hunters," Marcus replied.

"I didn't know that."

"They're bigger, and much more aggressive than the males," he added.

Keelin quirked her head. "Would ye be teasin' me, Marcus?" In all her life, she'd never thought of females as being the fiercer of the species, although she supposed it made sense. After all, 'twas the mother who had to see to the feeding and safekeeping of her young.

He shook his head as he lifted his hands to hers. "Open your hands," he said.

She did so, and he gently placed the nestling in the cradle she created next to her bosom.

"So soft," she said.

When Marcus did not reply, she looked up. He stood so close, and was gazing at her in a way that made her feel as if her bones were melting. Candlelight flickered and the tiny feet of the merlin in her hand tickled.

If only he would kiss her again as he had in the courtyard. Keelin could feel his breath, the heat of his body, standing so near. Aye, 'twas a wondrous thing to hold such a wild creature in her hands, but 'twas her heart that beat savagely in her chest. She knew that only Marcus's touch could quell the fierce longing that she felt.

Yet she knew it should not be. It *could* not be. She was destined to leave Wrexton and take *Ga Buidhe an Lamhaigh* to Carrauntoohil. She was Eocaidh O'Shea's daughter, and her clan needed her.

"Will you be puttin' leashes on these two?" she asked, her voice no longer her own, but unfamiliar with its soft and husky timbre.

"Yes," Marcus replied as he moved closer.

"And bells, as well?" she whispered, her body leaning toward his without the slightest conscious effort.

"Yes," Marcus replied, his lips so close to hers that she could feel his breath upon them.

"And will you be sealin' their eyes?" She protected the nestling she held as Marcus moved even closer, tipping his head toward her own, to meet her lips in a kiss.

"'Tis likely," he said absently. His mind was not on the training of his birds.

"What?" Keelin demanded, pulling back and looking up at him. "You'd sew their eyes closed in order to bend them to your will?"

Chagrined, Marcus realized he'd said the wrong thing. How was he to know she would be offended by birds having their eyelids sewn shut—if only temporarily. He put his hands on her shoulders to keep her from pulling away.

"'Twill be up to Gerald," he said firmly. "Occasionally it is necessary to seal the eyes. But not always."

"Oh," Keelin said, embarrassed. She glanced down at the wee thing in her hands. 'Twas not her business how he trained the poor creatures, and she should not have spoken out. "My pardon, m'lord, 'tis just—"

He captured her lips then.

Keelin was taken by surprise, but she quickly responded with all the passion that dwelt in her. She leaned into him, taking care not to crush the small bird in her hands, but allowing the tips of her breasts to touch his chest. The result reminded her of the extraordinary reaction she always had when she touched *Ga Buidhe an Lamhaigh.*

But this was ever so much more pleasurable.

Keelin wished her hands were free so that she could touch Marcus. She yearned to run her fingers through his golden hair, to learn the contours of his face by touch. She longed to feel the heat of his body against her own. Keelin knew, though, that if she moved away to set the nestling down, the mood would be broken.

So she contented herself with the feel of Marcus's lips on hers, the pressure of his hands on her shoulders. His scent, which was now so familiar to Keelin, was wholly Marcus's—clean, masculine. She heard his breath, coming no more easily than her own, and felt the texture of his skin. Keelin felt surrounded by him, by glorious sensations. She sighed into his mouth, and the kiss changed.

One of his hands moved to cradle her head. His lips opened, compelling Keelin to open hers. Without hesitation, he invaded her mouth, drawing a sensual moan from the back of Keelin's throat. She was floating in a sea of sensations.

Never before had she felt like this, as if she were cherished beyond reason, enfolded in Marcus's strength. 'Twas what she needed after years of forced isolation— years of loneliness and yearning.

'Twas what she would have once she returned to Carrauntoohil and wed the man to whom she was promised.

Abruptly, she broke away from Marcus. She could not do this with him—*to* him. She cared too much, both for

Marcus and for her own sanity, to allow their emotions to carry them away. Soon she would leave Wrexton, and she wanted to take her heart with her.

The short leather cord that belonged to Marcus—that even now lay between her breasts—would go with her, to remind her of what might have been, if she had not borne the responsibility of being Eocaidh's daughter.

Marcus stood alone in the mews, looking at the small merlin Keelin had awkwardly placed in his hands before she fled. He felt fortunate that his hands were not shaking, for he could not recall another occasion in which he felt his soul had been so completely exposed and vulnerable.

What witchery was this? How did Keelin O'Shea manage to pry him open and flay him raw time and again like a master tanner?

Marcus knew without a doubt what would have happened had Keelin remained with him in the mews. He had thought himself above such base behavior, yet he'd been more than ready to consummate their attraction for one another. What had happened to his honor, his sense of chivalry?

Sorcery, was it?

Marcus did not know whether it was sorcery or not, nor was there anyone whom he could trust with his questions. Normally, a man in Marcus's position would consult his priest. Wrexton's chamberlain, however, was not a particularly tolerant cleric. Father Pygott interpreted ecclesiastical law too literally, in Marcus's opinion, allowing no deviation from what he perceived as truth. And, as Marcus had often seen when his father or the steward conducted hallmote, truth was not always obvious.

The priest's judgment could be swayed either for or against Keelin, and Marcus was aware that the man had no love of "foreigners." He doubted Keelin would fare well under the chamberlain's scrutiny. Marcus would have to take care that Father Pygott did not get wind of Keelin's "magic" spear, or of her visions that predicted the future.

The more Marcus thought on it, the more he was convinced that Pygott would not accept any explanation of Keelin's talent, outside his realm of experience. She would be condemned out of hand.

Keelin was not in the great hall when Marcus went inside. However, Isolda and Beatrice stood in a far corner, talking together in hushed tones, while Beatrice's hands gestured emphatically.

A maid happened by, and Isolda immediately took her to task over some infraction, her voice rising harshly, loud enough for Marcus to hear. He winced at the severity of her tone, but had no interest in involving himself in their domestic difficulties. Soon enough, he would find a husband for Isolda, then she and her companion would be gone from Wrexton forever.

As he escaped up the great stone stairs, he only hoped that Wrexton's staff could hold out until then.

Chapter Twelve

Keelin was glad for once, that Uncle Tiarnan could not see her. She knew her lips were swollen and her cheeks flushed with the passion she and Marcus had shared in the mews. She doubted Tiarnan would approve of any sort of liaison with Marcus, and did not want him to see how foolish she had been.

She had no future here at Wrexton, and well she knew it. She raised a hand to her breast, where Marcus's leather cord lay nestled between her breasts, and acknowledged for the first time that she *did* wish it otherwise. But soon the twisted slip of cord would be all that she'd have to remember him.

"Keely lass?" Tiarnan said.

"Aye, Uncle," she replied, "'tis me." She hardly recognized her own voice, laced as it was with the tears she struggled so diligently to hold back. No doubt Tiarnan would hear the difference.

"What ails ye, lass?" Tiarnan asked.

"Oh, 'tis nothin'," Keelin replied. Now that she knew Marcus had *Ga Buidhe an Lamhaigh,* all should be well. She fought tears as she looked over at Adam, lying pale and weak in his bed. "How are ye, Adam?" she asked.

"Better, Keelin," Adam replied. "Uncle Tiarnan has been telling me all about Kerry and Carraun... Carrauntoohil. Is it really as magical a place as he says?"

"Ach, aye, lad," she said, smiling tearfully as she sat on the bed next to him. She took one of his hands in hers. "Every wee bit of it."

"Might I go there someday?"

"'Tis a long and arduous journey," Keelin said. "Not a voyage to be taken on a whim."

"Will you ever go back?" Adam asked.

Keelin nodded. "Aye," she said quietly. "I must. My people need me."

"Why?" Adam asked. "You've been away a long time. Can they not do without you awhile longer?"

Can they not, indeed? Keelin thought, then quickly corrected her thinking. The O'Sheas needed her now during these troubled times.

With Cormac's death, they would be feeling vulnerable and lost, especially without *Ga Buidhe an Lamhaigh*. The spear had seen Clann Ui Sheaghda through the worst of times across untold ages, even before Saint Patrick, when the *Tuatha De Danaan* still trod upon on Irish soil.

Keelin forced a smile onto her lips. "Ye know I wouldn't dream of leavin' until you're fully well again."

"You won't?" he said in a sad tone, with a wee bit of wariness to it.

"Nay, Adam. I promise I'll be here with ye until you're able to be up and about."

The promise seemed to placate the lad, and he relaxed enough to doze. Keelin knew it meant she'd have to stay on at Wrexton a good week or more, too many days of trying to avoid Marcus.

'Twas something her heart did not want her to do.

She sat near the lad and wondered about the spear. What had kept her from sensing its presence earlier? As soon as she'd come into the keep, she'd felt its presence again, and would have been able to locate it even if she'd not known that Marcus had it hidden somewhere.

A light knock at the door brought Keelin to her feet. A footman stood in the gallery with a message from Lord Marcus for Lady Keelin and Lord Tiarnan.

The honor of their presence was requested in the great hall for a feast in honor of Bishop Delford.

When the footman left, Keelin turned to look at Tiarnan. He was smiling. "Ah, 'tis a nice gesture, to be sure," he said, "but ye'll have to go without me, Keely lass. I'm not up to it."

Keelin thought of facing Marcus again so soon after their interlude in the mews, and did not know if she was up to it, either.

The gathering in the great hall was somber as would be expected after the death of Wrexton's lord. Only two musicians were present, playing the harp and the mournful viele. Marcus was grateful there would be no singing this night, for he wanted the meal over and done early, without any vocal lamentations of his father's death, no extended prayer ceremony by the bishop.

'Twas not that he did not mourn his father. On the contrary, Marcus felt Eldred's absence acutely, especially these last days since they'd returned to Wrexton. Marcus did not know if he could ever rule his domain as well as his wise and benevolent father had done.

Keelin and her uncle had not yet arrived in the hall. Marcus knew that his request for her presence had been issued late, though he doubted she would take offense at the breach of courtesy that was implied. Keelin's views on etiquette were quite different from those of the English ladies of his acquaintance.

All of Wrexton's high-ranking knights and their ladies were present in the hall, as well as several officials from Wrexton Town, including the reeve and sheriff and their wives. As the guests arrived and the hall became more crowded, Marcus positioned himself near the dais where he could keep an eye on the stone stairs of the keep, the place where he would see Keelin as she descended.

He craved her presence beyond all reason, sensing that she would support and encourage him through his first formal meal as Lord of Wrexton.

Father Pygott and Bishop Delford stood near Marcus, speaking of local church matters. Marcus paid little heed to the two clerics. He could think only of Keelin, and keeping her at Wrexton until he was able to sort out his feelings for her.

She was not indifferent to him, of that he was certain. He may not have kissed a multitude of maidens, but he was nonetheless capable of determining her interest, her arousal. He knew she hungered for *his* touch as greatly as he craved *hers*.

If only she did not feel compelled to return to Ireland so quickly, Marcus would have time to court her properly. He would present her with gifts befitting her station, and provide feasts where minstrels would sing her praises. He would win her and keep her at Wrexton.

Yet he understood duty. And Keelin's duty to her clan was clear—at least it was clear to Keelin.

Isolda hovered nearby. Marcus sensed that she intentionally avoided him, but he gave little attention to her slight. Instead, he noticed that she was more short-tempered than usual with the servants, causing at least one young maid to run out of the hall in tears.

No matter that he intended find another home for her, Marcus could not allow Isolda's abuse of the castle servants to continue. Her anger at him and her situation did not give her liberty to mistreat those below her.

Marcus took his leave of Bishop Delford and began to make his way toward Isolda, but Keelin suddenly appeared at the top of the stairs. Marcus halted.

She was breathtaking in her simplicity.

She hesitated for just an instant before she began to descend, but Marcus caught her eye and she started down, moving gracefully. She was nothing short of majestic. Wearing a simple velvet gown of a deep blue that hugged her slender frame, she was more elegant than any other lady in the hall. Her hair was bound at her nape, with a few sprigs of white and green somehow threaded there. Her head was bare otherwise.

A pattern of interlocking gold stitching trimmed her neckline, setting off the fine bones of her neck, and a modest décolletage. A golden girdle of the same pattern encircled her hips, swaying mesmerizingly with each step she took.

Keelin's skin was pale in the candlelight, though a flush of color graced her high cheeks. Her eyes glittered green fire, taking in all that she saw around her. Her mouth was full. It was red and inviting, and Marcus could think only of their softness, their sensuous heat.

Marcus guided her to him through the power of his will and his eyes on her.

He wanted to intercept her before introducing her to the bishop, in order to inform her of the expected protocol, but Isolda caught Keelin's arm and led her to the bishop herself. Isolda performed the introductions, as though Keelin were the honored guest, then took a step back and waited with an odd gleam in her eye.

Marcus saw Isolda stiffen when Keelin knelt to kiss Delford's ring and receive his blessing. He did not understand the subtleties of the interchange, but was pleased to see that Keelin followed the appropriate proprieties without having to be prompted. He should not have expected anything less of her.

Isolda recovered herself quickly and began to speak, awkwardly interrupting Keelin's compliment on the bishop's requiem for Eldred de Grant. "'Twas inspirin', yer eminence," Keelin said in spite of Isolda, "and an honor to share the Mass with all who mourn Lord Eldred."

Marcus saw Delford warm to the compliment. The bishop continued to converse with Keelin, much to Isolda's dismay, and turned to walk with her to their places at the main table on the dais. Marcus followed, as did the rest of the guests, and waited for the bishop to bless the meal while he puzzled over Isolda's behavior.

The music stopped as Delford stood to give his blessing. When the bishop finished, the music resumed, and servants began to carry in trays laden with food. Isolda reappeared, carrying a tray with four gold chalices, which she carefully set before Marcus, Bishop Delford, Keelin and herself.

In spite of himself, Marcus had to give credit to Isolda for her graciousness. She had been chatelaine of Wrexton a long time, and knew her role very well. No doubt the goblets were filled with the castle's best wine and Isolda would subtly hint for Marcus to toast Bishop Delford.

Keelin took a deep breath to steady herself. Uncle

Tiarnan had advised her to relax and be natural, and that all would be well. From the first, though, the evening had not boded well.

Earlier, Isolda had come to her chamber under the guise of seeing that Keelin's maid was performing satisfactorily. Isolda spoke to Keelin of English custom, and what she could expect during the evening's festivities. She instructed Keelin to perform a courtly curtsey for the bishop, and to remain silent unless the bishop or Marcus spoke to her.

She had eyed Keelin's gown and asked, "Have you no better apparel for Wrexton's great hall?"

Keelin had shaken her head self-consciously and Isolda had remarked that the blue velvet would have to do, but that Keelin could not enter the hall with her head uncovered. Before leaving Keelin, she sent the maid to fetch a headrail from Beatrice, and told Keelin to put it on before coming down to the hall.

When the maid brought it, the yellowed wimple smelled of onions. Even the maid wrinkled her nose at the distasteful thing.

Keelin had been shaken by the subtle hostility she received from Isolda. She had done nothing to warrant such ire, and she did not understand what made Isolda dislike her so. Dismissing the maid, Keelin went to Tiarnan for some reassurance before going down to the hall.

'Twas fortunate indeed that Uncle Tiarnan had taken her in hand, and spoken of what would be expected from an Irish princess. Had she followed Isolda's advice, she'd have made an utter fool of herself.

"Uncle, are ye certain I'm not to be givin' his eminence my curtsey?" Keelin had asked.

"Ach, no, child," Tiarnan retorted. "'Twould be a grave insult to do so. And mind, ye only be *sippin'* yer wine down there, Keely lass,'' he'd said. ''Yer not accustomed to strong drink and 'twill make ye silly.''

Keelin doubted anything could do that, for she'd never felt less silly in her life. She'd been intentionally tutored by Isolda Coule to appear the buffoon. Keelin could only guess at the reason why, and not very well at that. She had too little experience of the world's subtleties to understand why Isolda would wish her ill.

She'd walked down the gallery with her emotions in upheaval. 'Twas not a pleasant thing to be so disliked, especially when she'd spent so many years yearning for the company of others like herself—like Isolda.

When she reached the top of the stone stairs, a strong sense of foreboding had slammed into Keelin. She managed to keep her composure, but the ominous presentiment persisted, growing stronger with every step.

At first Keelin worried that something would happen to Adam. After all, his condition was still very precarious. He was weak and still feverish, although he showed definite signs of improvement. Yet that did not seem to be the cause of her uneasy feelings.

No, 'twas something else, but what it was, Keelin could not even venture to guess.

Isolda's place was at Marcus's left hand, and though Keelin thought she saw him pause when Isolda took her place, he said nothing. Food was placed on the table and Keelin took her seat next to Bishop Delford. The music, which had resumed after the prayer, stopped when Marcus raised his goblet to toast Bishop Delford. He said a few complimentary words, and then everyone in the hall stood and lifted their cups to the cleric.

Keelin stood with the rest and turned, then lifted her own goblet. Instantly, the thing slid from her hand, narrowly missing the bishop and herself. Splashing wine everywhere, it clanged to the table, causing a deep red stain to appear—both on the white cloth as well as on Keelin's face.

'Twas greased, she thought as she tried to maintain her dignity. She smiled and muttered an apology, but was mortified by the accident. Servants arrived with cloths to clean up the spill and Keelin rubbed her hands together. Though they were damp with the spilled wine, she was certain they were oily, too.

"'Tis no matter, my child," Delford said in reply to Keelin's apology. "No harm done."

Yet she could feel all eyes upon her. Everyone in the hall had to be aware of Keelin's blunder and it was all she could do to seat herself again and pretend that all was well.

"Lady Keelin and her uncle have agreed to remain at Wrexton until Adam is better," Marcus said, quickly speaking up to fill the silence caused by Keelin's disaster. "We have no healer here, and their skills have been well tested with my young cousin." His eyes were more than kind, they held the solace and succor Keelin desperately needed to see her through the calamity.

"Ah, yes," Delford said, "the boy was gravely wounded. 'Tis a blessing he yet lives."

"God's will be done," Isolda muttered.

"True enough, gracious lady," Delford said.

Keelin was churning inside. She rubbed her hands on the fine cloth that had been placed before her, and took meat from the platter that was passed to her. Her movements were perfunctory. She could not be at ease when Isolda's unexpected venom poisoned her so.

Keelin could only wonder what would happen next.

After the meal, Marcus had had no choice but to play the host to Delford, but he resented each minute spent away from Keelin's side. Isolda hovered nearby, quite aware that Marcus would say nothing of his plans to send her away in the bishop's presence. She engaged the bishop in lively conversation, her eyes flashing with life and gaiety, while something else lurked beneath the surface.

Marcus was not quite sure what she was about, but Isolda did nothing without purpose.

The meal had barely ended when Keelin approached Delford to bid him farewell and wish him a safe journey on the morrow. Then she turned and bid Marcus good night. Her attitude was quite formal, subdued even, with none of the graceful ease of her conversation before dinner.

Marcus did not understand what had happened to change her demeanor so dramatically. He could not believe that the incident with the wine goblet could have upset her so much, but, suspicious now, he wondered what else could have happened that he had not noticed?

The evening wore on interminably after Keelin retired. The food did not settle well, nor was the company especially exhilarating. Eldred's death had cast a somber pall over the evening, and the guests were quiet and appropriately respectful of their fallen lord.

The visitors from Wrexton Town departed early, and the castle guests retired as soon as it was polite to do so. Servants began clearing up the hall, carrying trays, cleaning up spills, and removing the trestles.

Marcus picked up a lamp and headed toward the stone steps, but he was waylaid by Sir William.

"A word, my lord," the knight said.

Chapter Thirteen

"What is it, Will?" Marcus asked. He was weary, but possessed of a strange restlessness. Even when he retired to his chamber, he was unsure he'd be able to sleep.

"My lord, I have never been known to mince my words," Will said, "and 'twould serve neither of us if I started now."

"Speak freely, then."

"'Tis pranks, Lord Marcus," Will said. "Pranks that'll do nothing but grow in severity until someone's hurt."

"Pranks?" Marcus asked, gaining a glimmer of what William referred to.

Will cleared his throat. He kept his voice down so that no others would hear him, but still, there was a hollow quality to the hall, now that it was nearly empty, and echoes emanated from every sound.

"Come with me to my chamber," Marcus said.

The man followed as Marcus led with the candle, and he did not speak again until they'd entered Marcus's room. The fire had been laid and the room was comfortably warm.

"My lord, do you recall yestermorn, when you and I came into the hall with Robert?"

Marcus nodded. He recalled the moment clearly. His eyes had met Keelin's and they'd made an instant connection to each other as if by some invisible thread that bound them. And the moment had broken when she'd fallen.

"Isolda tripped her."

Marcus frowned. "Are you certain?"

"'Tis not my way to go telling tales, my lord," Will said, firmly, "but like I said, this is bound to go further still. Tonight, Isolda greased the lady's cup so she'd drop it and make a spectacle of herself."

Marcus did not want to believe it, although it was all too easy to do so. He'd seen plenty of evidence of Isolda's tyranny at Wrexton, especially in the last few days since his return. Now his ire rose on Keelin's behalf, having to suffer Isolda's meanness without a word of complaint.

No doubt Isolda had meant for Keelin to spill the goblet of wine all over herself as well as Bishop Delford. What a sight that would have been! Keelin would have looked like a clumsy churl to all who were gathered in the hall.

Marcus should have realized that Isolda would feel threatened by Keelin's presence, but he'd been preoccupied with all that was required of him since his return to Wrexton.

And with Keelin.

He had not given any attention to Isolda or how she might feel about Keelin O'Shea. In fact, he had probably made matters worse by telling Isolda he intended to find her a husband and move her away from Wrexton.

"I thought nothing of all this until tonight, my lord,"

William added. "But there are bound to be more incidents...."

"You're right, Will," Marcus said.

"And Lady Keelin has done so much...first for Adam, then Edward's leg...."

"Yes, she has," he said, silently chastising himself for his oversight. "Concern yourself no further. I'll deal with Lady Isolda."

William lowered his head, then took the candle Marcus handed him. "Well, good night, then, my lord," he said as he turned and opened the door.

"Good night, Will," Marcus said. "And thank you for your vigilance."

Keelin passed the night in restless sleep. That strong, intuitive sense of foreboding had abated to some degree, yet she still sensed something amiss at Wrexton Castle.

If she'd had *Ga Buidhe an Lamhaigh* in her possession, she might have picked it up and gotten a clearer sense of what was wrong. Instead, she tossed and turned through the night, battling faceless demons in her sleep.

It was barely dawn when a light tap at her chamber door woke her. By the flickering light of the dying fire, she climbed groggily from her bed and opened her chamber door.

Marcus stood in the dark gallery, holding one candle. He did not speak for a moment, but cleared his throat and seemed to consider what he wanted to say. Finally, he spoke. "I did not want you to miss the hunt."

Through her haze of semiwakefulness, Keelin saw his eyes rove over her disheveled appearance. She knew her thin linen shift was hardly decent, but felt no need—or desire—to cover herself in Marcus's presence.

"Oh," she said as her mind cleared. Memory and

good sense returned. "Yes. With your birds." Marcus himself looked dangerous, if only to her peace of mind, Keelin thought as she crossed her arms in front of her.

He nodded, unable to take his eyes off her. He stepped into Keelin's chamber, pushing the door shut behind him. Then he held something out to her.

Ga Buidhe an Lamhaigh.

"Oh! Thank you, Marcus," Keelin said, taking the leather-encased spear from his hands. She turned away and Marcus followed her deeper into the room.

"Here's where I would hide it," he said, finding his voice again as he walked to the bed and picked up one edge of the mattress. The imprint of her body was still there, and the blankets were a tangled mess from her restless night. Her intimate presence could not have been illustrated more clearly, though Marcus gave no sign of noticing. "Lay it here, lengthwise along the frame. I doubt it will be disturbed there."

"Oh, aye," she said, putting the spear on the frame, just as he'd said. "'Tis likely the best place for it. I thank ye, Marcus for thinkin' of it. And for keepin' it safe for me."

Marcus dropped the mattress back into place and stepped away from the bed, his eyes never leaving her. They glittered darkly in the faint light of the room, and Keelin suspected that he was thinking of neither the spear nor the morning's hunt.

She felt more naked than ever, even though she was covered from throat to toes. Keelin doubted Marcus realized how he looked at her, or even that a heavy silence hung between them. Uneasily, she placed one hand at her neck, where the ties of her gown had loosened. Her fingers toyed with the laces.

Keelin felt the pull, the need to be desired and cherished. She knew that if she gave but one small tug on the laces, and then a tiny shrug, the gown would fall from her shoulders. She could finally learn what magical force urged her to seek Marcus's embrace time and again.

But she would not risk *Ga Buidhe an Lamhaigh,* or the welfare of the clan, to satisfy her own trivial needs.

Her decision to remain aloof was a sound one, and Keelin knew it was the only one she could make under the circumstances. 'Twould be a mere week or so, she told herself, that she would have to keep this potent attraction at bay. Then Adam would be up and about, and Keelin would be well on her way to Carrauntoohil.

Quickly, before she could change her mind, she raised both hands to Marcus's shoulders and turned him, pushing him out of her chamber. "Leave me now, m'lord," she said shakily. "I'll dress and meet you in the hall."

Marcus stood outside Keelin's door and forced his heart to slow, his breathing to return to normal.

Still, he could see the delicate bones of her neck, the sleek muscles of her throat moving as she spoke. Her hair was loose, as always, but this morning it had been tangled and mussed by sleep. Her eyes had been slightly swollen, leading him to believe she had slept no better than he.

The bed had nearly been his undoing. Still warm from her body, he could easily envision her lying upon it, her lustrous hair spread out like a sensuous blanket, her arms raised to welcome him.

He had his honor, though, and he meant to keep it, along with Keelin's.

He was aware of the impropriety of visiting Keelin's chamber, especially while she was undressed, but had been unable to restrain himself. Besides, it had been necessary to return the spear to her, and see that she was awake and ready for the hunt.

He had no intention of letting her run from him today, as she had done the afternoon before in the mews, and again after the supper with Bishop Delford and the rest of the castle guests.

Marcus walked the length of the gallery and went down to the great hall. There, servants were already preparing for the day's needs—food, laundry, fuel. Delford's men were making ready for the bishop's departure later in the morning.

Marcus went into the main kitchen and looked over the satchels of food Cook had prepared for the hunting party, as well as the baskets of food that would accompany the bishop and his men. He informed the servants that Lady Keelin would be out of the keep all day, but she was to be summoned if Adam's condition warranted her presence.

When all was satisfactory within the keep, Marcus braved the cold and crossed the bailey. Entering the mews, he found Gerald Falconer readying the birds.

"Will we take the dogs this morn, my lord?"

Marcus nodded. They would need meat, and plenty of it, to keep the residents of Wrexton fed through the winter. Since Marcus had the right to hunt deer and boar in the king's forest, he would attempt to bring back at least one of each, as well as plenty of small fowl and game.

"Lady Keelin will be joining us today," Marcus said.

"Ah," Gerald replied as he pulled a hood over Cleo's head. "The lady has a clear and healthy respect for your birds, my lord."

'Twas true. He'd seen that Keelin appreciated the falcons with a reverence that few people had. "Are the lads ready to go?'' Marcus asked as he gathered some fur pelts from a cupboard. They would need extra warmth once they were far afield and he did not want Keelin to be chilled.

''Aye,'' Gerald replied. ''They've been up awhile, making everything ready. We were just waiting to see if you wanted the hounds.''

''Very good.''

Marcus's next stop was the shed where many of the horses were temporarily being housed. He chose a gentle mount for Keelin, and had it saddled along with his own.

By this time, the rest of the hunting party was out in the bailey, creating a bit of a disturbance before sunrise. Marcus walked into their midst, looking for Keelin. She was not among the throng.

He looked through the darkness back toward the keep, and saw a tall shadow there, a woman draped in a warm, dark cloak. Keelin. Marcus handed the reins of both horses to Boswell, and headed to the place where she stood.

He clipped up the steps, taking them two at a time. When he reached Keelin, he saw that a bright excitement lit her eyes even though she was reticent to join the party in the bailey. Though Keelin had never struck him as timid or retiring, Marcus understood her hesitance in approaching a strange crowd of people. Especially after having been treated so poorly by Isolda Coule.

''Are you ready?'' he asked.

Keelin gave a shy nod. ''Are you sure I should be comin' along, Marcus?''

Pausing for only a moment, Marcus took her hand, then turned and led her quickly down the steps and into the bailey while a pale, pinched face observed from a narrow, stone arrow-loop high above them.

* * *

"Hold your arm out, Keelin," Marcus said, "and she'll return to you."

Keelin did as Marcus instructed, holding her thickly gloved hand out so that Guinevere would find her perch. Keelin watched as the beautiful gyrfalcon circled, riding high on the cold wind, until she was just above them.

She braced herself for Guinevere's landing as Marcus began speaking to the bird, using the familiar words and tones that calmed the creature. All at once, in a controlled and dignified descent, the gyrfalcon alighted on Keelin's forearm, and was rewarded with a bit of meat.

Keelin felt her heart tip as the graceful bird rested on her hand. She could not imagine anything more powerful or majestic as these beautiful birds in flight, or on the hunt.

And Marcus… His patience in handling the falcons made her wonder if he would show the same patience and joy in his children, when he had them.

Keelin looked up at him then, and saw pride in his eyes, along with something more. Her heart tipped again, and her eyes skittered away before she was forced to acknowledge what she saw.

Clearly, allowing Marcus's feelings to develop any further was wrong, when she intended to leave Wrexton as soon as Adam's condition improved. God and all His saints had to know that her own feelings had progressed well beyond what was prudent. As it was, Keelin did not know how she would manage to leave Wrexton— *Marcus*—when it was time.

Her eyes suddenly burned and she turned toward Gerald Falconer, mindful of the gyrfalcon still perched on her fist. What she really wanted was to run away, run back through the hills to Wrexton Keep.

Or throw herself into Marcus's arms and never let go.

"Will ye be takin' her now, Master Falconer?" she asked, her voice an embarrassing croak.

"Nay, my lady," Gerald replied. "This time, you'll be sending her to her real prey."

Marcus came up behind her. "Can you hold her any longer, or is your arm tiring?" he asked.

"N-no, I'm all right," she stammered. He was too close, and she was all too susceptible to him. She did not want to notice his thick, gold-tipped lashes, or the bright blue of his eyes. She *could not* acknowledge the admiration he had for her. She *would not* allow it to progress any further.

Marcus nodded to Gerald, who began to walk toward the lake where the large waterfowl fed. It was there that Guinevere and Cleo would hunt and bring cranes to their masters.

Keelin tramped through the woods next to Marcus, unable to trust her own voice. Once she'd started thinking about Marcus's children, all she could do was envision the lovely wee darlin's he would have one day. Without her.

"There'll be cranes in the water beyond the wood," Marcus said. "Gerald said there're enough so that we might bag a few without depleting the population."

"Depleting…?"

Marcus smiled at Keelin's puzzled look. "The huntsmen must take care not to kill off too many, else there won't be enough to populate the brooks and fields next year."

"And 'tis the same with the deer," Keelin asked, "as well as the boar?"

Marcus nodded.

"I never knew anyone kept count of the game in the forest."

"You would be surprised," Marcus said. "I am fortunate to have jurisdiction over Wrexton's forests, but most of the green land of the kingdom belongs to the crown."

"The dead king's son?" Keelin asked. "But he's just a wee lad, is he not?"

"Yes, he is," Marcus replied, "but he has a whole army of counselors to see to his interests."

"Hmm," Keelin replied. "And some of them see to their own, I'll wager."

Marcus laughed. 'Twas a wondrous sound to Keelin's ears. She had to steel herself against the seductive sound of his deep laughter and keep a distance between them. "That's a very astute observation for one who's never been to court...or have you?"

"Have I what?" she asked. "Been to court?"

"I was jesting, Keelin," Marcus said, watching deep color seep into her cheeks. He felt exhilarated, treading through the thick woods in the brisk morning air with Keelin O'Shea at his side. She was tall and stately, and kept up his pace as she carried Guinevere on her gloved fist, as if she'd been born and raised to do just that.

Yet something about her was different this morning. She was quiet, even wary. He had noticed it first thing, when he'd met her on Wrexton's steps, but had thought she would relax when she felt accepted as part of the hunting group.

But the sun had long since risen and they'd been out over an hour, and still Keelin remained uncharacteristically reserved.

"Have you tired of carrying Guinevere?" he asked.

"Ach, no, Marcus," Keelin said, her natural enthusiasm surfacing momentarily. "She's a marvelous bird and I fancy carryin' her as long as ye'll let me."

"The lake is not much farther. Once we get there, I'll show you how to release her."

"Ah, that'll be fine, Marcus," she said, speaking from her heart. He knew her experience on the hunt would become a memory she planned to take back to Ireland with her. He would not speak to her of this again, but hoped that by the time Adam had improved enough for Keelin to leave, she would be hard-pressed to do so.

Chapter Fourteen

'Twas well before noon when the members of the hunting party stopped to fill their bellies. Gerald found perches for the falcons, then covered their heads and attached their leashes to the branches. The dogs were led a distance downhill, then their leads were secured and they were given water and food. The huntsmen were then free to join the rest of the party for the meal.

Wrexton's cook had sent plenty of food in baskets, and the hunters unloaded plates and trays of meat pies and joints, cheese and bread, as well as some dried fruit, setting it all haphazardly on the back of the wagon.

"'Tis fitting that you begin, my lady," Gerald said as he handed Keelin a plate.

"I thank ye," she replied with a smile. Marcus was right behind her, and Keelin noticed him filling his plate quickly in order to make room for the others. He was a considerate man, knowing the hunters would never presume to push ahead of their lord.

The air was not as bitter cold as it had been earlier in the morning, and with a quick glance to the sky, they saw heavy clouds moving in.

"I'll hand over my firstborn son if we don't have

snow by morning," said one of the dog handlers as he surveyed the sky.

"Can't imagine who would want the lazy jacka-napes," Marcus teased as he helped Keelin to sit on one of the big fur pelts that had been laid out.

"Ow, I resent that remark!" the said firstborn son protested, gaining a laugh from all the men assembled.

Keelin laughed along with the others, appreciating the pure joy of being with Marcus as he bantered with these men and boys whom he'd known for years. She had never seen her father jest so easily with anyone, and in recent years, she had certainly not had any opportunities to make friends or indulge in such lighthearted diversions.

Marcus eased himself down to her side and crossed his legs, putting his plate on his lap. His knee brushed her thigh.

Though a lightning bolt of sensation coursed through her, Keelin kept her eyes on her plate and forced her hands to remain steady. She took a deep breath and made herself think of the morning's hunt, and her success with Guinevere.

"Are you too cold to continue with the hunt?" Marcus asked.

"N-no, m'lord," she replied, wondering if he had noticed her sudden tremor. 'Twould not do at all for Marcus to fully understand his effect on her. This pleasant interlude would be of limited duration. "But I should get back to the castle, and Adam—"

"We'll be summoned if he needs you."

"Lord Marcus," the huntsman's son said, "if I'm to become your huntsman, I'd best learn to shoot. My father says you're the only one to teach me."

"Aye, yer father's right, lad," one of the men said. "There's none better than Lord Marcus at the long-bow."

Sounds of assent ran through the group, and Marcus agreed to begin the boy's first lesson right after they had all eaten.

"Will ye show me, too, Marcus?" Keelin asked.

Marcus frowned when he met her eyes. Clearly, he'd never heard of a woman using a bow either for pleasure or need.

"'Twould be a skill of great value to me when I journey home." If only she'd known how to make arrows and shoot when she and Tiarnan had fled Ireland, she would have had a much easier time seeing that she and Tiarnan had had enough food. As it was, she'd had to snare whatever small game she could, and fish the rivers in order to eat. It had not been easy.

Keelin did not know what her circumstances would be when she traveled to Kerry, but she was well aware that every skill she acquired would only help her.

She could see that Marcus still had second thoughts about teaching her to shoot, but he tipped his head slightly and agreed. His face was ruddy from the cold, but his eyes were as clear as the Kerry sky. A few loose strands of golden hair blew over his forehead and Keelin felt an urge to smooth them back.

She resisted. 'Twould not do at all to touch the man any more than was strictly necessary.

"Yer leavin Wrexton, Lady Keelin?" one of the lads asked.

"Aye," she replied. "But not till young Adam is well, though." Keelin did not see Marcus's eyes darken at her words, but finished her cup of ale and stood.

* * *

"Lend me your longbow, Philip," Marcus said to one of the older boys. "It should be of a good length and heft for Lady Keelin."

The boy handed it to Marcus, who then picked up a bag of arrows and walked to the place where he would conduct the lesson. Keelin and the boy, Dob, walked alongside him while the rest of the hunters cleared up the remains of the meal.

"Take this cloth, Dob, and tie it to a branch on yon tree," Marcus said. "We'll use it as a target."

The boy ran to do as he was bid. "Have you ever shot an arrow before, Keelin?"

"Nay, Marcus," she replied. Her intensity and the lilt of her voice pierced through him.

"Here, then," he said. "Take hold of the bow in your left hand, and the arrow in your right."

Keelin did so, but awkwardly.

"Nay," Marcus said, coming close behind her. He put his left arm around her to steady her hand on the bow. With his right hand, he guided hers in the correct way to hold the arrow.

Her scent was as fresh as the outdoors, laced with the intriguingly spicy fragrance that was Keelin's alone. A few loose strands of her hair brushed his face and he inhaled deeply.

He felt a slight tremor run through her and he pressed closer to her.

"I-is this right?" she asked breathlessly.

"Better." Marcus's voice was a mere whisper in her ear.

"And the arrow? It goes—"

"Here. Nock it this way." Marcus kept his arms around Keelin and turned her body away from where Dob was tying the target to the tree. Marcus used the bow to gesture ahead. "See the young birch with the notched trunk?"

"Aye." Her reply was barely audible amid the sounds of the forest, and Marcus knew she felt his proximity just as potently as he felt hers.

"Take aim just below the notch."

She lifted the bow and Marcus felt her stiffen.

"Relax, Keelin," he said. "You're wound as tightly as that bow string."

She nodded stiffly, and Marcus could see that her joints were not about to loosen.

"Bend your knees, sweetheart," he said, "and roll your shoulders."

If Keelin noticed Marcus's use of the endearment, she did not show it. Instead, she followed his instructions and bent at the knees a few times, then rolled her shoulders, inadvertently pressing her back even closer to Marcus.

This time, the shiver ran through him, and 'twas all he could do not to drop the bow, turn her in his arms and meld them together with his kiss. But his men were all around, and Dob would be upon them in a few short moments.

"Now, take aim," he repeated hoarsely this time. "Be careful not to crush the fletching."

She moved her fingers so that they no longer rested on the feathers, then raised the bow again.

"Pull back on the string," he said, moving her arms slightly to correct the aim. "Now let loose."

Keelin released the arrow and watched it fly. She stood stock-still, waiting to see the results of her first attempt at archery. Hardly an instant passed before the arrow hit its mark. When it did, Keelin dropped her arms, then she turned and faced Marcus.

Her lips were but a breath away from his. Long black lashes framed eyes darkened with excitement.

"Good shot, my lady!" Dob said as he reached the spot.

"I thank ye, Dob," Keelin said without taking her eyes from Marcus's. "Your turn," she said then, and laughed.

Marcus could barely draw a breath.

They rode into Wrexton's bailey where grooms met them to take their mounts and the kill of the day, and the huntsmen herded the dogs to the pens. Gerald headed to the mews with the falcons, with Marcus and Keelin walking right behind him.

Keelin had had a marvelous day. She'd learned to hunt, had shot a bow and was fast becoming a decent horsewoman. She'd not had so much excitement since…well, she could not remember a more exciting time.

"Do ye mind if I help with this, Marcus?" Keelin asked. Though she was weary, she did not want to see an end to this day.

"Not at all, Keelin," Marcus replied. "Gerald will look them over to see if they sustained any damage while out on the hunt, and if not, he'll leave them on their perches for the night. There will be little to see."

"Ah, but 'tis not every day I'm given the privilege of huntin' with falcons, Marcus," she replied. "I would see them bedded for the night."

Keelin would have recalled those words if she'd been able to, for Marcus's eyes held a look that made her realize he was thinking of something altogether different than leaving falcons on perches. She was determined, however, not to succumb to any seductive looks or wishful thinking. She had worked too hard all afternoon to avoid falling prey to Marcus's powerful allure.

"Will ye be feedin' them again, Master Gerald?" Keelin cleared her throat. She turned away from Marcus and walked toward the falconer in the farthest corner of the mews.

"Nay, my lady," Gerald said. "They've had their fill. But if you would release Gwin's leash?"

"Oh, aye," Keelin said gladly. She needed a task to occupy her mind, her hands.

Marcus carried a lamp to the perch so that Keelin could see better to open the small buckles. She felt the warmth of his body so close to hers, just as she had during the archery lesson.

Even now, she could feel his warm breath in her ear, his strong arms around her, guiding her own hands and arms.

"'Tis a wee buckle, Gwin," Keelin said shakily, "but I've got it now."

The falcon took a step away on her perch, then ruffled her feathers and settled down.

Keelin wished it would be so easy for *her* to settle down.

Isolda met Marcus and Keelin just inside Wrexton's great hall, with footmen to take their cloaks, and goblets of warm, mulled wine to ward off the chill. The fire had recently been stoked, so the hall was warm and inviting.

Marcus would have enjoyed a few quiet moments with Keelin near the fire if only Isolda had not remained with them. Keelin appeared distinctly uncomfortable in her presence, and Isolda herself seemed somewhat ill at ease.

Marcus did not think he would ever understand

women. But at least he'd become more adept at dealing with them of late. He credited Keelin with the change. Somehow, his dealings with her had caused him to be less diffident, and more confident in his exchanges with the fairer sex.

Men's voices disturbed his train of thought, and he turned to see three of his knights approaching from the far end of the hall. 'Twas Sir William, along with two other knights who had been sent out early to scout the perimeter of Wrexton land.

Will and the others gave their lord a bow, then greeted the ladies.

"Anything to report, Will?" Marcus asked.

The knight shook his head. "Nay, my lord," he replied. "Nary a sign of any strangers on our boundaries. We ran across a peddler or two, but no other intruders."

Though Marcus would like to have had a swift and expeditious confrontation with the vicious Celts who'd killed his father, he had to admit he was glad of the reprieve. He wanted his knights in top form before taking on that barbarous army, and he wanted some solid plans in place to ensure his victory.

"Well, I must say, *that's* a relief!" Isolda remarked, drawing the men's attention to her. Her eyes were bright, as if she'd had one cup too many of the mulled wine. She rubbed her hands on her gown nervously, then turned to Keelin and smiled graciously. "You'll want to change out of that awful kirtle before we sup, Lady Keelin. We generally do not wear rags to table here at Wrexton."

Keelin's eyes lowered and her face drained of color. Everyone was silent in the wake of Isolda's insult. All the men, including Marcus, were struck dumb by Isolda's petty cruelty to the guest who had done so much for Adam.

Keelin quietly set her goblet down. Clearly, she did not know what to say, or how to react to the acerbic words Isolda had cloaked in a deceptive sweetness. As the men watched Keelin struggle for control, Marcus moved quickly to stand beside her, before she was able to bolt. Then he met Isolda's insolent gaze and spoke to her with a tone of authority that came from a source deep within.

"Since you will be sitting in Adam's chamber during the meal, Lady Keelin's attire should not bother you. It certainly does not offend me, nor will it offend anyone else who intends to join me at table."

"But my lord—"

"And in future, you will guard your tongue in the presence of my guest, Isolda," he added, touching Keelin's lower back. "I will tolerate no further discourtesy from you as long as you reside here at Wrexton."

Silence persisted as Marcus urged Keelin away from the group and walked with her to the stairs. He did not know what power possessed him to speak to Isolda the way he did, but he did not regret speaking out. Isolda's insolence was intolerable, and if she thought to use Keelin to punish him for sending her away, then she had better think again.

She was fortunate he was not a man who would ever consider using violence against a woman.

Keelin climbed the steps ahead of him, her spine straight, her bearing as regal as befit the Irish princess she was. She did not speak until they were close to Adam's room. When she turned to face him, her eyes were suspiciously bright and held none of their previous confidence. "I—I would ask that a tray be brought to

Adam's room for me, Marcus. I should be dinin' tonight with the lad since I promised—''

"You will sup with me," Marcus said gently. He traced the line of her jaw with one hand and smoothed a lock of hair back over her ear. Though Isolda's cruelty had cut *him* to the quick, Keelin bore the slight nobly. "How you are garbed matters not," he said. "I care only that you join me...."

"Marcus," Keelin said, stepping back to the wall, "I—I will not be the cause of a rift between you and Isolda. Soon I'll be leavin' Wrexton and Isolda—''

Marcus did not allow her to pull away. He let one hand drop to her shoulder. The other hand went to the wall beside her, bracketing her head. He hesitated only for an instant, then dipped his head and tasted her lips as he'd wanted to do all day.

The sound Keelin made gave him the impetus to seek more. He delved into her mouth and pulled her close, matching the hard planes of his body to her soft curves.

Keelin responded as though she could not get enough of him, the knowledge sending hot flames of arousal through him. He'd never experienced anything like this, and knew he never would again, without Keelin O'Shea.

Abruptly, and without warning, Keelin broke away. She gave a quick shake of her head. "Nay, Marcus," she whispered, working to regain her composure. "What I feel—'' She stopped, then began again. "'Tis no matter what we might want...." One crystal tear dropped past the barrier Keelin worked so hard to maintain. *"Please!"* she cried, then turned and hurried to her own chamber.

Marcus stood alone in the gallery and watched Keelin make her escape. He had not wanted to upset her, but only make her understand the depth of what he felt for her. She was his. If ever there was a woman made who was meant for him, Keelin O'Shea was the one.

He ran one hand across his mouth and over his whisker-roughened jaw. He knew the timing was bad—he should not be thinking of love and marriage when his father's body was barely cold in his grave. Yet Marcus knew Eldred would not begrudge him this. For years, his father had despaired of Marcus ever finding a suitable wife, one he could love as Eldred had loved Rhianwen.

Now that he'd found the right woman, Marcus was not about to let her leave without fighting for her.

Chapter Fifteen

Keelin dried her tears and looked down at herself. She was wearing the same plain, brown kirtle she'd worn on the hunt, and could see nothing wrong with it. 'Twas well made and clean.

To be sure, the gown was not in the height of style, nor would Keelin ever have considered wearing it to the earl's table. But it had been purely practical to wear while out on the hunt. 'Twould have been utterly foolish to wear one of her better gowns for tramping over the countryside with the falcons and dogs.

She sniffed again, and fought a new onslaught of tears. The ugly brown kirtle was the least of her worries.

Her growing feelings for Marcus would do nothing but cause further heartache for both of them. They both knew she had no choice but to return to Kerry. The clan needed her, never so desperately as now, with Cormac's death.

And there was a man in Ireland waiting to wed her. Keelin knew her father had chosen a fine, powerful chieftain for her husband, and 'twas her duty to go to him as soon as she was able. The O'Sheas would need every alliance possible in order to thwart Mageean and his plans to subjugate Clann Ui Sheaghda.

It did not matter that Keelin's heart was becoming too deeply involved at Wrexton. For the duration of her stay, she would take pains to avoid Marcus. No matter how difficult 'twould be, she would go out of her way to show Marcus that she was unaffected by him, by his kisses, his touch. She would discourage his attentions whenever possible.

The fire was nearly nonexistent in the grate, so Keelin added more peat. She did not doubt that Isolda had given orders to the servants to stay out of her chamber, for there were none of the usual amenities she had become accustomed to at Wrexton.

After all of Isolda's attempts to discredit her—and the lady had been quite good at it, if truth be told—Keelin finally understood how threatening her presence was to Isolda. The woman had a secure position at Wrexton, as long as the lord did not take a wife, and it probably seemed to Isolda that Marcus would soon remedy his bachelor state.

Keelin wiped the tears from her eyes and hoped Isolda would leave her alone once she learned her position was safe.

"Ye don't say, lad!" Tiarnan replied when Marcus told him of Keelin's exploits. He kept his voice down because Adam was asleep, but couldn't contain his joy for Keelin and the fine day she must have had. "She learned to shoot a longbow?"

Marcus smiled. "Yes, she did," he said. "And with some practice, she'll become quite adept."

"She's got the height fer it," Tiarnan remarked proudly.

True enough, Marcus thought. Her height was perfect. As were her eyes, her smile, her hair. Her hands were soft and feminine, yet strong and competent. And the rest of her...

"And what of the falcons?" Tiarnan asked. "Me brother never let her near his own birds, but Keelin had a passion for 'em. Sneaked into Eocaidh's mews whenever she was able."

"She did very well with the birds, Tiarnan," Marcus answered. "Handled them as if she were born to it."

"Well, that she was!" Tiarnan said. "If only me fool brother had realized what a prize he had in that lass. If only..."

Marcus frowned. "Keelin and her father were...at odds with one another?" he asked, anxious to learn anything he could about Keelin.

Tiarnan sighed, shaking his head. "'Tis not so easy to explain. Ye had to have known Eocaidh. Me brother was a born leader. He had a fierce devotion to the clan and to his duty."

Now, at least, Marcus could understand where Keelin got it. But doubted he'd accept any excuse for the man's indifference to his daughter.

"To Eocaidh, the good of the clan came before all else," Tiarnan said. "Even before the happiness of his only child."

Tiarnan stopped speaking for a moment and mulled over his words. By the old man's expression, Marcus could see that he was deep in thought. But the direction of those thoughts was a mystery.

"You spoke once of Keelin's brother."

"Aye, Brian," Tiarnan said. "All Eocaidh's hopes rested in the lad. The day he drowned...'twas as if Eocaidh lost all he'd had in the world."

"And Keelin?"

"It took a year or more, but Eocaidh finally realized that all hopes for his line rested in his daughter," Tiarnan said. "He began to look for a man who would be a suitable husband."

It was a long moment before Marcus could voice his question. "And did Eocaidh find one?"

"Aye," Tiarnan replied. "And to this day, the man awaits Keelin's return."

Tiarnan's health improved significantly in the days spent at Wrexton. The efficient chimneys as well as the freedom from worry had done wonders for him. He still coughed, but not with the same frequency as before, and it didn't rattle him so badly when he had one of his spells.

He'd begun to hope for a wee bit more time.

He damned his loss of sight and the fact that his blindness made it necessary to concentrate all the more on the subtler signs given by a person: tone of voice, meaningful pauses, sighs. 'Twas all terribly wearying.

The young earl stayed only long enough to satisfy himself of Adam's condition, then to verify that someone would be along to help Tiarnan to his room. Then he wandered out, most likely to seek his own chamber, and the necessary quietude to think over what Tiarnan had said.

Marcus de Grant had given him very few clues, yet the old man sensed clearly that the young earl was disturbed by the knowledge of a husband waiting for Keelin in Kerry. Mayhap there was hope here.

In the days since the Englishmen happened upon their wee cottage in the wood, Tiarnan had learned more than enough about the de Grant men, and life at Wrexton, to know that Keelin could be happy here. Even without having the second sight, he knew that nothing but pain and disillusionment awaited Keelin at Carrauntoohil. If Fen McClancy still lived, she would be forced to wed the old lecher and produce an heir joining the McClancy and O'Shea clans.

If not, then Clann Ui Sheaghda would make an oracle of her in the manner of the Druids, Tiarnan thought as he crossed himself piously, and Keelin would never have the things she longed for, the things she deserved for her happiness.

Either way, the lass would be thrust once again into a land deeply ravaged by warfare and strife. As before, she would be but a mere instrument used to bolster the clan's spirit. No one would recognize that she was a young woman with needs and yearnings of her own.

Ach, aye, Tiarnan wanted the clan to survive and prosper. He knew his duty was to return his niece and the sacred spear to Carrauntoohil. But not at the cost of Keelin's happiness...her very life. The O'Sheas could get along without the gift of Keelin's second sight. Mayhap someone else who had the skill to tap into the power of *Ga Buidhe an Lamhaigh* would surface.

With a decision not easily made, Tiarnan roused the footman who slept at the end of Adam's bed, and bid the man to help him to his chamber. He doubted he would rest easily tonight.

Morning brought a slightly warmer temperature, as well as an ankle-deep layer of snow. And while it made quite a beautiful scene as Keelin gazed out her chamber window, it would make travel difficult.

The strong foreboding was back, more potent than before. It crawled up her spine and gripped the back of her neck with icy fingers, just as it always did when some danger was upon them. But what was it now? Surely not Mageean's warriors, come to attack Wrexton? They would not be so bold, nor so foolish, she thought.

What could be making her feel so uneasy?

'Twas time, Keelin knew. Though touching it would make her weak and practically useless to Adam today, she knew it was time to use the power of *Ga Buidhe an Lamhaigh,* and try to discover what disaster was upon them.

She went back to the bed and pulled the mattress up, dreading, as always, the contact with the mysterious power within the spear. She hesitated a moment, and stood gazing at the leather-sheathed artifact. It was right where she'd left it, resting along one edge of the bed frame.

A quiet tap at the door startled Keelin and made her drop the mattress back into place.

"Begging your pardon, Lady Keelin," a young maid said. "I'd never be so brazen as to disturb you...." The girl glanced back into the gallery behind her, then twisted her hands, clearly ill at ease.

"Yer not disturbin' me, Lizzie," Keelin said. "What is it, then?"

"My sister's babe," the maid explained. "The child's got the ague and it worsens with every day. We're worried that—that—"

"Do ye want me to have a look at the babe, Lizzie?"

"Oh, please, my lady," the girl replied gratefully, "would you be so kind?"

"Ach, aye," Keelin said. She had mixed feelings about abandoning *Ga Buidhe an Lamhaigh* for the moment, but her aversion to touching the spear won out. "'Tis no trouble a'tall. Where is the child?"

"Down in the pantry with her mam," the maid said. "If you'd follow me…"

The pantry was a small and tidy room just behind the kitchen, kept warm by the adjacent cook fires. Lining the walls were shelves stacked with foodstuffs, crocks of spice and oil, bags of wheat flour, corn and barley. Barrels of ale stood along each wall.

Keelin could hear the wee babe's wheeze when she entered the room.

"Oh, my lady, 'tis good of you to come," the young mother cried. "I don't know what's to become of my poor little Peg."

Keelin went to the mother and child, and placed her hand on the infant's back. "Has she been wheezy all along?" she asked.

"Nay, for two days, she had a terrible wracking cough. Then last night, nigh on midnight, the wheezing started and then the fever, and she hasn't opened her eyes to me since."

Tears streamed down the mother's distraught face. Keelin could not deny that the illness was serious. 'Twas not a good sign that the infant had been insensible for hours. She had fever, and there was a swelling in the throat causing the harsh sound that came with every breath.

Keelin did not know if there was anything she could do for the babe that would help her.

Nevertheless, she would try.

"Do ye mind if I take her from ye for a moment?" Keelin asked, touching the child's downy blond hair.

"Please…"

With Eldred's death, all the lord's responsibilities became Marcus's. He had lived at Wrexton with his father all through the five years of Eldred's earldom, and the two men had learned together what was expected of the earl, what the earl could expect in return.

Marcus knew he would soon need to travel to the other estates of his domain, but there was more than enough business needing his full attention at Wrexton Castle for the moment.

Town affairs kept Marcus occupied most of the morning. He and Wrexton's steward had ridden out in the snow just after daybreak, to meet with the bailiff. By the time they returned to the keep, the morning sun was high and glistened brightly on the new snow.

'Twas cheerful looking—not at all the kind of setting he would have chosen to sit Isolda down and straighten her out. Yet it had to be done, and the sooner, the better.

Marcus headed for the keep, and the kitchen, where he believed he would find Isolda hounding the staff.

He was determined to speak to her now, before any further incidents occurred—either with the castle servants or Lady Keelin. For the duration of Isolda's time remaining at Wrexton, Marcus would not allow her to continue her blatant harassment of Keelin. He would deal with her now, directly, just as his father would have done, just as he should have done when he'd first spoken to her.

He was learning. Everyone tested his limits, from the town bailiff to Wrexton's steward. And they were learning that he was as reasonable as his father before him. And that his limits were not to be pushed.

Marcus entered the kitchen through the back entrance, and found a decided lack of activity there. Several servants stood about, yet no one seemed to be occupied with any of the tasks that were essential to feeding the multitude of people housed at the keep.

"What is it?" he asked Cook, certain that Isolda had caused yet another set of problems. "What's happened?"

"'Tis Annie's new babe," Cook replied. "The child has taken ill and—"

"Annie?" Marcus asked. "John's wife?" He remembered the occasion of the girl's marriage to one of Wrexton's footmen nearly a year before. It had been an opportunity for Eldred to ride Marcus, in a purely good-natured manner, about his own unmarried state.

Annie had grown big with child soon after, and Eldred had forbidden her to continue working so hard at the keep. He saw to it that Isolda found small tasks for the girl, to keep her occupied and happy.

Marcus knew Eldred had seen to a baptismal gift for the child only a few weeks ago.

"Yes, m'lord," Cook replied. "Lady Keelin is there, doing what she can for the little girl."

That Keelin was involved did not come as a surprise to Marcus. He'd taken note of her friendly interactions with the servants, and while the Wrexton staff remained respectful, they were agreeable and comfortable with her. 'Twas very different from their dealings with Isolda, especially of late.

"Where are they?"

Cook gestured with a tilt of his head. "In the pantry, m'lord."

When Marcus arrived and looked through the doorway of the small room, he saw Keelin standing in the center with her back to him.

Her hair was caught in a thick rope of braid that hung down the center of her back, and she was clad in the deep-green gown she'd been wearing when he'd first seen her. The fabric hugged her body closely, from her neck to her hips, then flowed loosely to the floor.

From where he stood, he could not see what Keelin was doing, but a strange odor permeated the room and there was steam rising from a large pan on the table.

"Take her now, Annie, and hold her over the pan," Keelin said, turning. She caught sight of Marcus and a sudden flush brightened her cheeks.

Keelin's reaction warmed him, too. For a moment, he imagined that everyone else was gone from the room, and he was alone with Keelin. He would touch her gently. Run one finger from the nape of her neck, down her spine, then brush his lips across the bright color on her cheeks. She'd be quick to respond, especially when he spanned her waist with his hands and met her lips with his own.

They had gone so far once before, in the inopportune location of the castle courtyard, with Keelin's breath catching in her throat, her desire for him as great as what he had felt for her.

Had they not been interrupted by Beatrice's untimely appearance, Marcus had no doubt they would have found a more private, secluded place. There, they would have explored each caress, each whispered touch. And Marcus would have been hard-pressed to honor his vow of celibacy.

He met Keelin's sharp green gaze. Confusion was in her eyes, as well as worry and concern. She ached for the poor child as if it were her own, just as she had for Adam, and she worked as hard as any servant to do what she could for the infant.

Hesitating only slightly, she stepped over to him and placed a hand on his arm. "Marcus, would ye mind finding someone to go up to Adam's chamber," she asked, ''and get my herb pouches? This wee lass is going to need more than what I've got here, if I'm to help her.''

Marcus did not dread his anticipated confrontation with Isolda as he had the last time, and knew the role of earl was coming more naturally now. 'Twas true, he had not yet tested his new standing in war, nor in any political dealings with the ruling council in London, but at least in his own domain, Marcus felt his competence growing.

He left Keelin and walked through the great hall, surprised that he had not yet encountered Isolda. Summoning one of the maids, he asked the girl to find Isolda and send her to the lord's study.

He walked to the far end of the hall and left, heading toward the chapel. There, a narrow, winding staircase took him to an upper level of the keep, just below the battlements. Marcus entered the chamber where all the past earls had dealt with Wrexton business.

The room was neither terribly small, for it served the Wrexton lords to hold meetings there, nor was it overly large. 'Twas a man's room, with furnishings and masculine appointments that had suited a number of Wrexton's earls before Marcus.

A handsome mahogany desk stood near the fireplace, with a large comfortable chair behind it. Mullioned windows provided better than adequate light during the day, and an iron ring holding several oil lamps hung over the desk so that it was possible to read or work by night.

The few books that Eldred had brought to Wrexton from Northaven Manor, as well as those belonging to the previous earl's collection were stored here under lock and key. There were ancient tomes, along with a few more recently copied volumes, colorfully illustrated and bound in leather. 'Twas Marcus's pride that he was able to read every one.

While he waited for Isolda, he carefully paged through the large volume that rested on the desk. 'Twas a religious tome, a work his father had recently acquired and was in the process of reading before they'd left Wrexton on their fateful journey.

A particularly vile but colorful illustration of Satan startled him. Portrayed as a lewd, grinning satyr, the devil stood in the pits of hell, watching as a witch was burned at the stake.

With uncharacteristic disregard for the value of the book, Marcus slapped it shut. He did not care to see the image of a dark-haired maiden being ravaged by fire. Nor would he entertain thoughts about witches and devils. If the rest of this volume contained similar topics and illustrations, Marcus would lock it away at the bottom of the cupboard, never again to see the light of day.

Still disturbed by the image he'd see in the book, Marcus stalked to the window and looked down on the courtyard. Dark clouds rode low in the sky, and it was snowing again.

Where is Isolda? he wondered impatiently.

He knew exactly what he intended to say to the woman, so he gave no further thought to it. He only wished he had an honorable offer of marriage in hand, and could get her settled somewhere soon.

Marcus wondered instead whether Tiarnan O'Shea supported or even knew of Keelin's decision to return to her home. He wondered if the old man knew Keelin intended to leave him behind at Wrexton, under the care of strangers.

Not that Marcus felt like a stranger to Keelin or her uncle. They'd spent too many days together in the crowded little cottage to be anything but familiar, and Marcus had developed a true fondness for the old man. He was unsure exactly what he felt for Keelin.

Was he a fool to discount the possibility of Keelin using sorcery? It had seemed entirely likely only a few days before. She had known about Edward's broken leg *before* he was carried into the cottage! She had healed Adam, when the boy's chances for survival had been utterly dismal.

What magic was at work through her?

Marcus went back to the desk and opened the offensive book. He turned the pages until he found the one with the illustration that had shocked him. Silently reading the Latin text, he soon found himself sitting down in the large chair, studying what was known about witches and their habits.

When he finished, he was shaken by what he'd read, but he knew Keelin was not one of them.

Marcus could not imagine her killing a child and sacrificing it, not after seeing how tirelessly she'd worked to heal Adam, or the way she cared so tenderly for Annie's infant. She prayed fervently and often, invoking the Irish saints as needed, never giving any sign of profaning the Eucharist or twisting the Mass to some evil purpose.

As for the Devil's marks on her body, Marcus had to assume there were none, although at his first opportunity, he would verify that with his own eyes.

With pleasure.

"Lord Marcus?"

"Enter," Marcus replied to the summons.

One of the footmen stepped inside the chamber and informed Marcus that Lady Isolda was nowhere to be found.

"The storm worsens by the minute, my lord," he added. "Baron Albin Selby and his family are here seeking refuge."

Marcus remembered meeting Selby a few years earlier, but he was not on familiar terms with the man. Nonetheless, Wrexton was known for its hospitality. That would not change with Eldred's death. "Find suitable chambers for them, Mathiew, and see that they are fed and made comfortable."

"Yes, my lord," Mathiew replied as he turned to leave. "Ah, Lord Marcus...there are others...several knights, a few peddlers...some freemen...."

"We've room enough, Mathiew, and stores to spare, I believe. See them situated in the hall."

Marcus stood and joined the servant as he headed for the stairway. He wanted to see the strangers in the hall for himself and assess the likelihood of trouble.

"Send one of the boys to fetch Sir Robert," Marcus said to Mathiew, "and ask him to join me in the hall." He intended to take no chances. Several Wrexton knights would remain in the hall until the storm passed and the strangers went on their way. Though he had no reason to believe any of his "guests" would be hostile, Marcus knew that with enough boredom and sufficient ale, the friendliest of males could become dangerous.

He did not forget about Isolda, though 'twas obvious his discussion with her would have to wait. Time enough to set her in her place.

Chapter Sixteen

The weather worsened as the day progressed. A fierce wind whipped around towers and battlements, and whistled through the courtyard and baileys. Brittle branches of centuries-old trees creaked and snapped in the gale, littering the frozen ground far below. An icy rain began to fall, pelting anyone who could not avoid outdoor commerce.

The river that flowed along the rounded curtain of Wrexton Castle slowed, dammed up by accumulating ice. 'Twas a sight not seen at Wrexton in more than a decade, but the signs of winter had been particularly severe this year. None of the old folk were surprised by the early storm, and many had remarked on the portents they'd seen ever since the autumn harvest.

By late afternoon, more weary, half-frozen travelers had arrived, seeking refuge within the warm walls of Wrexton Keep. Marcus accepted all, fully aware that any who remained out in such inclement weather did so at risk to their lives.

None of the servants grumbled over the extra work, for it took their minds from the dire plight of Annie's child.

Keelin, too, was glad of something to do, though it pained her that the activity was at the expense of the wee babe in her arms. She'd sent the infant's mother off to sleep awhile, along with her husband, John. The young couple had not had much rest in the last few days, and Keelin suspected that would continue until Peg was better.

Meanwhile, Keelin held the babe in the only position in which she was able to breathe. The child was not in quite so much distress now, thanks to the concoction of archangelica and lungwort that Keelin had steamed and gotten the child to inhale. And for good measure, Keelin had rubbed freshly churned butter into the babe's chest and made the sign of the cross three times over it. Now, all they could do was wait.

"How is she?" Marcus asked, startling Keelin. She hadn't heard him enter the pantry.

"A wee bit better, I think," she replied.

"You must be tired," he said, pushing away from the doorjamb and walking in.

"Aye," Keelin answered. "'Tis wearyin' to deal with a sick babe for hours. It wears on yer nerves, if ye know what I mean. Ye worry that ye haven't done all ye can...or that you've done it all, but it won't be enough...."

"Whatever happens, Keelin—"

"Don't be sayin' it, Marcus," she said fiercely. "I'll hear nothin' about what might or mightn't happen."

Marcus ran a hand across Keelin's jaw, cupping her chin. "You've done everything you can for now," he said. "Why don't you let me hold her awhile, and you rest your arms."

"Ye'd do that, Marcus?" she asked, surprised by his offer.

"Of course," he replied. "Hand her to me."

His big hands were awkward with the wee child, but with a minimum of fuss, he settled the babe against his shoulder. It took no stretch of the imagination to think of Marcus, one day nurturing his own child, a beautiful wee blond nursling like little Peg.

Keelin turned quickly away and busied herself with the pan of cooled water. She tamped down the flurry of emotions that flooded through her at the sight of Marcus, holding the child so gently, knowing that his own little towheaded darlings would be born and bred long after she returned to Kerry.

Until now, she had trained her attention solely on getting home to Kerry, and had avoided thinking of leaving Wrexton. And Marcus. Now, the thought of Marcus and the life he would pursue after she was gone caused overwhelming pain.

Duty had never been so onerous before. Even when Keelin had been required to flee her home and clan, she'd done so without question. Somehow, that had changed. For the first time in her life, her heart was no longer with Clann Ui Sheaghda. She did not dare think where it lay now.

"Keelin?"

She blinked back the tears that had started to form, and turned to him. "I'll just—"

"What is it?" Marcus asked, his dear brow furrowed with concern. "You're troubled."

"Nay, Marcus," she replied brightly, lifting the pan of water. "Will you open that door for me?"

"Only when you tell me what has upset you."

"'Tis just the babe…I'm worried…."

"Set the pan down, Keelin," Marcus said. "There is no rush to empty it, and I would have you rest a few moments before I must leave you again. The storm has brought both vagabonds and highborn to our doors, and soon I will have to deal with the chaos in the hall.''

Keelin swallowed the lump in her throat as she replaced the pan on the table. A flood of vague images clouded her vision, and she shook them away before they could cause her any further anguish. She had no desire to see the future, had *never* wanted this strange power that not only plagued and terrified her, but made her the repository of all her clan's hopes and dreams.

'Twas too much for one person to bear.

What of her own hopes and dreams, the secret desires she'd always nurtured in her heart? Did they mean nothing at all? Was she to deny her growing need and desire for Marcus de Grant, and all the love and security he could provide?

''We both have much to do, Marcus. I—I must go and see to Adam,'' Keelin stammered. ''I've not looked in on him yet, and he's bound to wonder.''

By the time Isolda made her appearance in the hall, the visitors had been fed and were settling themselves down to endure a long night. The Selby family— Baron Albin, his wife and two daughters—had retired to their chambers in the south tower. Marcus was about to look in on Adam, hoping he would find Keelin there.

He considered stopping to have words with Isolda then and there, but decided against it. Morning would be soon enough.

Marcus found Tiarnan sitting with Adam as the boy drifted off to sleep. He was sure the old man had been entertaining the boy again with stories of his youth, along with magical tales of Ireland's glorious, enchanted past. Keelin was not in sight.

"Yer lad is on the mend, Marcus," Tiarnan said quietly, "though it'll be a few more days before he'll be sittin' up without too much discomfort."

Marcus could see that that was true. The boy's color was nearly normal and he was resting peacefully for a change.

Marcus sat down quietly next to him and gently ran his hand over the sleeping boy's head.

"The lad's had a hard way to go," Tiarnan said.

"Yes, he has," Marcus said, thinking of the incident that had brought Adam to this state. "You and Keelin have done so much."

"Think nothin' of it, lad," Tiarann replied. "'Twas nothin' but our Christian duty. Though I'm glad things have worked out as they have."

"Meaning?"

"That Keely lass is safe here at Wrexton," Tiarnan said. "Mageean's mercenaries cannot harm her here."

True enough. The weather would hold them off for a time, but Marcus's army was well prepared, and he now knew exactly how he would deal with Mageean's men.

"You know she plans to return to Kerry," he said.

Tiarnan pursed his lips in thought. "I suspected the lass would get it in her head to go when she saw the vision of Cormac's death. She'll be certain the clan needs her now."

"But the weather will hold her here."

"Aye," Tiarnan replied. "Fer a time."

That was what Marcus feared. He knew there was a limited amount of time to win her, and to overcome her strong sense of duty. Deep in thought, Marcus did not notice that Tiarnan was preoccupied with his own thoughts. They sat together in silence until Tiarnan finally spoke.

"I...er...I'm hopin' no harm befalls the lass when she touches the spear."

Marcus jerked his gaze back to Tiarnan. "What do you mean?" he demanded. "When she touches the spear, will its power weaken her just as the vision did the night she saw Cormac's death?"

"Aye, lad," Tiarnan replied. The old man clearly sensed Marcus standing and stepping over to the door. "As soon as she touches *Ga Buidhe an Lamhaigh,* she'll become weak and insensible. I don't like for her to do it alone—"

Marcus was gone before Tiarnan could finish. He settled back in his chair to pass the hours at Adam's side and hoped he had done the right thing, leading the young lord to Keelin...

Ach, time was wastin', Tiarnan thought. Nothin' but duty and pain, and then more pain awaited Keelin in Kerry. 'Twas time to take action.

The servants practically begged to be allowed to carry water for Keelin's bath. She had worked so tirelessly from morning until night for Annie's babe, and the child seemed to be breathing easier now. Half the servants believed she was specially blessed with healing powers. Little Peg's parents thought she was a gift from God.

Keelin merely wanted to bathe and go to bed. Any thoughts she might have had about touching the spear had fled. She knew she had to be at her best when she tapped into the power of *Ga Buidhe an Lamhaigh,* and she was anything but at her peak.

Yet she was still troubled by the intuitive awareness that something was wrong, or something disagreeable was about to happen.

Footmen had stoked the fire and placed the tub near

it, so it looked warm and inviting. Keelin disrobed, then stepped into the tub and sat in the waist-high water.

She released a long, satisfied sigh and leaned back.

The only way she could sit was with her knees folded under her, which she did gratefully, since it was not often that the luxury of a full, hot bath was offered. She suspected the soap sitting on the lip of the tub had been purloined from another lady—Isolda perhaps—but Keelin was not about to question it now.

She took the lovely scented stuff and lathered up, fully enjoying the luxury of the bath and a few stolen moments of relaxation.

When the door to her chamber flew open, Keelin sat rigidly in place. Marcus could not have looked more startled than she felt. They were both transfixed, neither moving.

Until the chamber door shut behind Marcus.

Keelin suddenly came to her senses and attempted to cover herself with her hands. Marcus should not be in her chamber, especially under these circumstances. No man had ever seen her unclothed, and Keelin knew that was an intimacy reserved for the one who would be her husband.

He took a step toward her.

"Marcus..." she whispered, unable to keep from wanting what she could not have.

She had no will of her own when he looked at her that way. Her hands dropped to her sides when he reached for her.

"You are so beautiful," he breathed, taking her hand as she rose from the tub.

Nothing in Keelin's life had prepared her for the surge of emotions that coursed through her now. She felt feverish, though she knew she should have been cold after stepping out of the bath. Instead, she felt heat—nay, 'twas more than mere heat, 'twas a sweltering fire that consumed her now.

Keelin knew she should reach for the long linen drying cloth, but could not make her hands obey her will. Her gaze never left Marcus's cool, blue eyes now darkened with ardor.

"Keelin."

His hands were on her shoulders. When his head dipped and his lips caught her mouth, wild sensations careened through her. His scent filled her.

Keelin leaned into his body, shocked to feel rough cloth and leather against her naked skin. Still, 'twas more wondrous than anything that had ever happened to her before.

Marcus pulled the combs out of Keelin's hair, allowing it to fall free. He slid his hands down her sides, marveling at the softness of her skin, her quivering response to his touch.

With only the slightest coaxing, she opened her mouth to him, exploring him as he did her. He heard a sound and thought it might have been his own voice, though his mind was so far gone, he could not be certain of anything but Keelin. Touching her, loving her.

He felt powerful enough to enfold her with his body, to hold her and protect her always. But she began unlacing his tunic and suddenly he was pulling it over his head, then looking down at her breasts, the tips brushing lightly against his chest.

"Yer a beautiful man, Marcus," she murmured, kissing his throat. It became impossible to swallow. "When I first saw ye by the wee stream near my cottage," she said, her lips moving downward, "I knew I'd never seen anything as lovely as you, all muscle-bound and golden.''

As her tongue touched one flat male nipple, Marcus nearly lost control.

''I wanted to touch you then,'' she continued, ''but—''

''Keelin, you cannot understand what your words do to me,'' Marcus rasped. ''Or your touch, your body...so soft, so...''

Their mouths melded once again. Marcus inched away just far enough to slip his hands between them. He covered her breasts, then touched the sensitive peaks with his thumbs, making her tremble with sensuous delight. He shivered, too, and realized he was at the edge of his control.

This was not what he'd intended when he'd come to her. His vow of celibacy, made all those years ago in France, was not meant to be broken on a whim. He was a man of honor, a knight sworn to the Code of Chivalry. He would win this woman as his wife, and not seduce her like some lowborn camp follower.

He broke away from her, reaching for the linen towel. He wrapped it around her with care, avoiding her questioning eyes. A few small oil lamps were burning, and the fire glowed, lending a gentle radiance to the chamber. All was silent, but for the howling of the wind outside.

When Keelin was modestly covered, Marcus guided her to a cushioned chair near the fire. He made her sit, then knelt before her and took her hand.

''Keelin,'' he said, finally looking into her puzzled eyes. He let out one frustrated laugh in an anguished bark. ''You are more to me than any woman I've ever known,'' he said. ''I would not dishonor you by seducing you, here in your chamber where you ought to be immune from any such advances.

"Instead, I would ask for your hand in marriage, and pray that you become my wife."

Gauging by her expression, she was stunned.

Marcus could not blame her for her confusion—one minute he was devouring her like a starving man, then suddenly he had her covered, neck to toe, and was on his knees offering for her hand.

A single crease formed between her brows and pain took possession of her eyes. She started to speak more than once, but in the end, seemed incapable of it. Instead, she cupped the side of his face with one smooth palm, sending shivers of desire through him. He forced himself to maintain control, to do what was right and honorable.

"We are well suited, Keelin," Marcus continued. "If you agree, I will speak to your uncle—"

Keelin dropped her hands and gave a quick shake of her head. "Marcus, I cannot," she said, unaware of the tears that began to spill from her eyes. Her chin quivered, but she did not allow her emotions to decide the moment. "Ye know that I am committed to returnin' to Kerry."

"Keelin, we—"

"My duty is clear," she said, brushing at her tears. He watched the movement of her throat as she swallowed. "I cannot abandon my clan now, at the moment when they've the gravest need for *Ga Buidhe an Lamhaigh.*"

"Is there no one else who can guide your clan, Keelin?" Marcus asked dolefully. "No other way than through the power of the spear?"

"Not for the O'Sheas," she whispered unhappily. "Never for the O'Sheas."

"You would sacrifice what we have—and a future between us—for the clan?"

She pulled her hand away and stood abruptly. "Do ye not see, Marcus?" she cried. "'Tis not my choice. Clann Ui Sheaghda has always had *Ga Buidhe an Lamhaigh*. And a soothsayer. My mother, and her mother before her…"

Marcus remained silent as he knelt in the place where she left him. He sensed that there was naught he could do to change her mind…at least not yet.

But he had a few ideas.

Gathering his tunic in his hands, he stood. He considered taking the few steps that would lead him back to Keelin, but decided against it. 'Twould be all or nothing between them, and he was counting on *all*.

Deep in thought, and profoundly frustrated, he left her chamber quietly. He closed her door and made his way to his own chamber, unmindful of the intruding eyes that watched from the darkened end of the gallery.

One thing he knew for certain, though. There was no devil's mark upon her body.

Keelin gave up her mien of composure when she heard the door latch. She crumpled to the floor and allowed her tears to flow freely.

Emotions warred within her. She could not give Marcus what they both wanted, not when what they desired most would come at the cost of the clan's security, of its most treasured traditions.

Yet what was she to do, when his offer was what she most craved in all her life: to be a valued and cherished wife? There was no reason to assume that the husband chosen by Eocaidh would be at all pleasing to her. A coarse and corrupt chieftain would have suited Eocaidh if only the man wielded enough power, controlled enough land…hated Ruairc Mageean. Her prospective bridegroom's regard for her would have no bearing on his suitability.

On the contrary, if she remained at Wrexton as Marcus's wife, he would care for her as no one had ever done before. She would share his hopes and dreams, would bear his children, and grow old with the lord of Wrexton.

She would be his lady, not merely his chattel.

This line of thinking was fruitless, she thought dejectedly, and unworthy of a Kerry noblewoman. She dried her eyes, then went to the bed where a delicate linen gown had been laid out for her. Slipping it on, Keelin crawled into bed and struggled to settle her mind.

She knew that was only the first of her battles. She had to try to settle her body, too, a difficult task after Marcus's sweet seduction.

Chapter Seventeen

"Who do you think has become chieftain in Cormac's place, Uncle?" Keelin asked, pacing before the fire in Tiarnan's chamber. 'Twas early yet, though the servants had been stirring quietly for quite some time. The worst of the storm had passed sometime during the night, and men were already clearing the baileys and courtyards of snow.

"Ach, lass, I could not say," Tiarnan replied from his bed, "though Eirc and Laoghaire are worthy men."

"But Uncle Tiarnan, Eirc and Laoghaire are mere lads! The O'Sheas need—"

"They were lads when we left Carrauntoohil, Keely," Tiarnan retorted. "They're men now."

She was silent as she considered his words. True enough, four years was a long time. An eternity, Keelin thought, without friends or family. And in four years both of the O'Shea cousins mentioned by Tiarnan would have become men. Especially if the raids and warfare had continued.

Terrible times had a way of maturing the shallowest youth.

"And how do you suppose the clan fares without *Ga Buidhe an Lamhaigh?*" she asked speculatively.

"About as well as any clan does without it," Tiarnan answered. "They'll be usin' their wits and good sense to get by."

Keelin traced the carved wood of the mantel with one finger, unaware of the satisfied expression on Tiarnan's face.

"And how long do ye suppose they'll be gettin' by without the spear?"

Tiarnan shrugged. "Fer as long as necessary, I imagine."

"And what about me?" she asked, returning to the bed and sitting next to the old man. "How long can they manage without the O'Shea seer?"

"Keely lass," Tiarnan said. "Are ye gettin' at somethin' here? Are ye so anxious to leave Wrexton and get back to—"

"No!" she replied, standing abruptly. "I mean…oh, Uncle, I don't know what I mean anymore."

"Keelin…"

"Everything seemed so simple before…"

"Before…?"

"Before Marcus," she replied quietly.

"Do ye care for him, lass?"

"Oh, aye," Keelin replied, dashing stupid tears away. "I care. But my duty to the clan couldn't be clearer. I cannot stay at Wrexton."

"And does Marcus want ye to stay?"

Keelin nodded. "He asked me to."

Tiarnan sighed. Four years ago, he'd have stood up and insisted that Keelin return to Carrauntoohil with *Ga Buidhe an Lamhaigh* as soon as it was possible.

However, Tiarnan's perspective had changed drastically over time. In his four years of travels, he'd seen and experienced so much that was beyond the realm of his life at Carrauntoohil, he could easily imagine his people learning to function without the spear. *Or the seer.*

Even now, without the vision of his eyes, Tiarnan could see that life at Wrexton agreed with Keelin. Marcus de Grant cared for the lass, something Fen McClancy would never do, nor could McClancy treat Keelin to the kind of life she would have here at Wrexton.

Tiarnan could not bear to think what would become of the lass if she fell into Mageean's hands. And there was grave danger of that if she left the protection of Wrexton to journey all the way to Kerry.

Yet who was he to say? Keelin was the one with the gift of the second sight. 'Twas her judgment that had to be trusted in this instance, and not the sentimental yearnings of an old man.

For, as much as he wished that Keelin's happiness and well-being could take precedence, he knew they did not. 'Twas the welfare and prosperity of Clann Ui Sheaghda that had to come first and foremost.

"Keely lass," he finally said, his brow furrowed and troubled, "I'm wishin' I had the answer fer ye, but I don't. When all is said and done, ye must follow yer heart."

"Nay, Uncle," Keelin cried. "I cannot trust my heart."

The loud crash of a slamming door startled the two, and Keelin went to see what was amiss. A short way down the gallery, in front of Keelin's chamber door, stood Annie with her infant in her arms. Her eyes were downcast, and the babe was wailing. Isolda towered over her, with hands on her hips, and rage in her eyes.

"Your employment is belowstairs, is it not?" the chatelaine demanded in a clear, even tone.

"Yes, my lady, but—"

"Lady Isolda, please," Keelin interjected, coming to Annie's rescue. She took the babe from the servant's arms and turned to face Isolda. "'Tis no trouble fer me to look at the wee—"

"I'll not have servants pestering the guests abovestairs," she hissed, barely containing her ire.

Annie sputtered, "Oh, but—"

"And no impudent speech from—"

"I'd rather be pestered by servants," Keelin said evenly, "than wrongly instructed on the true protocol for approachin' a bishop."

Isolda's mouth opened, then shut. She raised her chin defiantly, then let it drop as she lost some of her cocky confidence. Her eyes darted to one side, then the other, finally resting on Marcus, who had suddenly appeared in the gallery behind Keelin. In a panic, she quickly withdrew before he could confront her as he was wont to do of late.

"Ye're lookin' fer me, Annie?" Keelin said, turning to the young mother. She was unaware of Marcus's presence behind her.

"Yes, my lady," she whispered, unsure now, how to behave. With the mistress angry and off in a huff, and the lord bearing down on them from—

"How's our wee lassie this morn?" Keelin asked, cuddling the child, who had finally quit her clamoring. "She's not so wheezy today."

"No, sh-she's much improved," Annie said, "but I was hoping you'd have more of that archangel powder you put in the boiling water, ma'am."

"Ach, aye," Keelin said offhandedly, as though nothing untoward had happened, though she was unsettled by the interchange with Isolda. She opened the door to her chamber. "I've plenty of it, as well as the lungwort, and yer welcome to it, Annie."

"Oh, my lady," the servant said, tentatively following Keelin into her chamber, "you've been so very kind to me and mine. If there's ever anything—"

"Nay," Keelin replied wistfully. "Just be gettin' our wee Peg well again. That'll be enough for me."

Estate business kept Marcus occupied for a goodly portion of the day. He welcomed the activities that kept him from acting precipitously with Keelin, and gave him time to reflect on his course of action with the stubborn Irishwoman.

He considered ignoring Isolda's behavior, then concluded he had no choice but to speak to her about her treatment of Keelin, and of the servants. There was no telling how long it would take to find her a suitable husband, to get her wed and settled in her own home. No matter how much he dreaded having to deal with the woman, it was his duty to do so, and to do it soon.

Rather than sending servants to look for the chatelaine, Marcus climbed a back staircase and headed for the solar, where he knew Isolda spent much of her time. He reached the heavy oaken door and heard voices raised within. Female voices, raised in anger. His hand hesitated at the door latch, but he steeled all his newfound courage and lifted the handle.

There was a sudden silence when he opened the door and stepped in.

Isolda was sitting in a chair near the fire, hastily wiping tears from her cheeks. Her companion, Beatrice, stood nearby, with her back to Marcus, so he was unable to see her expression.

Isolda stood suddenly, knocking over the small embroidery frame where a partially finished altar cloth was draped.

"Marcus! I—I— Was there something you needed?" she stammered. Clearly, it was an effort for her to regain her usual composure.

Marcus moved farther into the room and righted Isolda's sewing. He did not know what had just transpired between Isolda and Beatrice, nor did he think it concerned him. But as Beatrice turned to leave the solar, he bid her to remain and hear what was said.

"This will concern you as well, Beatrice," he said. "Please remain and hear what I've come to say."

The older woman bowed her head and folded her hands under her sleeves. Marcus was still unable to read any expression on her face, though it was no matter to him. He intended to make himself absolutely clear to both of them. If it helped to have Beatrice present, then so be it. Surely, her presence would not hinder his purpose.

"Isolda, your treatment of Lady Keelin is abominable," he began. "You have maligned and insulted her— No," he said, negating her attempt to dispute his words, "do not deny your wrongdoing. I have seen your petty meanness with my own eyes." And from this morning's confrontation outside Keelin's room, he deduced another slight of which he'd been unaware until now.

He did not care to think what other objectionable incidents Keelin had suffered and not mentioned to him.

"My lord, Isolda has—"

"I will be heard on this, once and for all," Marcus interjected when Beatrice tried to speak. "If you do not cease in your efforts to discredit Lady Keelin, then I will be forced to send you away *before* a suitable bridegroom is found for you.''

''But Marcus—''

''Nay, I do not wish to be unkind, Isolda,'' he said firmly, ''but you leave me little choice. I cannot—I *will not* allow you to offend my guests any further.''

''I beg your pardon, Marcus,'' Isolda said. Her eyes were downcast and, other than the white-knuckled grip she had on her own hands, she gave all outward appearances of calm. ''I—I never meant... That is, I...''

''Please. Do not offer any excuses at this late date,'' Marcus said. ''Just bear in mind that I will tolerate no further unkindness toward Lady Keelin or her uncle, nor will I allow you to continue tyrannizing the servants as you've done since my father's death.

''A suitable husband will be found for you, Isolda. As I told you before, I will provide a generous marriage portion for you, so you need not worry that you will be shabbily wed.''

Neither woman said anything in response to Marcus's dictum, but stood silently with eyes downcast.

''It may be some weeks before a suitable husband is found,'' he said in closing, ''but in the meanwhile, I would expect that you comport yourself more kindly and benevolently than you have done of late.'' He remained only a moment more, considering whether to add anything more. Deciding he'd said enough, he turned and exited the solar.

As anxious as he was to leave the women's domain, he took no notice of the inflamed insolence that crossed Beatrice's face when he closed the door after him.

Chapter Eighteen

"**Y**ou are not too cold for our lesson?" Marcus asked Keelin as they walked out to the shooting range. She had been reluctant to come out and practice shooting the bow, but somehow, he'd talked her into putting on a warm cloak and traipsing out to the area where his men did their target practice.

Most of the walkways had been cleared of ice and snow, so it wasn't difficult to get to the remote area behind the keep, where no one could be hurt by a stray arrow.

"Nay, Marcus," Keelin replied honestly. "'Tis good to be out of doors for a change."

In truth, the last two days' confinement had chafed at Keelin, even though the company had been highly entertaining.

Among the various travelers who'd come to take shelter from the storm was a troupe of mummers. These men, along with some of their families, were in the process of making the rounds of the wealthy western estates, putting on plays for the approaching Yule season. They were en route to Wrexton when the storm came upon them, and they trudged ahead, making it to the keep just as the worst of the weather befell them.

Since that time, they'd performed twice for the gathered company, to the delight of all.

And all the while, Marcus had kept his distance. He had made no further advances toward Keelin since the night of their encounter in her chamber, though her emotions were in just as much turmoil as before.

She missed him.

Oh, aye, she'd kept herself busy. After all, Adam still needed her careful tending, and so did wee Peg. But no amount of work could keep her thoughts from returning to the intimate moments they'd shared by the fire in her chamber, when she'd all but given herself to him.

"See the red cloth tied around that big oak?" Marcus asked, stopping Keelin where she stood.

She nodded, squinting, looking into the distance. "Aye."

"'Twill be your first target," he said. "After you master this one, we will move on to the farther ones."

Keelin wet her lips nervously. She brushed her hair back, then lifted the bow and nocked the arrow just as Marcus had shown her before.

"Nay, Keelin," he said, coming around behind her. "You are too tense. Remember how I showed you before? Loosen your joints." He put both hands on her shoulders, sending a thrill of anticipation down her spine. She forced herself to concentrate on the bow, the arrow, the target, but all she could think of was Marcus: his touch, his taste, the texture of his skin.

"That's better," he said, though Keelin did not see any improvement. If anything, she was more tense. "Now train your eyes on the target. Raise the bow a bit."

Marcus leaned close and put one hand on her bow arm, pulling up slightly to correct her aim. Keelin felt his rough jaw as it brushed her cheek. She closed her eyes and inhaled, relishing his scent, and the feel of his strong arm around her. Her heart pounded in her chest and she was certain Marcus could feel it if only he would lean a wee bit closer.

Marcus was not unaffected by her nearness, but he was determined to remain in safe territory with Keelin. Instinct told him he would have to hold back in order to win her, though every minute away from her was pure torture.

They'd sat through hours of the stranded Baron, Albin Selby's, anecdotes, and though the stories were pleasing enough, Marcus would have preferred to spend as many hours alone somewhere with Keelin. He could think of nothing but peeling away her clothing and then tasting every inch of her.

If he thought the time away from her was torture, the minutes *with* her were worse. He did not know how he would manage to keep to his plan when she tempted him so.

"Let it loose," he said quietly in her ear.

The arrow flew, and met its mark an instant later. It did not quite hit the target, but at least it was close.

He had not moved away from her, and had no intention of doing so, either. At least not until he was certain his proximity was having the desired effect.

"I missed," she said, turning slightly. Her lips were achingly close to his. When he felt her breath coming in short pants, he let her go.

Marcus cleared his painfully thickened throat. "'Twas not bad," he said, reaching for another arrow, "for a novice."

Keelin did not reply, but turned back to the target and, if Marcus was not mistaken, she had to force herself to concentrate on the target ahead. She took the arrow from him and they repeated the process, only this time, Marcus pressed himself more closely against her body. He breathed his instructions into her ear. He called her sweetheart when the use of her name would have sufficed.

She missed the target again.

In frustration, Keelin turned around and reached for her own arrow this time. From her fierce expression, Marcus could not be sure she would not turn and shoot *him,* but she lined herself up with the target again, concentrated on her stance and her form, took aim.

Marcus smiled.

Keelin shot.

When the arrow hit the target, Keelin gave out a cry of glee, turned and threw her arms around Marcus. ''I did it!''

''That you did, love,'' he replied, giving a quick kiss to her nose. 'Twas all he could do to stop there. Nonetheless, he managed to force himself.

Detaching himself from her embrace, Marcus asked, ''Will you try it again?''

''Aye. I will.''

Snow began to fall again an hour later, and since it interfered with the visibility of the target, Marcus and Keelin had to abandon their target practice.

'Twas none too soon for Marcus. He'd had difficulty keeping his hands to himself even after she'd mastered the technique necessary for shooting. She had a way of muttering to herself that made him want to laugh, but he'd been prudent enough to keep his mirth to himself, especially after he sensed her rising frustration with the tactics he was using on her.

Marcus smiled to himself as he picked up the quiver of arrows and his own longbow. His onslaught of Keelin's senses was working just as he'd planned—even better, if he considered the effect it was having on *him.*

Well aware that he'd only won a small skirmish, Marcus turned and headed back to the keep beside Keelin. He placed one hand at the small of her back, enjoying tremendously the sense of possession that gesture gave him.

He felt a tremor sweep through her when he touched her. *Ah,* he thought, *victory will be truly sweet.*

"Do ye mind if I bring in some of these holly sprigs, Marcus?" Keelin asked, stopping by a stand of the evergreens. "I know ye mourn yer father, but 'tis nigh on Yuletide and...well, I wouldn't mind hanging a few to remember the season."

"Not at all, Keelin," Marcus replied. "In fact, when we return to the keep, I'll send some of the men out to bring in a few pine boughs for the great hall as well."

Keelin smiled with delight.

"We have another custom here in England," Marcus said. "We gather mistletoe, and hang it from the lintels—"

"Oh, aye," Keelin said with enthusiasm. "In Kerry, we gather it, too, and its magic protects the children."

"How is that?"

"Well, ye hang it over the wee babes' cradles and the faeries won't steal them."

Marcus raised an eyebrow.

"And 'tis common for folks who're out late at night to wear it in an amulet to protect them from the— Nay,

I should not be smilin' that way if I were you, Marcus de Grant. Ye have no idea how many innocent travelers have been saved from the terrible creatures that lurk in the dark.''

Marcus shook his head. ''At Wrexton, 'tis a different kind of magic.''

Keelin looked at him skeptically.

'''Tis true,'' he said. ''Come.''

He took her hand and they walked along a narrowly cleared path in the garden, until they reached a few small juniper trees. ''Do you see the mistletoe growing there?'' he asked.

''Aye,'' Keelin replied, looking at the familiar leaves.

Marcus set down his bow and the quiver, then reached up and snapped off a branch of mistletoe with his fingers.

''It makes a good decoction for delirium, too,'' Keelin remarked as Marcus gazed at the plant in his hand. Keelin easily understood his hesitance to speak of its magic. She found it difficult to speak of *Ga Buidhe an Lamhaigh* and the special powers it possessed.

He raised the plant high, then looked at Keelin. The heat of desire burned in his eyes, and Keelin felt it singe her to the roots of her soul. Time stood still as he moved closer. Keelin's breath caught in her throat and her heart thudded painfully in her chest. Her breasts throbbed with the need for his touch and an ache that centered in the core of her being spread out to the rest of her body.

Keelin's eyes fluttered closed as his lips came closer. She inhaled and caught his essence as she waited for that first tempestuous touch of his mouth.

He did not touch her.

Keelin's eyes flew open as Marcus suddenly turned, retrieving his bow and arrows from where he'd left them. He seemed to steel himself for some difficult task, saying hoarsely, "When the time is right, Keelin O'Shea, I will show you the magic of the mistletoe."

Keelin's head spun. If there was more magic than what she'd just experienced, she did not know if she would survive it!

Marcus took Keelin's arm and started walking down the path. He cleared his throat. "We'll have to seek a Yule log soon, too," he said, as if to dispel the power of the last few minutes. "My father would have wanted all of Wrexton to enjoy the mirth and gladness of the season."

It took Keelin a moment to adjust to the change of topics. This would be the first time Marcus would celebrate the Christmas season without his father. 'Twould be difficult for him, for all of Wrexton, for she had seen that Eldred had been much loved by all the people here.

But Keelin had no opportunity to comment, for one of the young grooms was bounding down the path toward them. "Lord Marcus!" he cried. He was excited and a little frantic.

"What is it, Dob?" Marcus asked.

"'Tis Frieda! Marshal Boswell sent me to fetch you! He needs you!"

Marcus shoved his bow and the quiver of arrows into the boy's hands. "Stay with Lady Keelin," he said, setting off at a run, "and see that she gets safely inside."

"Yes, m'lord!"

They watched as Marcus disappeared down the path, surefooted and fleet. Then Keelin turned to the lad at her side. "What happened?" she asked. "Who is Frieda?"

"She's Lord Marcus's mare," Dob replied, trying to subdue his excitement. "Tryin' to foal, she is, but havin' trouble."

Keelin remembered seeing two beautiful mares, one a

chestnut, the other a gray palfrey, both huge with pregnancy, when they were led from the burning stable. She was chagrined to learn of Frieda's difficulty, and considered following Marcus to the stable. She thought better of it, however, when she recalled what her father's reaction would have been to her "interference" where she did not belong. 'Twas likely Marcus would not care to have her in the way, either.

"And Lord Marcus will help Marshal Boswell with Frieda?"

"Well, yeh," the lad replied. "Lord Marcus knows everything there is to know about horses. And he's teachin' me."

"That's commendable," Keelin said absently. Her nerves were raw, thanks to Marcus. She should be grateful he'd kept his distance, but instead, she was frustrated and tense.

They had almost reached the keep when Keelin realized she would likely meet Lady Isolda in the hall. With so many travelers stranded, 'twas up to the chatelaine to supervise activities in the hall. Dreading another confrontation with the woman, she asked Dob, "Would there be a staircase 'round back o' the keep?"

"Yes, m'lady," the boy replied. "It's this way."

Keelin went along with him, skirting the path that followed the high wall of the keep. She looked up at the windows and the battlements that edged the perimeter of the building as well as the castle walls, and realized what a massive fortress Wrexton really was. Truly, Marcus was lord of as fine a fortress as she'd ever seen. Carrauntoohil Keep was a crude stone stronghold compared to it.

With the snow tapering off, Keelin thought she saw a figure move in one of the upper windows. She could not see who 'twas, nor did she know what rooms overlooked this part of the bailey.

Shuddering, Keelin moved closer to the curtain wall. She did not like the feeling that overtook her just then.

"The river flows under the wall up there," Dob remarked, pointing ahead. "Lord Marcus was once kept prisoner in the rooms down below by the old earl."

"Eldred kept his own son imprisoned?" Keelin asked, startled by the boy's words.

"Oh, nay, m'lady," he replied. "'Twas the old earl, the one before Lord Eldred. It be quite a story if you'd care to hear it."

Keelin was certain 'twould be a good story, but she was too preoccupied to enjoy it now. Something was about to happen, some disaster was about to befall her, though she could not say exactly what it would be. She felt an urgency to get inside quickly, to Uncle Tiarnan's chamber. "Nay, not now, Dob," she said as she picked up her pace, "but later on, if you've a mind to tell it, I'd be willin' to listen."

The lad smiled at the promise of further congress with the lady Keelin. "There's the buttery," he said, taking his task of escort and guide seriously, "and if you walk just a little past it, there's steps leading down to the lord's quay."

"And is there a stair back here where I can—"

"Yes, m'lady," Dob said, pointing ahead. "If you go in through that doorway, there's— Look out!" he cried, shoving Keelin off the path.

A large slab of stone and mortar glanced off her shoulder and crashed to the ground next to her. Dob knelt in the snow next to Keelin. "My lady! Are you all right?"

Keelin sat up. She frowned and shook her head in confusion. "What happened? I...that noise..." She looked up to the top of the wall, then at the block of stone on the ground nearby. "This is what hit me?"

Dob gave a shake of his head, clearly puzzled by the event. He looked up at the keep, then back at Keelin. "I—I don't know how it could have fallen, m'lady," he said in astonishment, "but it did. Are you hurt?"

"Nay," Keelin replied, wincing as she shrugged. "Just bruised my shoulder a wee bit, I think."

"Let me help you up."

The lad gave her his hand and Keelin pulled herself up. It had been close. One more inch either way and the heavy piece would have done serious damage. It might have killed her.

She wondered if *this* incident was what had her intuition humming with apprehension or if something worse awaited her.

"I—I'll see you inside and then I'll run back and get Lord Mar—"

"Nay, Dob," Keelin said. She could see that the lad himself was quite shaken by the experience, and Keelin did not want him to feel responsible. She merely wanted to get to Tiarnan's chamber where all would be well. Surely no harm would come to her when she was with her uncle. "If ye'll just take me to the steps and walk along with me to my chamber... No need to be disturbin' Lord Marcus over this. No harm was done as ye can see."

"But m'lady..." he said, clearly unsure what to do.

"No arguin', lad," Keelin said firmly though she felt quite wobbly inside. She took the boy's arm. "Come. Walk with me."

Keelin found Tiarnan sitting with Adam. She had dropped off her cloak and changed into her green gown, and felt marginally better. By the time she arrived in Adam's chamber, her intuition warned her of no further danger, and she did not intend to upset either Tiarnan or Adam by speaking of the incident on the path. She would simply take what comfort she could from their presence.

Adam was laughing when she entered the room.

"Oh, Lady Keelin!" he said, grinning. "Lord Tiarnan was just telling me of the time when you tied together the boot laces of all the men sleeping in your father's hall and—"

"Uncle Tiarnan!" Keelin cried. She pushed the frightening incident to the back of her mind for the moment. "Ye know better than to be regalin' the lad with such wild tales. I've always behaved as a proper Irish—"

"A proper Irish rascal!" Tiarnan declared.

Both Adam and Tiarnan burst into laughter with Tiarnan's description of her, and she could not help but smile, too. In spite of all of Keelin's difficulties at Wrexton, Tiarnan had found contentment and a return to good health. He had all the companionship he needed with Adam and Marcus, and the knights who had sheltered with them in their poor cottage.

He would be happy here, Keelin thought. With a clear conscience, she could leave him at Wrexton, knowing his days would be safe and comfortable.

Adam's wound was healing well, too. He was gaining strength every day and would soon be able to move in and out of his bed without assistance. He would begin taking solid food and his recovery would be nearly complete.

Though all these things meant she would soon be able to leave, thoughts of her return to Carrauntoohil gave her no joy. On the contrary, Keelin felt nothing but misery at the thought of going away. Yet she schooled her expression and her voice so as not to betray the sorrow she felt within.

"I'll have ye know, Master Adam," Keelin said with feigned indignation, "that I am the daughter o' Eocaidh O'Shea, High Chieftain of all o' Kerry. 'Tis not fittin' to mock such a high personage, if ye catch my meanin'."

"Keelin!"

Just when Keelin thought she'd regained her equilibrium, Marcus flung the door open and stepped inside. His clothes were a mess—a combination of mud and blood, Keelin thought, and his face was drawn.

Clearly, he'd heard of the incident on the path, and suddenly Keelin had a desperate need to feel his protective arms around her.

"Ah, Marcus," she said instead, standing up from her place on the side of Adam's bed. She clasped her hands together in front of her, and sent him a forbidding expression. She did not want Tiarnan's peace shattered by a discussion of the accident on the path. "How fares Frieda?" she asked quickly. "Has she foaled?"

For a fair man, Marcus's face darkened perceptibly, but he went along with Keelin, clearly understanding her intent. He replied that the mare had delivered a fine colt, but not without difficulty. It remained to be seen whether or not the horse would recover from the birth, or if she'd ever bear any more young.

"Will she die, too, Marcus?" Adam asked, his voice small and troubled. It had not occurred to either Marcus or Keelin that the boy would take Frieda's condition to heart.

Keelin sat back down next to the lad and glanced up

at Marcus, hoping that her eyes did not betray her need for him. She knew he was torn between the need to stay and offer reassurances to Adam, and hauling her out of the room to question her on what had transpired outside.

She hoped he realized Adam needed him more than she did.

"Nay, Adam," Marcus said, kneeling next to the lad, "trust that Marshal Boswell will take excellent care of her. And just wait until you're able to go out and see the colt. He's a fine lad—has the look of his sire."

Adam relaxed some with Marcus's words.

"But Frieda," Adam persisted. "She will be all right?"

"Adam...I can't promise you," Marcus said, "but she seems so. The birth was not easy, but I believe Marshal Boswell will see that Frieda recovers."

"Might I go and see her, Marcus?"

"Absolutely not," Marcus replied. "You are not yet healed, young man, and I would not have you leave your warm chamber—"

"But Marcus—"

"Nay, I'll hear no more," Marcus replied as he got up. "I will check on the mare often and let you know of her progress. When you are fully healed, you may visit Frieda and Isabella in their temporary stable, but not until then. Keelin," he said, turning, "I would have a word with you."

He took her by the elbow and began to usher her out of the room. Completely attuned to each other, neither of them took note of Adam's pout or the puzzled expression on Tiarnan's face as they left Adam's chamber.

Marcus kept one hand under Keelin's elbow until they reached her room and entered. Marcus closed the door and latched it.

Keelin turned, pressing her cheek against Marcus's chest. His arms went around her.

Neither spoke.

'Twas the first time Keelin had ever felt fragile to Marcus. For all her height and strength, she was still a woman, in need of his protection. And he had failed her. First when she'd been injured in the stable, and today, on the path.

Never again, he vowed.

"Keelin," he said, "where were you hurt? Dob said the stone hit you, knocked you down."

"Aye, it did, Marcus," she replied. She started to shake all over again, thinking about her close call. And then there was Marcus, so near, his effect on her so profound... "Dob pushed me from the path, so it barely hit my shoulder."

"Thank God for that," Marcus said.

"And for Dob."

"Yes," Marcus replied, his throat thickening with emotion. "He'll be well rewarded." Had Dob not been so quick, he might have lost her. All he could do now was hold her, and reassure himself that all was well.

He pulled away slightly, moving his hands to the laces that held her bodice together. Keelin did not stop him, nor ask what he was about. Proper or not, he would see with his own eyes that she was truly unhurt.

When the bodice was loosened, Marcus gently pulled it off Keelin's shoulders, leaving her barely clad in her white chemise. She looked even more vulnerable than before, with so much soft, white skin exposed. He longed to touch her, to pull her close, but he dared not, for fear of injuring her. "Which shoulder was hit, Keelin?" Marcus asked, his voice a quiet rasp.

"My left," she replied, turning slightly.

Gently he pulled the thin chemise down. Keelin stayed still, though she was unable to conceal a slight tremor, and the way her breasts rose with quick, nervous breaths.

He had vowed to remain chaste, yet he could not resist touching her. The sight of her graceful neck and delicate collarbones evoked something totally male and primal inside him, responding to her utter femininity. He ran the tips of his fingers gently across her fine bones and could not suppress his own tremor.

A nasty red scrape marred Keelin's shoulder, and a large bruise had begun to form around it. Marcus knew it had to hurt with every move she made, but he doubted any bones were broken.

Goose bumps appeared on her skin and when Marcus turned his gaze to Keelin's face, her cheeks were flushed and her eyes closed. He felt every bit as aroused as she looked.

One long lace held the gathered chemise together. Marcus gave a half-hearted attempt to resist, but lost the battle. He gave the cord a slight tug, and the fine linen fabric slipped. *It will do no harm to look,* he told himself, *and mayhap touch. But no more.*

As it was, he'd gone too far.

Chapter Nineteen

"Marcus," Keelin said. It might have been uttered as a question, or an answer, Marcus thought. Mayhap even a prayer.

"You are so very beautiful," he said. He took one hand and raised it to his lips, and when he lowered it, he dropped a soft kiss on her injured shoulder, causing Keelin's breath to catch.

Her reaction inflamed him. He put his hands on her waist, then slid them up to bear the weight of her breasts. With thumbs extended, he touched her nipples, causing the tips to bead, and making her gasp with the impact of his featherlight touch.

Marcus had never touched anything so fine. He circled the deep pink skin, then bowed his head in order to taste her. Taking one breast deep into his mouth, Marcus felt Keelin's hands in his hair, and heard her gasp with pleasure.

He released her.

"Marcus!" she cried breathlessly. "Please…"

Marcus pulled the chemise back up to cover her. He could take no more, and knew she could not, either.

"Keelin, I must go before I do something I will regret."

"No—"

"Yes," he said, summoning the strength to retie the lace. "I will leave you now and go to my bath. But we will sup together in the hall."

"Marcus—"

He cut her off with a quick kiss on the lips.

"In the hall," he said. "At supper."

Marcus might have smiled at the expression on Keelin's face when he left her, but he knew his own was no better. Still, he did not regret leaving her. Honor demanded it.

Water had been brought to his chamber for his bath, and he wasted no time getting to it. He stood upright in the tub, sluicing the warm water over his body. It did not help to ease the arousal that was nearly painful, but at least some of the day's grime rinsed off. Looking down at his body, Marcus did not know how long he could live with the tension. The way he wanted Keelin was beyond what he'd ever felt for any other woman, and he had vowed to take his passions no further than chivalry allowed. Already, he'd stretched the boundaries.

But the relief of finding her relatively unhurt had been too great. He'd had to touch her, he'd needed the reassurance of her body against his, the taste of her skin on his lips. She had needed him just as badly.

With a frustrated groan, he forced his thoughts away from Keelin. 'Twould not serve either of them if he could not keep his emotions, as well as his physical reaction to her, in check.

He rinsed the soap from his body and stepped out of the tub. There was much to do before supper.

Marcus dressed quickly and threw a warm cloak around his shoulders. It was full dark now, so he picked up an oil lamp to light his way. He did not meet anyone in the gallery as he walked toward the stairs that led to the parapet.

'Twas just as well. Marcus would see how and where the stone had come loose and fallen on Keelin before bringing workmen up to make repairs. He'd been unaware of any weak areas where the stone and mortar were deteriorating, but he supposed the storm could have knocked something loose.

The stairway was dark and cold. Marcus climbed the steps, and when he reached the top, he saw snow on the ground inside. He frowned. Unless there was a space under the door for snow to blow and accumulate inside, there was no logical reason for it to be on the steps inside.

He pulled open the door that led to the parapet. The small lamp and the unearthly glow of the snow provided the only light.

Yet Marcus could see tracks.

The footprints were obscured by the newly fallen snow, but clearly, someone had walked out there, and returned. Hence the snow inside, on the top step.

There was no reason for anyone to have been out there. Unless...

Nay. He refused to even begin thinking of such a thing. Someone must have decided to investigate the falling stonework in order to prevent any further mishap. Tonight he would talk to the men who were stationed inside the keep and find out which of them had heard of Keelin's accident and had gone up to the parapet to look.

Marcus held the lamp up and walked to the wall overlooking the path. 'Twas a clear shot straight down, with no trees or other obstacles to impede the path of a falling object. He looked along the crenelated wall, searching for a space where the stone had become dislodged.

He found the spot. And it was not in the vicinity where Keelin had been injured.

Keelin's insides were shimmering. 'Twas the only way to describe how she felt. And now she was seated on the main dais at Marcus's right hand, while servants brought course after course of beautifully prepared food. Keelin could barely sit still for all the agitation she felt.

She had yet to recover from their moments together in her chamber.

Looking back on it, the whole day had been heavily charged. Marcus had touched and teased her while they were on the archery range, until she was nearly out of her mind with need. Even now, as he sat beside her, Keelin could not remain unaffected.

She tried not to take note of his hands as he cut their meat in the trencher, or when he held his cup. She avoided inhaling too deeply, to avoid sinking into the clean, masculine scent that was Marcus. She tried not to become too accustomed to the extraordinary sense of safety she felt whenever he was near.

She shut out thoughts of leaving here, and the pain that was certain to accompany her departure and took a sip of wine to settle her nerves.

Baron Selby and his wife sat at Marcus's far side, along with his daughters. He was a jovial fellow, and seemed not at all put out by the storm that delayed their return home from a journey to visit Lady Selby's parents.

''I never expected such harsh weather this far before

Christmas," he said. "Else we'd never have left Rentford Manor, the estate of my wife's father."

Lady Selby just rolled her eyes.

"Papa," Selby's younger daughter said, "Grandsire warned you of the—"

"Now, now, Elga," Selby scolded. "'Tis rude to contradict your elders. Your grandsire was not entirely certain that the weather would change so drastically after the rain."

The friendly banter continued as they ate, and Keelin relaxed. It seemed strange that Isolda, who seemed set on controlling every aspect of life at Wrexton, was not in the hall. However, the meal was far more pleasant without the chatelaine's disapproving eyes constantly glaring at her, without having to be continuously on her guard.

Someone had seen that trestle tables were set up to accommodate the rest of Wrexton's visitors, and they feasted nearly as well as the lord of the castle. While acrobats in gaily colored costumes began tumbling at one end of the hall, the visiting mummers prepared to entertain the company again. Musicians were tuning up and making ready to play as two wandering minstrels walked among the tables singing and harmonizing songs of valor and romance.

"Have you mastered the bow yet, my lady?" Sir Robert asked from his place farther down the dais.

Keelin laughed. "Far from it, Sir Knight," she said. "But I'm makin' good progress, I think."

"Lord Marcus is a good instructor," Sir William remarked. "Without fail, his aim is true."

Keelin thought she detected a twinkle in the knight's eye, but could not be sure. "Aye," she replied, "but is he as good with a target that moves?"

''Well, that remains to be seen,'' Robert said, ''does it not, my lord?''

''I've been tested both ways, gentlemen,'' Marcus said dryly, ''and never found wanting.''

''Lady Keelin,'' a feminine voice interrupted. Isolda had come up behind her and spoke quietly. Her expression was one of distress, and her hands twisted in front of her. ''May I speak with you for a moment?''

Keelin hesitated, but Isolda seemed quite upset. Without a doubt, something was wrong and Keelin worried that it was Annie's babe again, or another one of the castle children fallen ill. Pushing herself away from the table, Keelin stood, causing Marcus to notice Isolda for the first time.

''Where are you going?'' he asked.

She shrugged, wincing with the movement of her sore, stiff shoulder. ''Not far, Marcus,'' Keelin replied. ''Don't be mindin' me. Just continue with yer meal and I'll be back when I can.''

Marcus shook his head. ''If you don't mind, I'll come along.''

Keelin could see from his expression that he would brook no resistance, even though his tone was mild. He intended to accompany her wherever she went and Keelin had to admit that his big, solid presence was comforting, even if 'twas unsettling at the same time.

They walked a few steps from the dais and Marcus stood behind Keelin. She resisted the urge to lean into him as Isolda spoke.

''Lady Keelin,'' she said, taking care to avoid looking at Marcus. ''I—I just want to say how regretful I am to have been so...unkind to you since your arrival here at Wrexton.'' Her manner was awkward, though she seemed sincere.

Her words were so unexpected, though, that Keelin was caught speechless for the moment. 'Twas no matter, though, for Isolda continued.

"Those incidents…they were childish and mean," she said. "I cannot tell you what came over me, but I sincerely regret causing you any embarrassment. Please allow me to—to bid you a belated welcome to Wrexton. I intend to do all in my power to see that you are made comfortable."

Isolda glanced quickly at Marcus, then back at Keelin.

"I thank ye, Isolda," Keelin said, extending her hands in a friendly gesture. Isolda took hold of them and squeezed once. Then she turned and walked away in haste.

Keelin stood watching Isolda as she made her way through the throng of people, then turned back to the table. Robert and William had both witnessed the chatelaine's apology, and while Robert smiled broadly as a result of it, William's visage was dark and forbidding, as if he did not believe in Isolda's sincerity.

"'Twas a very gracious thing," Keelin said to Marcus as she seated herself. Her words were for William's benefit as well, for Keelin truly believed Isolda was remorseful for her unkind behavior.

Marcus did not know what to believe. He shared Will's skepticism, yet he'd seen Isolda's eyes. He did not detect any deceit there.

Questions remained regarding Keelin's accident, however, and whether or not it was in truth, an accident. Isolda was the likeliest villain in the scenario, yet Marcus had learned she'd been occupied in the hall at the time Keelin had been hurt. They could not be Isolda's footprints on the parapet.

Yet who else felt threatened by Keelin? The castle

servants had come to love and respect her, especially since she'd cured Annie's babe. Not one of the servants missed an opportunity to sing Keelin's praises for the fine job she'd done with Adam and little Peg. And Marcus had seen them coming to her at all hours to ask her advice for one malady or another.

Mayhap the stone and mortar incident was truly just an accident, though come daylight, Marcus intended to investigate further. 'Twas quite possible he'd missed something in the dark.

Keelin knew that the frivolity in the hall bothered Marcus. After all, his father was only recently buried, and such merry activity had no place at Wrexton now. 'Twas one thing to hang a little pine and holly about the keep in order to commemorate the season, and yet another thing altogether to engage in boisterous fun.

Still, the stranded travelers needed diversions to keep their interest—and the peace. So Marcus did not object to the plays or the dancing, although he refrained from joining in, as did Keelin.

Of all the visitors in the hall, only two made Keelin uneasy. They were knights, brothers by the look of them, and not as old as their first impression gave out.

Both men had brown hair, worn long. The shape of their chins was the same, long and pointed, and one of them had a deep dimple piercing the center. The same brother was cursed with eyes of two different colors, brown and blue. Keelin was unnerved whenever his gaze caught hers.

They'd let it be known they were on an errand for their lord, a viscount from Lincolnshire, when they'd been caught by the storm. Keelin thought the viscount must have fallen on hard times to have outfitted his knights so poorly, for their armor was tarnished and their livery frayed.

Keelin noticed that the women of the castle avoided both brothers. She planned to do likewise.

The weather turned even colder, and it kept everyone indoors another few days, bundled in extra clothes and cloaks.

Tempers flared among the visitors in the hall, and Marcus and his men were well occupied keeping the peace. The servants were overtaxed, as well, and Marcus solved the problem by seeing that the burden of maintaining the hall was shared by all, including the visitors.

Though 'twas a blessing that the inclement weather would not last much longer, Marcus knew that when it became possible to travel, Keelin would make haste to return to Kerry. After all, she'd only promised to remain at Wrexton as long as Adam needed her, and the boy's condition was improving steadily. In another day or so, the boy would be able to leave his bed unassisted.

Marcus had not pressed Keelin for the last few days. He'd been acutely aware of her whenever she was near, and his hands fairly itched with the need to touch her. He realized, however, the benefit of allowing Keelin to stew alone over her feelings for him. If he had accurately read the look in her eyes, then she was feeling equally frustrated.

He judged it was time to act. All was quiet in the hall for the moment, with Marcus's most trusted knights present to keep watch on things.

Knowing that Keelin would not refuse an opportunity to visit the falcons, Marcus invited her to join him to see how the nestlings progressed at their training. He had spoken to Gerald on several occasions and knew the small merlins were ready for company.

"Ah, my lord!" Gerald said as he and Keelin entered the long building. "I—I was just about to take my leave—"

"Nay, Gerald. Not yet," Marcus said, suppressing a smile. The falconer had not forgotten Marcus's instruction to vacate whenever he and Keelin arrived. "Stay and show us the nestlings."

"Very good, my lord." The falconer smiled. "'Tis a fine pair of merlins you've got. They took to the hood and bells, and they've been out at night."

"Then they're nearly ready for the lure."

"Yes, my lord."

"What is the lure, Master Gerald?" Keelin asked, a curious line furrowing her brow.

Marcus followed Keelin and Gerald deeper into the mews as the falconer explained Wrexton's method of training the birds. Knowing that Keelin shared his enthusiasm for the falcons, he had hopes of taking her out to the fields when these merlins were taught to hunt.

He only had to convince her to stay long enough.

They reached the perch where the two newest birds sat together, with jesses and bells on their legs. "Stay quiet, if you please, my lady," Gerald said, using soft, even tones. "They're accustomed only to me as yet, and my voice...."

The falconer took one of the birds onto his gloved hand and held her close enough to pet her gently. He cooed and spoke affectionately to the bird and the merlin remained calm, her eyes darting around in the semidarkness of the building.

Marcus picked up one of Keelin's hands and slipped

a glove onto it. Then Gerald transferred the falcon to her. Keelin's eyes lit with excitement.

"Speak to her in a soft voice like this," Gerald instructed as he continued to stroke the bird.

"Ach, yer a fine lass," Keelin said, taking up after the falconer left off. The merlin ruffled her feathers slightly, but settled right down when Keelin continued speaking.

Her voice had the opposite effect on Marcus. He eased up behind her, standing as close as possible without touching more than her cloak, though he would have preferred to press the length of her back against him.

Instead, he listened while she cooed to the merlin.

"I'll take my leave now, my lord," Gerald said. "Their hoods are on the bench...."

Marcus nodded, giving the man his leave.

He could feel her warmth. As she spoke to the bird, Marcus did not hear her words, only the soft cadence of her voice, the wonderful lilt of her speech.

The door latched tightly behind Gerald as he left, and Marcus leaned slightly forward, catching a few strands of Keelin's hair on his chin. He inhaled deeply of her scent, taking care not to startle her or the falcon.

Only one torch glowed near the door of the mews, so the light was faint, but all the rest of the birds were dimly visible on their perches. Some were at shoulder height, and others down low. Beyond the perches was a large, open area where the training took place, and the birds could fly.

"Ach, I love the trill of your wee bells, my beauty," Keelin said. "Marcus, why do they wear the bells?"

"To alert the falconer of their movements," he replied. "Gerald or one of the other falconers, stays here at all times."

"I didn't realize..." Keelin said, keeping her voice down. "Of course I should have known...they're valuable birds."

"Will you come with us when we train them to the lure?"

Keelin hesitated. Marcus came around to face her, taking the small merlin from her and replacing it on its perch.

"When the weather clears, we'll take them out to the fields for a couple of hours and see what they can do." He took her chin between his thumb and forefinger. "Say you'll come, Keelin."

She seemed mesmerized by his gaze.

The hot yellow flame of the torch flickered in her eyes, but then she closed them. "Aye, Marcus," she breathed. "I'll come with ye."

Pleased by her answer, he watched the smooth muscles of her neck as she swallowed hard. "Keelin," he said, tipping her head back slightly. "Look above you."

She raised her eyes and looked at the dark beams overhead. "What, Marcus? Ah, 'tis the mistletoe."

He nodded, taking notice of the way Keelin's eyes widened at the sight of the plant. Several sprigs had been hung from the beams in the mews, and Marcus had hoped for an opportunity to demonstrate how the mistletoe tradition was kept in England.

"'Tis magic, you said," Keelin remarked, her voice small and doubtful in the hollow expanse of the building.

"There are many who say so," Marcus said. He stayed close, taking a lock of her silken hair between his fingers.

"And all ye must do is hang it above?" Keelin asked.

One side of Marcus's mouth quirked up. "Yes," he said. "And...have a lover at hand."

"A—a lover, ye say?" Keelin whispered.

"Aye," Marcus replied, and without further ado, he took possession of Keelin's mouth.

Keelin had been both hopeful, yet afraid that something like this would happen. She'd done her best to avoid Marcus and the potent attraction that shimmered between them. Her heart was already impossibly tied to Marcus and to his home, and no matter how many ways she considered it, she could not find a reason to abandon her duty to Clann Ui Sheaghda.

She had no choice but to leave Wrexton.

Something that felt frighteningly like despair welled in Keelin's throat and she made a sound. If only the mistletoe possessed some magic that could keep her here at Wrexton Castle with Marcus.

She clung to him, relishing the sensation of his hands in her hair, on her shoulders, along her spine. She allowed him to pull her close, knowing this could very well be their last intimate moments together, for surely the weather would soon break and she would be compelled to leave.

"Ah, Keely," Marcus whispered as he nuzzled her ear. His lips moved down her neck, his hands pushing aside the bulky cloak. "Have you any idea how much I want you?"

Aye, I do, she thought, as one wayward tear slid down her face. *About as much as I want you, but I dare not say it.*

She threaded her hands through his hair, that gilded mane she so admired, and pulled him even closer while his lips drove her to distraction. She could not think while he touched her so…could not muster the power of will she needed to refuse him.

"Marcus," she murmured.

He pulled her even closer, pressing their bodies together, sending sparks of need through her. His lips teased an exquisitely sensitive area below her ear.

"The magic is very potent," she said breathlessly as his touch wreaked havoc with her senses. She was certain that even without the mistletoe, her feelings for Marcus could not be any stronger. The tiny magical plant had not been necessary to bind her heart any tighter.

'Twas pure torment, though. No matter how much she cared for Marcus, regardless of what they two might want, she had to return to Carrauntoohil.

Abruptly, she pushed away from him.

"Keelin?" He'd thought she was equally enthralled.

"Marcus," she said in a quavering voice, "we cannot...'tis not possible for us..."

"Keelin, I don't—"

"Please, Marcus," she cried, turning away from him. "Do not make this any more difficult for me. I must return home."

"No." His voice was harsh and full of frustration.

"I cannot stay," she said quietly, walking away from him, "no matter how I might wish otherwise...."

Keelin pulled her cloak tightly around her and skittered out of the mews. It took every dram of willpower in her body to keep her legs moving, walking away from Marcus. If she allowed herself half a moment to think, to feel, she would turn and go back to him.

She lifted her skirts and ran back to the keep as if the very devil were biting at her heels.

Chapter Twenty

"**Y**e cannot leave in this weather, lass," Tiarnan said as he sat listening to the activity in Keelin's chamber.

"It's bound to improve soon, Uncle," Keelin said as she folded another gown and put it into her satchel. She would leave the wooden trunk for Tiarnan to keep his things in, and take only what she needed for her journey.

"And what of *Ga Buidhe an Lamhaigh?*" he asked. "Who will protect you and the spear as you travel?"

"I will find a way, Uncle Tiarnan," Keelin replied, resolved as she was to leave as soon as possible, before her heart suffered irreparable damage. Before too much harm came to Marcus's. "Mayhap I will pay some Wrexton knights to accompany me."

"Have ye yet spoken to Marcus about that?" Tiarnan asked, the anger and frustration in his voice nearly palpable. He never raised his voice to her, but Keelin knew he was close to it now. Did he not understand how important it was to get *Ga Buidhe an Lamhaigh* to Carrauntoohil?

"Nay," Keelin replied.

Tiarnan slapped one hand impatiently on his thigh. "If all is so settled then, why do ye weep?"

Keelin sniffed and brushed away her tears. She swallowed and tried to make her voice clear so that her uncle would believe the lie. "I—I do not weep. I merely…"

"Ye merely *what*, lass?" Tiarnan demanded. By rights, he could not fault Keelin for her loyalty and sense of duty to the clan. But Tiarnan was convinced that returning to Kerry now would not be the best thing for the lass. Besides, it was dangerous to travel at this time of year.

And travel with *Ga Buidhe an Lamhaigh* would be doubly dangerous. If Mageean's men came upon her… ach, by the saints, if *any* group of unscrupulous men ran across her while she traveled… Nay he could not bear to think of it.

Nor could he bear to think of her leaving Marcus de Grant. 'Twas obvious the lad cared deeply for her, and he was a fine young man. There wasn't a better one in all of Kerry, either young or old, and that included Fen McClancy, Keelin's intended bridegroom.

Mayhap it took the hindsight of a lonely, solitary old man to see the folly of living life for a principle, an ideal. All Tiarnan knew was that he'd been alone his whole life, and that if he had the chance to live it over again, he'd have found someone to share it. Someone to care for, who would have loved him in return.

'Twas a shame Marcus hadn't hauled Keelin off to some secluded place and had his way with her. Tiarnan had done what he could about the matter, sending the lad to Keelin's chamber when she was bathing, knowing full well that Marcus would barge in when he believed Keelin faced the danger of handling *Ga Buidhe an Lamhaigh* alone….

Well, that hadn't worked, at least not that Tiarnan was aware of. Ach, aye, *something* had happened, but the result had not been a betrothal, as Tiarnan would have wished.

Nay, the lass's heart was breaking and there was nothing he could do to help her.

"Uncle," Keelin said as she raised the mattress and dropped the leather-encased the spear on the bed, as if she could not bear to touch it. "I *must* leave. I've been feelin' a premonition that comes and goes—somethin' terrible will happen soon. I must take the spear and return to Kerry before the O'Sheas suffer another disaster."

"But Marcus—"

"It does not matter what I feel for Marcus, or that I'll never love another," Keelin cried, whirling away from Tiarnan. He could feel her erratic movement about the room and felt the pain of her decision. "I have no choice! 'Tis my duty to take the spear back to Clann Ui Sheaghda! Ye know how precious the spear is, and 'tis irreplaceable. The clan depends on it! There is no other who can do this!"

"Keely lass—"

"Uncle!" Keelin rushed to his side and knelt next to him. "Hush...someone is..."

"What is it, lass?"

Keelin shivered. "I—I don't know why it should bother me, but someone's heard us."

"Who?"

"I do not know," Keelin replied. "But I sense clearly that someone listened to everything we said...about the spear, about my returning to Kerry...and it feels wrong. Someone wishes us—*me*—ill."

"The chatelaine?"

She looked inward, trying to see more. "I do not know."

Tiarnan knew Keelin's first thought would be to take the spear and suffer whatever visions it offered her. Yet the experience would weaken her substantially. And if an enemy was near, Keelin would need all her physical and mental strength to protect herself.

"What of your premonition?" Tiarnan asked quietly. "Could it not be about Wrexton? Your heart is tied here as strongly as to Carrauntoohil."

Keelin shook her head. "I do not know, Uncle," she whispered. "I do not know."

Keelin did not come to the hall to sup with all who were gathered there. Annoyed with himself for missing her so acutely, Marcus sat at the dais with Selby and his family, tending his cup of ale, and watching yet another of the mummers' plays.

In this, a "wooing" play, a clown in ridiculous garb courted a woman. Naturally, there was a mighty knight slain early in the story, but the wooing by the fool progressed. Marcus was oblivious to the laughter of the audience, but fully attuned to the clown and the object of his desire.

Never had he felt so clownish himself. In all the years of his awkwardness with women, of the brutal shyness that had plagued him, Marcus had known how unlikely 'twas to find a woman with whom he could share his life.

Yet now that he'd found her, he had to let her go.

He took a long draught of ale and watched as the mighty knight was restored to life by the blessed water poured over him. His wounds now gone, the character took up his wooden sword and traveled through sleet and storm to return to his true love—the one now pursued by the clown.

Marcus could watch no longer. He drained his cup and stood, taking his leave of the company. In his present mood, he was not fit for them at the moment, anyhow.

His temper now as fierce as the weather, he stormed out of the hall, pulling on a cloak as he went. He did not know where he would go, for he had no wish to unleash his ill humor on anyone, neither man nor beast. Yet he felt too savage to keep up his civilized demeanor.

The weather was too foul for a mind-numbing ride, so Marcus stalked through the freezing rain and wind to the mews. There, he knew he could find work to occupy him. There were always leashes to cut, jesses to mend. Perhaps he would work a bit with the new birds.

Anything, he thought, to keep his mind from dwelling on Keelin's disavowal of all they felt for each other.

A terrible westerly wind blew the door open when Marcus unlatched it, allowing rain and wind inside until he could slam the door closed against the elements.

It was suddenly dark again, though Marcus quickly lit the lamp that hung near the door. When he did, he was astonished and dismayed by the devastation within.

Gwin and Cleo were not on their perches. Nor were the two nestlings that were just being trained.

And where was Gerald?

Marcus took the lamp and walked tentatively through the mess on the floor—through bits of leather, tools, candles, broken lamps and lamp oil. One workbench had been overturned, as well, with the contents of its drawers strewn about.

"Gerald?" Marcus called. He walked farther into the long, low building, glancing as deeply into the darkness as his vision allowed.

There was no reply, so Marcus continued his search.

Two more birds were missing, one goshawk and a merlin. All in all, the missing birds were the most valuable in the mews.

Deep in the shadows, Marcus caught sight of a long, dark shape on the ground. Knowing full well it was a body, he dreaded what he would find. He hurried over, set the lamp on the floor, then turned the falconer over. There was a bloody wound on the man's forehead, but he was breathing.

"Gerald!" Marcus called.

The falconer groaned but did not open his eyes. Marcus gently shook him, and after several trics, the man finally looked up with unfocused eyes.

"Lord Marcus," he rasped.

"What happened here?" Marcus asked. "Are you hurt anywhere besides your head?"

"Nay, my lord," Gerald replied as Marcus helped him to sit up. "I don't think so. Just bruised a bit."

"Tell me what happened. Who did this?" Marcus looked around the shattered mews.

"Two men," Gerald replied, gingerly touching the injured spot on his skull.

"Who were they?"

"I couldn't say, my lord," Gerald replied. "They were not from the village, nor the castle. I'd guess they were a couple of the stranded ones. I mean, men staying at the keep...out of the weather.... Sorry, m'lord. My head's a bit muddled."

"Don't fret, Gerald," Marcus said. "Stay here. I'm going for help."

Marcus braved the icy cold again, rousing the grooms and huntsmen, who followed him back to the mews. One of them saw to Gerald, while the others began cleaning up the mess.

Marshal Boswell stood amidst the chaos with his hands on his hips, shaking his head. "What happened to the falcons?" he asked.

"They took them," Marcus replied, coming to the only conclusion possible. The intruders had wrought utter devastation to the mews, but had left no falcon carcasses. "If they can get far enough away, those birds will be of untold value to whoever stole them."

"Should we organize a search?"

Marcus shook his head. "Send someone to the gate first. See if anyone has left the castle. Then we'll search the grounds—we'll look through all the buildings and cellars."

"Do you really mean it about leaving, Keelin?" Adam asked, his face a long mask of woe.

"Aye, Adam," Keelin replied, her own sad expression no better. "As soon as the weather clears, I'll be off. As I told ye, my clan needs me."

"But *I* need you!"

Twas not like Adam to whine, but he'd used every other tack to convince Keelin to stay at Wrexton, and no argument had yet worked.

"And Marcus," Adam continued. "What do you think he will do when you're gone?"

"Sure and he'll manage once I've gone, laddie," Keelin retorted, struggling to hold her emotions in check. "A man like Marcus will not remain unmarried for long, and he has Isolda to—"

"Ah, but you're wrong, Keelin!" Adam cried. "He has never looked at Isolda the way he looks at you. As often as Uncle Eldred urged him to wed Isolda, Marcus refused as many times."

Keelin looked down, embarrassed. She did not like to

think what else Adam had observed while lying idle on his sickbed.

"'Tis true," Adam said. "And I've seen how *you* look at *him*."

"Adam, ye're young yet," Keelin said. "Ye do not yet understand the weight of responsibility and duty, but one day, ye will. And—and—"

Keelin's breath was suddenly, shockingly knocked out of her as if she'd been punched. She struggled for air, and began to shake as a vision took shape....

There was a broken-down barn in a wintry dell. Snow drifted in deep swirls around the stone structure, and thick daggers of ice hung from the trees all 'round. Blood stained the snow on the ground, and Ga Buidhe an Lamhaigh *was in danger of being lost forever....*

The feeling of dread that accompanied this vision was akin to the feelings she'd had in recent days...a certainty that some evil was to befall her. Yet she could not pinpoint exactly what was to happen. If only—

"Keelin?" Adam asked. "What is it? Are you all right?"

Keelin gave a quick shake of her head and came to her senses. She did not want to alarm Adam. "Ach, aye, lad," Keelin said shakily. Her mind was immersed in worry and her body slowly recovered from the shock of the vision. "I just thought of somethin' I must do. Well, 'tis late," she said lightly. "Time for ye to be catchin' yer rest now. I'll say good night to ye."

She had not planned to touch the spear until she was back in Kerry, but she had to clarify what she'd seen. 'Twas imperative to find out *now,* what she could do to prevent the loss of *Ga Buidhe an Lamhaigh.*

Only by touching the spear—and suffering the consequences—could she do so.

The sounds of revelry in the hall were clearly audible when she walked through the gallery to her chamber. After all the minor disturbances that had occurred throughout the past few days, Keelin knew Marcus would not leave the hall until everyone had retired. 'Twas comforting to know he was nearby.

Keelin would not tell Tiarnan of her intention to draw on the power of the spear, because the old man did nothing but worry when she did so. Instead, she went straight to her own chamber, lit the lamps and lifted the mattress.

Ga Buidhe an Lamhaigh was not there. Nor was the pouch of gold coins she had hidden with it.

Keelin lit another lamp and began to search her chamber. She clearly remembered returning the spear to its hiding place next to the coins before walking Tiarnan to his chamber. Certainly her uncle had not returned and taken the spear and the coins—he would have had difficulty finding his way. Moving the mattress and finding the precious items would have been nigh onto impossible for him.

No, it had to be here somewhere, her mind insisted, even though she could not sense its presence.

Keelin spent precious minutes searching. The spear was not in the chamber, nor were Keelin's other valuable possessions, a small gold brooch that had belonged to her mother, and a jeweled dagger that her father had owned all his life. The coins had disappeared as well.

An intruder must have gone through all her things and taken whatever seemed valuable. Yet that explanation did not feel quite right. Intuition told her there was more to it than that, but Keelin could not quite see what it was. Whatever was going on here, however, *Ga Buidhe an Lamhaigh* was missing. That was all that mattered.

She had to find Marcus.

Keelin had vowed to redouble her efforts to avoid him, knowing that being with him was pure torture. She was certain he must be angry with her for running from him that afternoon, but now she had no choice but to enlist his assistance. She could not go after the spear alone.

She left her chamber only to collide with Beatrice, Isolda's companion. She'd never exchanged words with the woman, but had sensed an unexplained hostility from her, ever since the day Beatrice had interrupted her and Marcus in the garden.

The old woman gave Keelin the impression of a spider under attack, all curled up upon itself. The comparison made Keelin shudder. "Is aught amiss, my lady?" Beatrice asked.

Immediately, Keelin was suspicious of the woman, but she doubted Beatrice was so foolish as to steal a guest's belongings. Nor would she have knowledge of the spear, unless...*Beatrice* must have been the one who'd listened at the door. She would have learned of the spear from overhearing Keelin's conversation with Tiarnan. It took no second sight to know that Beatrice was not innocent in this.

"Aye," Keelin demanded, facing the woman, "and I'll have an answer of ye, Beatrice. Now."

The old woman's eyes darted in the darkness. Eyes that Keelin had often felt upon her, though she had not realized it until now. "There was a man," Beatrice said boldly. "One of the visitors, a knight...a strange one, he...one blue eye, one brown...went looking for things to take...valuable things, like Lord Marcus's books...."

Goods that were easy to carry.

"Came out of the lord's study and nearly knocked me

down...went to your chamber, and when he came out, said he'd be a rich man...."

"What else, Beatrice?" Keelin demanded. "What more did he say?"

"Nothing, really," Beatrice replied. "Only that he knew a better place where he could wait out a storm, with none the wiser and no way to find him."

"Well, he must have taken a likin' to ye, to be so free with his tongue."

Beatrice shrugged. "Mayhap," she said.

"So, what else did he tell ye?"

"Why should I tell you?" Beatrice asked, backing up to the gallery wall. She clenched her fists, gathered all her bitterness about her, and snarled, "You've ruined everything by coming to Wrexton, and now Isolda and I are to be cast out."

"Cast out? What do ye mean, woman?"

"The lord will wed ye," Beatrice said angrily. "Isolda and I will be useless to him then."

Keelin shook her head impatiently. Everyone knew she planned to return to Kerry. Regardless, this discussion had no bearing on the thief, on *Ga Buidhe an Lamhaigh*, or where the man had taken it. By all the saints, the villain could keep the brooch and the knife, but she had to retrieve the spear.

"Tell me about the thievin' maggot who sole my things," she demanded, leaning threateningly toward the woman.

"He said there's a place, an old barn in a little dell west of the castle—"

The vision. Keelin's premonition had showed her the place. 'Twas a broken-down building made of stone and timber, with a leaky thatched roof. She wondered if she could find it.

The woman sniffed, but said nothing more of importance, and Keelin shuddered at the malice she sensed from the old woman. She took a few deep breaths to calm herself, then turned away and went down to the great hall in search of Marcus.

She did not witness the gleam in Beatrice's eye as she walked away.

It looked as if the mummers had performed again, but they were now finished, and the minstrels had taken up their instruments and were playing halfheartedly. Some of the visitors were dancing, others were making up sleeping pallets near the fire and putting the young ones to bed. Baron Selby and his family were not in sight, and Keelin assumed they must have retired for the night.

Neither Marcus, nor any of his knights were in the hall.

Frantic now, Keelin asked several servants if they'd seen Lord Marcus, but the reply was always negative. She could not imagine where he and his most trusted knights had gone.

Finally finding a footman who knew more than most, she learned that an emergency had drawn Marcus and his knights out to the mews. Worried over what other disaster had occurred, Keelin quickly returned to her chamber to add a layer of clothes, and put on her cloak.

When she was warmly dressed, she hurried down to the mews, and found neither Marcus nor any of his knights, though there were many men working inside.

What would she do now?

"Ach, Gerald!" she cried when she gained entrance to the building. Eyeing the devastation all around her, and Gerald's bloodied forehead, she cried, "Saints above, what happened here?"

"Thieves, my lady," Gerald answered as Keelin

peeled away the stained cloth that the falconer used to dab at his wound. "They took Guinevere and Cleo, and a couple of the smaller birds...."

"Ach, no..." Keelin said as she dropped down on the bench next to Gerald. Marcus would be devastated by the loss of his prized birds. If the thief's intent had been to hurt Marcus, besides stealing something of value, he could not have chosen better.

Had *Ga Buidhe an Lamhaigh* been taken by these same thieves? Keelin thought 'twas likely. After all, how many thieving strangers had Wrexton taken in? Most were honest men who'd come to the castle with their families for shelter, and were even now bedding themselves down in the great hall.

Keelin shook her head in shock. If the same man who'd burgled her chamber was responsible for the disaster here in the mews, his method had changed drastically from one place to the other.

Nevertheless, no matter how many thieves there were, Keelin burned with the need to act. She, Keelin O'Shea, was guardian of the spear. *Ga Buidhe an Lamhaigh* was missing, as were the rest of her valuables, along with Marcus's precious birds.

There was nothing to be done here. Keelin saw that the gash on Gerald's head needed no sewing, and several men were at work cleaning up the damage done.

She would be of greater assistance to Marcus. The thief had the spear and the birds. To find the birds, 'twas necessary to find the spear.

She had to believe the power of *Ga Buidhe an Lamhaigh* would draw her to it.

Chapter Twenty-One

'Twas not difficult to leave through the castle gate. Keelin was not questioned as she rode through—she figured the guards were unable to see her clearly, and must have assumed she was part of Marcus's party.

She rode through the village, following Marcus's tracks southward. The wind blew through her layers of clothes, but Keelin continued on, undeterred. She had no choice but to recover the spear. She could not count on Marcus or anyone else being able to find it, for the thief might be clever enough to cover his tracks.

She continued to ride until she reached a low wooden bridge over a narrow stretch of frozen river. The wind was fierce here in the open, and Keelin hunkered down on her mount to make herself smaller, and to sap up some of the horse's warmth.

Marcus had to be quite a distance ahead of her, because his tracks were barely visible in the blowing snow. Keelin could barely make them out, and she hoped it was easier for Marcus to keep the thieves' tracks in sight.

She got to the other side of the bridge and had just started to urge her horse forward when the first clear sense of *Ga Buidhe an Lamhaigh* came to her. The spear was not straight ahead, toward Marcus's tracks. The power of it came from the west, toward the hilly country beyond Wrexton lands.

She looked to her right, toward the desolate hills, and knew the spear traveled in that direction. Yet Marcus's tracks continued south.

Keelin knew she had no choice. She had to follow where the spear led her, and hope that Marcus would eventually catch up to her. If she did not, the thief could travel so far ahead, she would never recover *Ga Buidhe an Lamhaigh.*

The thieves had either gotten away from the castle much sooner than Marcus thought, or they were riding incredibly hard and fast. It was unbelievable that they were managing to elude him this long.

He continued southward in his pursuit, accompanied by William and Robert, following whatever faint tracks remained. He was as angry as he'd ever been, his hospitality having been violated by a couple of rogue knights. They could have taken what gold he had locked in his study, or any of the precious cloth stored in his father's trunks.

But in taking the falcons…Marcus's wrath knew no bounds. He would catch up to the bastards and see that they paid the penalty for endangering the birds.

"Lord Marcus!" Sir William called. "We must rest the horses soon. They cannot continue at this pace."

And the weather had taken a turn for the worse. Snow, light flurries at first, was now coming down in a torrent. It was nearly impossible to see ahead, and the thieves' tracks were lost. Still, Marcus knew the knights could not be far ahead. They rode a couple of run-down horses, and they were burdened with the birds. They could not possibly continue to make good time.

"We keep on," Marcus said, pulling his wool muffler tightly against the brutal wind. He took some comfort in the knowledge that Keelin was snugly lodged in her chamber at Wrexton.

She was likely in her bed now, wrapped in thick wool blankets, listening to the wind whip around the turrets and battlements of the castle. What he wouldn't give to be wrapped in that bed with her, the heat of his body warming hers.

Idiot! he thought, berating himself. He was like the fool in the mummery play, pursuing her when she'd made it quite clear that she would soon ride out of Wrexton Castle and return to her home. Would wed a man whose name she did not know. Bear children—

Hell and damnation! He could not let her do it!

He was no fool in a play. If anything, he was the warrior knight, restored to life. *He* was the man for Keelin, not some Irish chieftain she had never met. And he would do all in his power to see that she understood that.

"My Lord!"

Marcus halted at the top of the rise and looked down the narrow valley below. Two dark shapes were barely visible in the distance. *Men on horseback.* And when he listened very carefully, Marcus could hear the sound of their voices, carried on the wind.

"They're shouting at one another," he said, keeping his voice low.

"Won't hear us coming," Sir Robert remarked.

"At least, not until it's too late," Will added.

"Let's go!"

They rode ahead, and their prey remained oblivious

until they were within bow range. When they realized they were being followed, the two tried to increase their pace, only to get bogged down in the accumulating snow. One thief fell from his horse, the other dropped his bundle.

All the while, Marcus and his men continued in steady pursuit.

"Devil rot yer, Ned," the man on the ground cursed. "I thought yer brother said there was a place to hide on this gleekin' road."

"There was—*is!*" the other man grumbled as he dismounted and tried to gather what he'd dropped. Eyeing the knights behind them, he said, "We can still lose 'em if we—"

"Halt!" Marcus shouted, watching the two bumblers as they tried to lead their horses and carry the squirming birds in the sacks. If any damage came to them... "Nay, Will, do not shoot." The knight lowered his bow and awaited the lord's orders.

"The louts are going to try to run for it," Robert remarked.

"Come on," Marcus said disgusted by the sight of the bickering thieves. "Let's be done with it."

The rogues berated each other and argued viciously as they tried to put distance between themselves and their pursuers. "...and I suppose the old woman told yer cockeyed brother there was a good hidin' place for the spear, too, eh?"

"What's it to *you,* you cowardly maltworm. 'Tis not as if you—"

Marcus dismounted and grabbed the first man by the throat, while William subdued the other robber. "What about a spear?" Marcus asked.

"Nothin'. I know nothin' about it," the thief choked.

Marcus forced the man to his knees in the snow. He had yet to do any damage to him, but the knave quivered in fear. "Answer me. You spoke of a spear."

"It weren't me, m'lord," the man choked as Marcus pulled tighter. "My brother's got it."

"Where?"

The thief pulled at Marcus's hand, trying to free himself of the choke-hold. Marcus threw a savage punch that caught the man in the jaw. "Answer!"

"I don't know!" he cried. "The old woman at the castle told him to take the spear and whatever else he could find in the lady's chamber and go!"

"Where?"

"Anywhere, she said, just out in the cold, and far away," the rogue moaned as he struggled to get loose of Marcus's grasp. "She said the lady, the young one, would—"

The knight stopped abruptly, realizing he'd said too much, believing he could get away with saying no more.

"*What?*" Marcus demanded, shaking him. "The lady would *what?*"

"Nothin'! I don't know! I weren't there!"

"Who was the old woman?" A sinking suspicion was beginning to form in the back of Marcus's mind. "*Who?*"

"'Twas the one what wears the white headrail," cried the other thief, the one who was pinned by Sir William. "She wanted to be rid of the young one!"

"Is that it?" Anguish roared through Marcus's chest as he shook the knight. "Did Beatrice put you onto the spear so that Lady Keelin would go in search of it? *Is that it?*"

The man pulled away so violently, he fell from Marcus's grasp and rolled to his belly. Marcus caught him as he started to scramble away. This time, Marcus did not go easy on the man.

"I'll have straight answers of you," Marcus declared after blows had been exchanged. *"Now!"*

"I tell you, I weren't there!" the rundown knight protested. One of his eyes was bruised, and his lip was split. "All I know is we was told to grab the falcons and run with 'em. Bren—my brother—was gonna steal the spear, and whatever else he could find, then go off in another direction."

"What was the old woman's part?" Marcus asked. "Did she say anything about it?"

"Nay," the man replied, afraid of bringing on any further wrath. He spit out a bloody tooth. "Just that the young one would come out looking for the spear, and if she met up with Bren, he could do what he liked with her."

Chapter Twenty-Two

Keelin's bruised shoulder throbbed with every move. She desperately wished she had put on another layer of clothes. Her mittens were soaked through and she could no longer feel her fingers. Her nose was frozen and her ears numb, even though her head was well covered by the hood of her cloak.

The cold went bone deep. She shivered with it, but forged on, aware that her own personal discomfort was nothing compared to the loss of *Ga Buidhe an Lamhaigh*. She tamped down her misgivings about pursuing the spear on her own, and concentrated on keeping herself from falling from her horse.

'Twas full night, though the landscape was lit with an eerie light. The snow was coming down so hard, it was difficult for Keelin to see even a few feet ahead of her. 'Twas fortunate the power of the spear still drew her, because the robber's tracks had disappeared miles back.

She trudged on, forcing herself to think only of the spear, and not the cold, nor the biting, freezing snow that pelted her face and froze her lashes. She could only hope *Ga Buidhe an Lamhaigh* would continue to guide her to it.

She visualized the ancient, obsidian spear that had been handed to her ancestor eons ago at Loch Gur, and knew that she had no choice. *Ga Buidhe an Lamhaigh* and her powers of second sight had dictated the course of her life so far. As guardian, she was compelled to risk life and limb for it. Nothing had changed. The burden was hers and hers alone.

Burden?

Aye. She'd been burdened with the ancient power since she was but a wee lass, and it had never brought happiness or contentment. *To anyone.* To be sure, Clann Ui Sheaghda believed that possession of *Ga Buidhe an Lamhaigh* somehow made them greater than all other clans.

Keelin was the only O'Shea who knew otherwise.

Still, she had no choice but to return the spear to Kerry. What she felt for Marcus could not enter into the decisions that had to be made.

The course of her life was set. She would wed the man waiting for her in Ireland. It did not matter that she had no feelings for him, nor could he possibly have any for her. Marriage among the nobility was not based on fleeting emotions, but contracted to provide strategic alliances.

Keelin swallowed the lump that had formed in her throat and struggled to hold the reins. Survival was more important than these foolish mental meanderings.

Her hands barely functioned now and she did not know how much longer her legs would have the strength to keep her astride. Nor did she know how long her horse would last under these severe conditions. Ice was building up on his mane and his eyelashes. She would soon have to find shelter for herself and her mount, even if she did not soon encounter the man who'd stolen *Ga Buidhe an Lamhaigh*.

She hated to think it, but mayhap 'twould be better to return to Wrexton and wait for Marcus. She halted and stood in the blowing wind, attempting to get her bearings.

There were no landmarks, other than the hills around her, which she could barely make out in the distance. Her tracks were covered almost as quickly as she made them.

She was lost.

Her only hope was to continue following her sense of the spear, and find that the man who'd stolen it needed her help as much as she needed his.

Two of Wrexton's knights met Marcus at the edge of the village. They appeared to be supplied for a long expedition.

"My lord, we were just coming in search of you!"

"Will and Robert, take the prisoners to the sheriff and make the charges against them," Marcus said, then turned to the newcomers. "You two, take the falcons back to the castle and get them settled. I'll—"

"Your pardon, my lord, but Lady Keelin is missing!"

Marcus's heart dropped. His worst fear, that the thief had told the truth about Keelin, had come true. She was out in the storm, in pursuit of her spear.

The little fool! What had possessed her to go alone?

"Give me your extra cloaks—"

"We brought blankets, my lord," the knight said, pulling the bundle off the rump of his horse and handing it to Marcus. "And some provisions."

"Good. Return to Wrexton," he said. "See that order

is kept in the hall, and find Beatrice. Lock her up some-where.''

''But, my lord—''

''Do as I say,'' Marcus commanded as he turned his horse and set off on another course. ''Keep all secure at the castle,'' he shouted as he rode away. ''I'll return as soon as I have Lady Keelin.''

West was the only direction to take. He'd traveled south once this night, and knew the thief who had stolen Keelin's spear was not there. To the north were high cliffs that would be difficult, if not impossible, to climb in this weather, and the river was eastward. A crossing would not be feasible now.

He could see no trail in the oddly reflected light of the storm, but there was a slight indentation in the snow that might once have been tracks. Marcus followed in hopes that it was Keelin's path.

He had never felt so terrified in his life. Was she dressed warmly enough that she would not to freeze to death? Was she riding in circles, lost in the storm, unable to find her way to shelter?

Worse yet, had she met up with the thief?

Marcus knew who the miscreant was. The man and his brother passed themselves off as knights, but he'd had his doubts about that. More likely they'd run afoul of the law and were on the run. Marcus had considered throwing them both on the mercy of the weather, but he preferred to keep them close, where he could keep an eye on them.

Well, so much for that theory.

Now Keelin had put herself at risk for the sake of that damnable spear, the object that would take her away from Wrexton and back to Ireland. Yet, if the damnable spear were lost to her forever, would she still feel so compelled to return to her home? Marcus was certain he could convince her to remain with him as his wife if there was no spear.

Mayhap he should wish the thief luck.

Nay. Knowing how she felt about the spear, 'twould kill Keelin to lose it. Marcus would do all in his power to see it recovered and returned to her.

So that she could return to Carrauntoohil with it.

She would not go alone. When the weather cleared, and travel became possible, Marcus would go with her. He would travel to Ireland with Keelin and do whatever was necessary to keep her from marrying some barbaric Celtic chieftain.

He grudgingly admitted that the husband chosen by Eocaidh O'Shea might not be a barbarian like Mageean's mercenaries. He could be a handsome and charming young fellow, or a wise young man as Tiarnan must have been in his youth. Would Keelin be happier in the bosom of her clan, than if she remained exiled in England?

As he searched for the trail that would lead to her, Marcus knew he could not give her up without fighting for her.

He picked up his pace. Regardless of her ultimate decision, his first battle would be here, in England. He had to get to Keelin before the bastard with the mismatched eyes could cause her any harm.

Keelin realized she'd made a terrible mistake in coming out on her own. Not even her prayers to Saints Bridget and Patrick could save her now. She would freeze to death in the hills so close to Wrexton, that if it were a summer day, she could probably run to the castle on her own two legs in half the time it had taken to ride this far.

Keelin wanted to weep, but knew that tears were useless. She was well and truly lost, and there was nothing to do but go on, as long as her poor horse could continue. If she had any kind of luck, they would go on until dawn, and perhaps there would be enough light to find some kind of shelter.

In the meantime, there was no choice but to—to— Keelin shook her head. She squinted her eyes to clear her vision. Something tall and dark loomed in the distance. 'Twas larger than a man on horseback...a building...but Keelin could not see if it was the barn she'd seen in her premonition.

She felt danger all around, the same as she had sensed in her vision, and knew this was the place. The spear would be here. She hoped the villain who'd stolen it, was not.

Glancing 'round as she approached the neglected barn, Keelin saw no one. The horse, sensing shelter, plodded ahead with a lighter step and quicker pace. When they reached the yard, Keelin was frozen too stiff to move right away. Shivering violently, she made slow, deliberate movements, and finally managed to dismount.

The door was shut, but the place was quite obviously deserted. Bare trees surrounded the barn, with branches laden with long icicles, just as she'd seen in her vision.

The only thing missing was the blood on the ground.

Keelin desperately hoped she would be gone before any blood was shed. Feeling more fortunate than she had any right to be, Keelin waded through a deep snowdrift until she reached the door. It was stuck shut.

Besides being frozen to the core, she felt weak and exhausted. She had little strength left. Pushing with all her might, she could not manage to get the door open. Unaware that she was weeping, Keelin knew her one chance for survival was in getting that door open, getting herself inside and making a fire.

With renewed strength and determination, she threw herself against the door once again, and when it burst open, Keelin fell in a heap on the packed dirt floor. She felt immediate relief, however, in getting out of the wind, and knew she had to get her horse inside, as well. Once she got a fire started, there would be a chance of survival.

Sounds of movement behind her startled Keelin and she whirled around, only to find that her horse was pushing his way inside. She gave a tremulous smile at his good sense, then got to her feet and shoved the door closed behind him. Then she started looking for fuel.

There was absolutely nothing of value in the barn. A few sticks of broken wood lay strewn about the floor, so at least there was something to use for making a fire.

Still chilled to the bone and shivering beyond control, Keelin managed to gather some of the scraps and toss them into the fire pit. Once she got a fire started, she stood close and tried to warm herself.

Steam rose from her wet clothing. She would have to remove it soon, but could not face doing it until the barn warmed up. 'Twas, unfortunately, a rather large room, and would be difficult to heat. Especially with holes in the thatching and cracks in the walls.

An old, rusted anvil lay on the floor near the fire pit, along with some useless, broken tools. Rotting leather straps hung from hooks on one wall. Looking 'round, Keelin could see that a smith had once worked here. Fleetingly, she wondered what had happened to him.

The horse nickered and shook himself, throwing wet chunks of snow all over the room, forcing Keelin's attention on her present situation. ''Aye, well, 'tis sorry I am that I haven't any grain for ye, lad,'' she said with chattering teeth. ''I've nothin' for myself, either, ye know.''

The horse snorted and shook again, as if unsatisfied with Keelin's answer.

Keelin glanced around again. While there was nothing to eat, at least she could quench her thirst with melted snow. And besides, she did not intend to stay long, only until daylight, when she would return to Wrexton and get help. At least that was—

The door whipped open.

At first thought Keelin believed she hadn't closed it well enough against the wind, but quickly realized her error.

The thief had arrived.

''Well, well, well...'' His voice echoed ominously in the cavernous space.

Keelin recognized him at once. He was the knight with the strange eyes. One blue, one brown. She shivered, and not only with the cold.

''Lost my way for a bit back there,'' the man said as he came into the humble shelter. ''But I caught onto your tracks and followed you here.''

He looked too cold to be a real threat to her now, but Keelin knew that could change at any minute. Her eyes darted around for something to use as a weapon, but there were only the rusted, broken tongs on the earthen floor next to the anvil. She was at the thief's mercy.

He threw his pack down beside the fire pit, and approached.

Keelin stepped away, eyeing the pack. Her spear was there. She had only to circle around the man and grab it. Then... What? She could not go back out in the frigid weather, even if she could get her horse out with her.

She was trapped. By the weather as well as the man.

"Ain't it just cozy-like?" the knight smiled unpleasantly as he sidled up to the fire. "Right nice of you to heat the place up."

As long as she kept her distance, she did not see how the rogue would be able to harm her. At the very least, she should be able to keep the horse between them.

But she had to get to the spear.

"The old hag was right about this place," the man said as he reached into his pack. He drew out a tin cup and set it on the hearth, acting as if all was well with the world.

His confidence shook Keelin. "Wh-what old hag?" she asked.

"The one what wears the white headrail," he answered, rummaging through his belongings. "Acts like some kind o' saint, she does."

"Beatrice?" Keelin asked. Isolda's companion was the only old woman at Wrexton who always wore a white wimple.

"Yeh. That was her name, all right."

"Beatrice sent you here?"

The knight barked out an obnoxious chortle. "Sent me here? Yeh, that and a bit more."

Keelin eyed the fire and wished the thief would move away so she could get closer to it. "Wh-what more?"

In reply, he dumped a handful of coins on the stone hearth. Grinning broadly, he added Keelin's jeweled knife and brooch to the pile. Keelin shuddered at the look of blatant glee in those disturbing eyes.

"Might take a while to get rid of that spear," he said. "Don't know of anybody who'd want it. But these..." he said, gesturing toward Keelin's valuables.

"You can have it all," Keelin said, "but the spear. That's the only thing I—"

His peel of laughter stopped her. "I can have it all?" he asked in a derisive tone. "My dear lady, I *do* have it all. Even more than you've guessed."

Keelin swallowed hard. How could she have thought she had any bargaining power with this man? He had the advantage—in every way.

"But Lord Marcus won't—"

"Aw, but the earl is out chasing his falcons!" the man laughed. "Won't be available to rescue his poor lady."

"You!" Keelin cried. "You took the falcons?"

He shook his head. "My brother and some fool he found to help him. Quite a nice diversion, wouldn't you say?"

Keelin shook her head in dismay.

"The old lady had everything figured. Once Ned has gone far enough, he'll leave the birds for the earl to find." The man started to move toward Keelin again, and she backed away, circling the room. "He'll be so occupied with his precious falcons that by the time he checks on you…ah, well…"

"No."

The thief merely chuckled at Keelin's denial of all he'd said, and continued to stalk her. "Ah, good. All this talk has warmed me up."

Chapter Twenty-Three

The snow let up just enough for Marcus to increase his pace. He rode toward a deserted dell that lay just outside Wrexton property, across the Welsh border. There was a deserted old barn there, and with luck, Keelin's horse had made for the shelter, as cold and unwelcoming as it might be.

At worst, it was the place where the thief had sought refuge, the only place for miles where Keelin could also find shelter.

After too many hours in the saddle, in the worst weather Marcus could remember, it was still deep night. At least, it seemed to be night, though Marcus was not sure morning would look much different if the storm kept up.

He rode on, oblivious to the cold, worried to the depths of his soul for Keelin's safety. He prayed as he'd never prayed before, that she was safely situated in the old barn in the dell, and that the rogue knight, Bren, was nowhere near.

The miles passed at a crawl and the chill finally penetrated Marcus's layers. His face was numb and his brows caked with snow by the time he reached the rise that overlooked the barn.

All Marcus's battle instincts came to life.

A horse, still saddled, huddled close to the building. It could not be the one Keelin had taken. Marcus knew she would not have left the animal untended in the harsh weather.

His heart sank. He must have missed her somehow.

Marcus drew his sword and approached quietly. The only person likely to be in the barn was the thief who'd stolen Keelin's spear.

That thought was contradicted by a sudden scream that pierced the night. *Keelin!*

Marcus spurred his horse forward, dismounting as he reached the entrance. He fairly flew through the tracks in the snow and flung the door open. The flickering light was just enough for Marcus to see Keelin sprawled out on the floor near the hearth, with her clothes in tatters, and her attacker hovering just over her.

The man roared up at Marcus's interruption and tried to yank Keelin up in front of him to use as a shield. She resisted, barely evading his grasp.

"Marcus!" she cried. Her chest heaved with terror as she held the shreds of her gown in place. She was effectively cornered, though, and unable to get to him.

Marcus's blood boiled with rage. How dare the knave lay his hands on Keelin!

Keelin tried to move away from behind the knight, but he spread both arms and leered at Marcus. "I could do her a fair amount o' damage b'fore I go, m'lord."

"Let her step away," Marcus said threateningly. His sword was drawn and poised, but 'twas not his way to skewer an unarmed man. Still, if he made one move toward Keelin...

"*Don't move,* m'lady," the rogue commanded. His strange eyes darted around the room, looking for some solution to his predicament. He could not move away from Keelin without risking a confrontation with Marcus. Yet if he harmed the lady…

Clearly the man understood his peril. There was naught for him to do but lower his arms and allow Keelin to move, else feel the point of Marcus's blade.

Suddenly, and without warning, the man swooped down and grabbed the jeweled knife he'd dropped on the hearth. In one motion he stood, arcing the knife toward Marcus, in a desperate attempt to render a killing blow.

The knife glanced off Marcus's chest and it fell to the floor with a thud. The thief quickly bent over and retrieved the knife, lunging at Marcus from his crouched position.

Marcus dodged the blow, but as the man fell to the ground, he wrapped one arm around Marcus's legs and tried to pull him over, thrusting with the knife at the same time. Marcus was taken off balance, and as the thief jabbed the knife, Marcus ran him through with his sword.

There was not a sound in the barn until Marcus heard a small whimper. Looking up at Keelin, he threw down his sword and went to her, gathering her into his arms, drying her tears with his cloak.

"Oh, Marcus," she whispered into his chest. "I was never so frightened—"

"Hush," he said, pressing his lips to her forehead. "'Tis over now. You're safe."

"Aye," she sniffed. "Safe. But what of you? Your leg—"

"'Tis naught," he replied quietly, though the rage of battle still rushed through his blood.

Marcus calmed himself with the knowledge that the primary danger was past. True, they still had to survive the storm that raged outside, and naught had changed between him and Keelin. She had her precious spear back, and would return to Kerry as soon as she had the chance.

Marcus remained silent, not saying any of the things that burned in his heart, but merely holding her close, relishing the softness of her body, the gentle purity of her soul. Mayhap there was something he could—

The horse snorted, startling them both, and Keelin let out a sobbing laugh. "I brought him inside with me," she said against his chest. "There was nothin' else to do with him."

Marcus nodded. Then Keelin began to weep in earnest, though she hardly made a sound. He rubbed her back and whispered comforting words as he absorbed her tears, praying with every fiber of his being, that he would find a way to convince her to stay.

"Oh, Marcus," Keelin finally said. "Can ye forgive me for bein' such a fool?"

Marcus took her face in his hands and looked into her eyes. Then he tipped his head and kissed her. "My only care is that you're safe. The rogue did not harm you?"

"Thanks only to you," she said. "I should never have left the castle. But I was so afraid I would never get *Ga Buidhe an Lamhaigh* back, and you were gone."

Marcus turned away and surveyed the room. He did not want to think about the damnable spear now, nor the risks Keelin had taken to recover it. He could not dwell on the fact that she intended to leave him to carry the spear to her homeland.

"Keelin..." he said, looking back at her. He swallowed and considered what to say. He pulled off his glove and ran one hand along her jaw, one finger across her quivering lips. "Wait here while I deal with all this," he finally said, his emotions too raw to talk rationally with her now.

He let her go and walked over to the man who lay dead near the fire. Grabbing his hands without ceremony, Marcus dragged him outside.

He pulled him to a snow-covered mound that looked like it had once been a building—probably a cottage, but at least it had been made of stone and wood. Here, he would do what was decent, covering the man, protecting his body from wild animals.

A sound made Marcus turn toward the barn, and he saw Keelin outside in the snow, leading the horses toward the door. There would soon be quite a crowd inside.

Keelin looked at the bloody trail in the tramped-down snow and shuddered. She drew the horses inside, then closed the door against the wind and added a few more sticks of wood to the fire. She picked up her belongings, the knife and the pin, and the pouch of coins, and put them with *Ga Buidhe an Lamhaigh* in a corner.

Keelin herded the horses to the back wall where they stood patiently, resting and gathering warmth from each other. She did not begrudge sharing the space with the animals, especially since their heat helped to make the drafty old barn seem snug. She hauled their saddles off and dried them with their thick blankets, and wished there was more than a few handfuls of old straw to give them.

Inside the thief's pack, Keelin found some bread,

along with a block of cheese. There were two bottles of ale and some dried apricots and apples. Along with the blankets and other supplies Marcus had brought, they should be able to survive there for several days.

Keelin hoped that would not be necessary. She knew that by morning, Tiarnan would know she was missing and assume the worst. She did not want him to worry longer than necessary.

And Marcus… She knew now that she could never leave him.

When the thief had grabbed her knife and gone for him, Keelin had experienced a terror unlike anything she'd ever known. The thought of Marcus dying had taught her that life would not be worth living without him.

She would see to it that *Ga Buidhe an Lamhaigh* was restored to Clann Ui Sheaghda, but afterward, Keelin fully intended to return to Marcus. She would live out her days as his wife, at Wrexton.

That is, if he would have her. Mayhap Marcus would not want a wife who behaved as foolishly as she. She knew he was angry—he'd hardly spoken a word to her, and his body had seemed as tense as a coiled spring.

She could not blame him. She had been worse than foolish to go out in the storm alone. *Witless* was the word that came to mind.

The door blew open just then and Marcus appeared. He picked up one of the saddles and propped it against the door to make it difficult to open from outside, then he joined Keelin by the fire.

Wordlessly, he pulled off his wet cloak and tunic, and stood in the firelight wearing only his hauberk and chausses. Keelin watched as he unbuckled the fastenings of the hauberk and pulled it off, leaving him in his plain, white linen shirt.

Keelin's throat went dry. She had fought against her attraction to Marcus from the beginning. She'd resisted taking note of his broad shoulders and narrow waist, his tight hips and powerful thighs. But in the space of the last hour, all that resistance had vanished.

"Marcus—"

"Keelin—"

They spoke at once, then stopped, awkwardly.

"Please," Marcus said quietly. "Go on."

Keelin blushed then. She took a step closer, until she could feel his breath on her face.

"I was wrong," she said simply, looking into his eyes. They were hazed with puzzlement, but he did not speak. Nor did he touch her.

With her fingers, Keelin brushed his hair back off his forehead. "I cannot return to Carrauntoohil," she said without taking her hand away. "At least, not without ye, Marcus."

"Keelin...what are you saying?" he rasped, taking hold of the hand that caressed him.

"That I love ye with every drop of my blood, every beat of my heart," she said quietly. "That I cannot bear the thought of leavin' here without ye—"

Marcus's lips interrupted her flow of words. In one motion, he slid an arm around her waist and pulled her to him, then kissed her as if he could absorb her into his being.

Keelin felt the rasp of his whiskers against her tender skin, the strength of pure muscle as he held her close. He smelled like the cold air, like leather and man. *Her* man.

Keelin threaded the fingers of both hands through his

hair, pulling him ever closer. She parted her lips and then Marcus was there, tasting, exploring, ravishing.

"Keelin," he said, trailing hot kisses down her throat.

"Aye, m'lord," she breathed, and tipped her head back to give him full access.

"I've longed to hear you say it," he said. He opened the laces to her cloak and let it fall. Her torn surcoat and kirtle followed.

The storm outside was nothing compared to Marcus's effect on her. 'Twas as if the combined forces of nature were acting on her now, causing a torrent of emotions and sensations to flow through her. She should have felt icy cold, standing in her thin chemise, but Marcus's touch ignited a fire in her that seemed impossible to quench.

His lips burned a trail along the sensitive skin at the edge of the chemise, making the tips of her breasts flame in response. When he finally parted the cloth and put his mouth to one tingling peak, Keelin's knees buckled.

"What's this?" he asked, discovering the leather cord Keelin always wore near her heart.

"'Tis yours, Marcus," she said breathlessly. He nuzzled one breast as his hand closed around the other, along with the cord. "I've…kept it over my heart…. I had to keep somethin' of ye…for when I left…."

"Tell me again," Marcus demanded gruffly. "Tell me you'll not leave."

"Oh, Marcus," Keelin cried, "'Twould tear my very heart out to leave ye."

"We'll be wed as soon as the banns can be read," he said, gently taking her shoulders in his hands.

"Aye, Marcus," she squeaked as he drew the chemise over her shoulders and let it fall.

"But I give you my vow here and now," he said as

he lay her down on the blanket near the fire, "to love and honor you always with my heart and soul and my body."

He threw off his own shirt and lowered himself over her, placing one hand on either side of her head. "I love you, Keelin O'Shea," he whispered. "I would do anything for you."

"Then love me now, Marcus," Keelin murmured, kissing the sensitive flesh below his ear. She relished the sensation of Marcus's powerful body all around her. "Make me your wife, m'love."

She moved her hips against his loins and felt his surging response. Desperate to feel him, flesh to flesh, Keelin unfastened his points, divesting him of his chausses.

"I should be frightened, yet I am not," she whispered, pressing kisses to his chest, to the small beading nipples hidden in the mat of golden hair.

The sound Marcus made was unintelligible, but he moved one knee to rest between hers, opening her, making her as vulnerable as she'd ever been. Yet she trusted Marcus entirely. He would never hurt her.

Trailing her hands down his taut belly, she touched him timidly, then more confidently when he made a low growl of approval.

"*Keely.*" His mouth came down on hers and once again, she reveled in the taste and texture of him.

Marcus could not get enough of her. Every move she made taunted him with promises of more, and he wanted to make it last for hours. Yet he knew that if she continued her sensual assault, he would last a mere minute or two.

Her beautiful eyes, hazy now with passion, were entirely centered on him. He watched them as he slid one hand down her body, stopping only to learn her most responsive areas.

"*Oh!* Oh, Marcus!" she breathed when he touched the essence of her heat.

He caressed her, teased her, and took her to the brink. Then he made her his own with one swift stroke, a fiery joining of their bodies as one.

"Oh, aye," she whispered as Marcus began to move.

He worried about hurting her, but if he caused any pain, she did not show it. She moved with him in a rhythm their hearts knew without prior tutoring. Bodies shifting, hearts pounding, nothing in Marcus's life had ever felt so very right.

Suddenly, she arced against him, and he felt the waves of pleasure course through her. He saw the wonder in her eyes and emotion overcame him. Feeling as if he'd found the other half of his being in Keelin, ecstasy shattered through him, taking him to heights he had never imagined possible.

Chapter Twenty-Four

The fire burned steadily in the pit, and Keelin slept with her head pillowed on Marcus's chest. They were well insulated in the blankets he'd carried with him, and the heat generated by the animals made their shelter tolerable. Marcus closed his hand around the leather thong Keelin had worn all these days, and cherished the knowledge that she loved him. That she would stay with him.

The sun may have risen on a new day, but there was no reason to rouse themselves to return to the castle. 'Twas still dark, and freezing rain pelted the rickety old building viciously.

Nay, 'twas better—and more pleasurable—to stay cocooned together in the warmth of the wool blankets. Soon she would wake and they would make love again, just as they had done during the night.

Marcus gazed at Keelin's dark lashes, curved over beautifully sculpted cheekbones. They'd stay the day here, without a care as they waited out the storm and enjoyed the luxury of being alone together. The barn was sound, if a bit leaky, and Marcus could think of no better place to spend the day with Keelin.

Just then she moved her legs restlessly and groaned in her sleep.

Marcus smiled, and thought of all the years ahead, sleeping with Keelin. He would quickly become accustomed to sharing a bed with her, and never—

"Mercy!" Keelin cried out.

"Hush, sweetheart," he soothed, kissing her temple. "'Tis just a dream. Sleep."

"Ye'll fall! *Stop!*"

"Wake up, sweetheart," Marcus said gently.

"Nay! It cannot be!" she cried out, neither asleep nor fully awake. "Please God, let it be—" Her eyes suddenly flew open and she sat up. She turned to Marcus. "'Tis Beatrice," she cried.

"Beatrice?"

"Aye," she whispered shakily. "She was up on a high ridge somewhere. Walking. Running...getting away..." Her brow furrowed as she recalled the vision that had come to her in her sleep. "But the rain and snow made it so slick..."

"What happened, Keelin?"

"Ach, the poor thing," she said, taking great, heaving breaths. She covered her mouth with the fingers of one hand. "She's fallen... There's a river...."

"I know the place," Marcus said. "Beatrice is there? She's fallen?"

Keelin nodded. "Aye, Marcus," she said. "She's dead."

Marcus had not told Keelin of his suspicions regarding Beatrice. He'd hoped to deal with Beatrice personally when they returned to Wrexton, but he had no doubt that Keelin's vision was accurate. Somehow, the woman must have left the keep during the storm and managed to kill herself falling off the ridge that overlooked the river.

'Twas an unfortunate turn of events, but if what Marcus suspected was true, Beatrice had been the cause of much of Keelin's grief since their arrival at Wrexton.

"There's more," Keelin said. "'Tis naught but a feeling, but..."

"I know," Marcus said as he pressed a kiss to her forehead. "I have it, too."

"Ye do, Marcus?"

He nodded. "But only because I learned a few things yesterday from the men who stole the falcons."

"What?" she asked.

"That Beatrice got them to take the birds so that I'd be occupied when she sent you out into the storm for the spear," he said. "She intended you harm."

"But why?" Keelin asked, truly puzzled. "What reason could she have—"

"She knew that I loved you," Marcus said. "And that I intended to make you my wife."

"But— Ach, Isolda."

"Exactly. But I don't believe Isolda was the one who decided to drive you away."

"Nay," Keelin said. "She tried a few little tricks, but I doubt Isolda could be truly vicious."

"I told her I intended to find a husband for—"

A loud pounding at the barn door, along with voices interrupted Marcus. He wrapped the blanket around Keelin's shoulders and went to the door.

"William?" Marcus asked as he pulled the saddle away from the door.

"Yes, my lord," said a relieved voice.

Marcus pulled the door open to see his favored knight

standing in the freezing rain, along with several other Wrexton knights mounted behind him.

"I brought the men along to..." He caught sight of Lady Keelin standing behind Lord Marcus, wearing naught but a blanket, and coughed. "I...er...was not sure whether you'd need..."

Marcus suppressed a smile at his confident, straight-spoken lieutenant, and stepped into the doorway to impede his view. "We're fine here, Will," he said. "Give us a moment, then you and the men can come in and warm yourselves before you head back to Wrexton...."

Two days in a wretched, broken-down old barn, and they were heaven to Keelin. Marcus had sent Sir William and his men back to the keep with word that all was well, and instructions on where to find Beatrice's body.

Keelin knew that Beatrice had been responsible for putting Isolda up to her tricks, and when those had not worked, the old woman had tried to separate her from Marcus by more dangerous methods.

Marcus and Keelin returned to Wrexton in the cold, but at least it was no longer raining or snowing, and the journey took merely a few short hours.

They were welcomed with mixed reactions—primarily relief, but sadness and regret colored their homecoming.

"My lord," Sir Robert said, as he greeted Marcus in the hall, "I would speak with you in private." Isolda stood beside the knight, with eyes downcast, her shoulders slumped. Keelin felt sympathy for the grief the woman must be suffering.

"In my study," Marcus said as he placed one hand on Keelin's back and walked toward the stairs. "Right after we see Tiarnan and Adam."

As always, his touch sent a thrill of anticipation through her. Though 'twould be difficult to steal any time alone together, she knew they would manage somehow. After the last two days they'd shared, she could not imagine leaving him for any length of time, much less sleeping alone, though she acknowledged that would be necessary until they were wed.

Then they would make plans to travel to Kerry.

From Marcus's glance around the hall, she could see he thought there were still too many people around, although many were making ready to take their leave now that the weather had cleared. She and Marcus learned that Baron Selby and his family had left earlier in the day, and the mummers were about to clear out.

"Find Father Pygott for me, Bill, and send him to my study, as well," Marcus said to a footman, then headed up the steps.

They found Tiarnan in Adam's chamber. The boy was sitting on a low settle near the fire, with Tiarnan right beside him. The two were head to head, speaking of some serious subject.

"Marcus! Keelin!" Adam cried when he saw them.

Keelin went to Tiarnan's side and kissed his cheek before doing the same to Adam. "Well, I see ye've healed up fine without me!" she said happily.

"Aye, the lad has done his part," Tiarnan said, looking toward her with his piercingly blind eyes. "The question is, how do ye fare, Keely lass? Ye survived the storm, but—"

"But nothing, old man," Marcus interjected. "My lady survived her ordeal—"

"And then you rescued her from the evil knight, didn't you, Marcus?"

"Aye, he did," Keelin said fondly, taking Marcus's arm. "He saved me from a terrible fate."

Keelin felt him straighten. "Lady Keelin has agreed to be my wife, Lord Tiarnan," Marcus said. His tone was formal and respectful, in spite of Adam's whoop of joy. "If she is not formally betrothed—"

"Nay, Marcus," Tiarnan replied, smiling broadly. "There was no binding betrothal agreement." *And with luck,* the old man thought, *old Fen was long dead and buried.*

"Good. I'll not wait the customary period for the banns to be read, Tiarnan," Marcus said, "so I'm sure Father Pygott will want to talk with you."

"Send him to me," Tiarnan replied. "I'll vow there are no impediments to the marriage."

Keelin accepted Adam's embrace, and that of her uncle. Then she stepped out into the gallery with Marcus. He pressed her up against the wall and kissed her.

"I've been wanting to do that ever since we arrived."

"Sure and that's not all you've been wantin', I vow," she said breathlessly.

"Nay." His hand covered her breast and teased her mercilessly. "There's more…" He nuzzled the sensitive spot he'd discovered at the base of her jaw. "You, naked…in my bed."

She ran her hands over his buttocks and pulled him tightly against her. "'Tis similar to my own secret wish."

"Ahh," he groaned, "and what would that be?"

She smiled. "'Twould not be a secret if I told ye, now, would it?"

"And what must I do to discover it?" he asked.

"Take as little time as possible with Sir Robert and Isolda…." was her whispered promise.

* * *

Every nerve in Marcus's body was humming as he entered his study and found Robert in the act of gently touching a tear that had dropped onto Isolda's cheek. 'Twas as erotic a thing as he'd ever seen, and he wondered why he'd never noticed the attraction between them before.

He cleared his throat and the two split apart guiltily.

"Lord Marcus," Robert said, clasping his hands in front of him. "I...er, I've come to ask your consent to wed Lady Isolda."

Marcus raised an eyebrow in astonishment.

"I realize it seems sudden," Robert continued as Isolda stepped up to him and looped her arm through his. "But I have admired the lady for a long time...longer than I care to think about."

Marcus had been blind to the attraction, though now that Robert spoke of it, he realized that what the knight said was true. And Robert had obviously kept his feelings in check in deference to his lord, who might have chosen the lady for himself. "And Isolda? What say you?"

Isolda looked at Marcus's shoes. When she spoke, her voice was soft, though not uncertain. "I have always held Sir Robert in high esteem," she said. "But 'twas not until after Beatrice..." a tear slid down Isolda's face, but she continued. "When Bea disappeared, I was frantic. We'd quarreled—over what she'd done to Lady Keelin. Oh, Marcus," she wept, looking him in the eyes, "I am so ashamed I did not realize to what lengths she would go...."

"As you've probably surmised, Beatrice pushed the stonework from the parapet in hopes of injuring Lady Keelin," Robert said.

"She also set fire to the haystacks behind the stable," Isolda added tearfully. "She only told me this before she disappeared, so I did not know…. Marcus, you must believe I did not know."

"But why?" Marcus asked, his expression one of sheer puzzlement. "What purpose—"

"To keep you from Lady Keelin. When the stable caught fire and Lady Keelin was there, Beatrice hit her. Whether she hoped to kill her or just scare her off, we'll never know," Rob said.

"Bea sent Lady Keelin out in the storm, too, hoping she would perish…all done so that you would lose her, and wed *me*," Isolda said sadly.

Marcus shook his head. He did not understand why the old woman would go to such lengths to eliminate Keelin when he'd made it clear that he had no intention of marrying Isolda. 'Twas a tragedy that she'd brought upon herself, to be sure, but a tragedy nonetheless.

"My father is aging, Marcus," Robert said. "I would take Isolda and move to the family estate, if you would release me from duty."

"Isolda," Marcus said. "Is this your wish?"

"Yes, my lord," Isolda replied. "I care deeply for Robert. If only I'd—"

"Hush, love," Robert said. "'Twas not your fault."

"I feel so ashamed," Isolda said sadly. "I behaved so badly toward Lady Keelin. Beatrice said no harm would come to her…that she would leave Wrexton and we would stay."

"'Tis over now, love," Robert said. "You've made your apologies to Lady Keelin and Marcus."

"You have my blessing," Marcus said absently, still in shock over the extent of Beatrice's betrayal.

"Enter!" Marcus called in response to the tap at the door. "Ah, Father Pygott..."

Keelin did not know how Marcus managed to convince Father Pygott to forgo the usual three weeks necessary for the reading of the banns, but in three days, she would be Marcus's wife. The ceremony was to be a simple one, in deference to Marcus's father, with no guests other than the dignitaries of Wrexton Town. Later, Marcus would send messengers throughout the shire to announce his marriage to Keelin.

'Twas nearly Christmas, and the hall was decked out in sprigs of pine and holly. There were bits of mistletoe hanging from the lintels of doorways, and Marcus never failed to make use of them, whenever he had the chance.

"Lady Keelin!"

She was standing on a stool in the solar, with Isolda and one of the maids, who were taking fittings on the gown she would wear for her wedding. Keelin turned to look at the maid who had entered, calling her name.

"Men have arrived in the hall," she said breathlessly. She must have run up all the stairs, Keelin thought. "*Irish* men! They're asking for you...and Lord Tiarnan!"

A terrible sense of dread should have come upon her, but there was nothing. There'd been no premonition of visitors from Kerry or anywhere else, only a strange and puzzling sight she'd seen a few days before, a vision of Carrauntoohil at peace—her people cooking and preparing for the holy days that were nigh.

"Go and fetch Lord Marcus—"

"He's already there, my lady," the maid answered. "He sent me for you!"

Puzzled by this turn of events, Keelin slipped off the gown and put on her old blue one. Then she made her way to the hall with the maid.

Four O'Shea men stood near the fireplace with Marcus and two Wrexton knights that Keelin did not recognize.

"Connor? Donncha?" she asked, addressing the two elders of Clann Ui Sheaghda.

"Aye, lass!" the two older men replied, grinning happily. "And we've brought Donal and Laoghaire."

Marcus slid one hand around her waist and gave her the support she had not realized she needed.

"When we first returned to Wrexton, I sent two of my men to Kerry," Marcus said, "to see what they could learn of Mageean, and the O'Sheas."

"'Twas a fairly short journey by ship," one of the Wrexton knights said. "The weather was fair enough as we traveled west, but we were delayed on the return."

Donncha took one of Keelin's hands. "'Tis glad I am to see ye, Keelin O'Shea, and glad to know that ye did not perish when we sent ye away."

Keelin was still recovering from the shock of seeing her countrymen here in Wrexton's hall. The hand that Donncha held trembled, she looked up at Marcus more than once to verify that she was not dreaming.

"Aye," she said in a small voice, "we're still alive."

"The wars between the O'Sheas and the Mageeans is over, lass," Connor said.

"Over? Ye mean Mageean—"

"Aye. 'Twas a sad day for all of Kerry when Mageean murdered Cormac," Donncha said.

"But at least Eirc O'Shea put the bastard in his grave before Cormac's dead body could grow cold."

"Mageean is dead?"

"Aye, lass," Connor said. "That's what we've been tellin' ye."

"Eirc is chieftain now," Laoghaire said. "And with Mageean gone, he's rebuilding Carrauntoohil. The keep, the church, the town—'tis all improvin' with his leadership."

"And with Ruairc Mageean gone," Laoghaire added.

Keelin realized then what her vision of Carrauntoohil meant.

"Eirc's sister has the gift, Keelin," Connor said. "She's got the second sight and can use *Ga Buidhe an Lamhaigh*. The elders have decided ye've devoted enough of yer life to defendin' the spear."

"And since yer plannin' to wed Lord Wrexton," Donncha added, glancing at the big Englishman who hovered over Keelin, "we'll take the spear back to Kerry and let yer cousin use it to hone her skills."

Rather than feeling a sense of panic at losing the spear, Keelin felt relief. 'Twas a heart-shattering, lung-bursting relief! She could relinquish *Ga Buidhe an Lamhaigh* without guilt.

Before she could reply, all attention turned to the staircase where Tiarnan was being helped down by Bill, the footman. Tiarnan's expression was one of shocked delight.

The O'Shea elders walked over to greet him as he arrived, and the three men hugged and clapped backs while Marcus pulled Keelin closer. "Do you mind?" he asked. "Giving up the spear?"

"Ach, no, Marcus," she said. "'Twill be my greatest pleasure to hand it to Connor and Donncha...well, perhaps my second greatest pleasure," she added, smiling wickedly.

* * *

"Adam is pleased that Tiarnan decided to stay at Wrexton with us." Marcus lit a few more of the candles that had been placed around the bed.

"Aye," Keelin said as she watched her husband. His movements were controlled and elegant. Mere moments before, he'd shed his wedding tunic and was bared to her view from his waist up. The flickering light caught on the golden hair on his chest, and with his every move, defined the muscles of his chest, his arms, his abdomen.

Keelin shivered with pleasure at the view.

"And what do you think, Keelin?"

"I think yer still wearin' too many clothes, Marcus," she replied.

He gave her a rakish smile and began to walk toward her, unlacing the points of his chausses. "What about you?" he asked. "You're still in your wedding gown."

"I need yer help to get out of it."

"Then, by all means," he said as he touched his mouth to hers, "let me assist you."

Keelin could hardly breathe as he teased her lips with his own, until she opened for him, allowing him entrance. All the while, his beautiful hands worked at her laces.

His tongue barely touched her, yet Keelin felt waves of pleasure crashing through her. Anticipating how his hands would feel when he finally removed her gown was pure torture.

He rained kisses down her throat, then pushed her gown from her shoulders. Standing nearly naked in a thin white chemise, Keelin touched Marcus intimately for the first time as his wife.

He threw his head back and reveled in her touch, while Keelin took pleasure in his response to her.

"Did you know I once thought you a sorceress, my love?"

"Nay," she breathed, scorching the length of him with hot fingers. "Ye never said. What changed yer mind?"

Marcus could barely speak, but managed to say, "Who says I ever did?"

* * * * *

MONTANA MAVERICKS HISTORICALS

Discover the origins
of Montana's most popular family...

On sale September 2001
THE GUNSLINGER'S BRIDE
by **Cheryl St.John**
Outlaw Brock Kincaid returns home to make peace with his brothers
and finds love in the arms of an old flame with a secret.

On sale October 2001
WHITEFEATHER'S WOMAN
by **Deborah Hale**
Kincaid Ranch foreman John Whitefeather breaks all the rules when
the Native American dares to fall in love with nanny Jane Harris.

On sale November 2001
A CONVENIENT WIFE
by **Carolyn Davidson**
Whitehorn doctor Winston Gray enters into a marriage of
convenience with a pregnant rancher's daughter, only to
discover he's found his heart's desire!

MONTANA MAVERICKS

RETURN TO WHITEHORN—WHERE LEGENDS ARE BEGUN
AND LOVE LASTS FOREVER BENEATH THE BIG SKY...

Harlequin Historicals°
Historical Romantic Adventure!

TRAVEL TO A LAND LONG AGO
AND FAR AWAY WHEN YOU READ
A HARLEQUIN HISTORICAL NOVEL

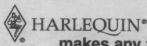

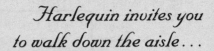

Harlequin invites you to walk down the aisle...

To honor our year long celebration of weddings, we are offering an exciting opportunity for you to own the Harlequin Bride Doll. Handcrafted in fine bisque porcelain, the wedding doll is dressed for her wedding day in a cream satin gown accented by lace trim. She carries an exquisite traditional bridal bouquet and wears a cathedral-length dotted Swiss veil. Embroidered flowers cascade down her lace overskirt to the scalloped hemline; underneath all is a multi-layered crinoline.

Join us in our celebration of weddings by sending away for your own Harlequin Bride Doll. This doll regularly retails for $74.95 U.S./approx. $108.68 CDN. One doll per household. Requests must be received no later than December 31, 2001. Offer good while quantities of gifts last. Please allow 6-8 weeks for delivery. Offer good in the U.S. and Canada only. Become part of this exciting offer!

Simply complete the order form and mail to:
"A Walk Down the Aisle"

IN U.S.A
P.O. Box 9057
3010 Walden Ave.
Buffalo, NY 14269-9057

IN CANADA
P.O. Box 622
Fort Erie, Ontario
L2A 5X3

Enclosed are eight (8) proofs of purchase found in the last pages of every specially marked Harlequin series book and $3.75 check or money order (for postage and handling). Please send my Harlequin Bride Doll to:

Name (PLEASE PRINT)

Address   Apt. #

City   State/Prov.   Zip/Postal Code

Account # (if applicable)   **097 KIK DAEW**

HARLEQUIN®
Makes any time special ®

Visit us at www.eHarlequin.com

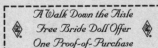

A Walk Down the Aisle
Free Bride Doll Offer
One Proof-of-Purchase

PHWDAPOPR2

COMING SOON...

AN EXCITING
OPPORTUNITY TO SAVE
ON THE PURCHASE OF
HARLEQUIN AND
SILHOUETTE BOOKS!

*DETAILS TO FOLLOW
IN OCTOBER 2001!*

YOU WON'T WANT TO MISS IT!

PHQ401

HARLEQUIN®
Makes any time special®

Silhouette®
Where love comes alive™

In August look for

AN IDEAL MARRIAGE?

by *New York Times* bestselling author

DEBBIE MACOMBER

A special 3-in-1 collector's edition containing three full-length novels from America's favorite storyteller, Debbie Macomber—each ending with a delightful walk down the aisle.

Father's Day
First Comes Marriage
Here Comes Trouble

Evoking all the emotion and warmth that you've come to expect from Debbie, AN IDEAL MARRIAGE? will definitely satisfy!

New York Times bestselling authors

DEBBIE MACOMBER
JAYNE ANN KRENTZ
HEATHER GRAHAM &
TESS GERRITSEN

lead

TAKE5

Covering everything from tender love to
sizzling passion, there's a TAKE 5 volume for
every type of romance reader.

Plus

With $5.00 worth of coupons inside each volume,
this is one deal you shouldn't miss!

TAKE5

5 Quick Reads. *5* Great Escapes.

Look for it in August 2001.